D1302289

Praise for R.J. Pine

"Grisham fans will enjoy this well written version of The Pelican Brief meets The Net."
--Austin American Statesmen on Exposure

"Pineiro boosts the action level and goes international."
--Publishers Weekly on Firewall

"Move over, Tom Clancy, there is a new kid on the block."
--Library Journal on Firewall

"Fascinating, stupendous, and terrifying."
--Douglas Preston, New York Times bestselling author, on Havoc

"The purest technothriller I've seen in ages."
--Stephen Coonts, New York Times bestselling author, on Ultimatum

"Firewall is a finely spun tale as you are likely to read. The well-executed plot twists keep you riveted. Fiction of the first order."
--Clive Cussler.

"A lickety-split new novel . . . Keeps the action churning and the suspense on high."
--Publishers Weekly on Exposure

Books by R.J. Pineiro

Siege of Lightning (1993)

Ultimatum (1994)

Retribution (1995)

Exposure (1996)

Breakthrough (1997)

01-01-00(1999)

Y2K (1999)

Shutdown (2000)

Conspiracy.com (2001)

Firewall (2002)

Cyberterror (2003)

Havoc (2005)

Spyware (2007)

The Eagle and The Cross (2008)

Meltdown (2010)

Truth be Told (forthcoming)

For more information visit www.rjpineiro.com

MELTDOWN

Copyright © 2009 by Rogelio J. Pineiro

A Wired Writer, LLC Book

ISBN: 1453742808
Library of Congress Card Catalogue Number: 0007141986

www.rjpineiro.com

First Edition: August 2010

In memory of Julio Gomez.
Vaya con Dios, my friend.

And,

For St. Jude, for making it all possible.

ACKNOWLEDGMENTS

Marty Greenberg, president of TeknoBooks came up with the idea to write a thriller that explored not just the dangers of global warming but the potential threat multiplier of eco-terrorism. Together with my agent and long-time friend Matt Bialer, we carved out an outline that became this book. I am grateful to both for their guidance throughout this project.

Thanks also go to my wife, Lory, for her unconditional love and friendship through the years. None of this would be possible without your constant support and words of encouragement during those long nights and weekends writing and rewriting this story. You shall always be the wind beneath my wing.

A note of appreciation goes to Michael Wiltz, for his thorough review of the manuscript.

Thanks go to my son, Cameron, now a sophomore at Wake Forest University, for making me so proud with your kind heart and academic and social achievements.

Finally, a warm note of appreciation goes to all of the men and women around the globe who devote their time and energy to the preservation of our natural resources. They are indeed the true heroes of our world.

MELTDOWN

R.J. Pineiro

"The supreme reality of our time is . . . the vulnerability of our planet."
--John F. Kennedy, 1963

"The Earth provides for every man's need, but not for every man's greed."
--Mahatma Gandhi

PROLOGUE

JAKOBSHAVN ISBRÆ GLACIER.
GREENLAND.

August 18, 2018.

The helicopter cruised over the deep fjord at thirty feet amidst towering flotillas of silvery icebergs drifting in the half-light of a summer evening in southwestern Greenland.

A full moon hung high in the star-filled, indigo sky, its gray light fusing with the wan orange glow from a sun that refused to set in the distant horizon, casting an amber double shadow of the helicopter across the surface of the fjord.

The winds were light this evening, and that suited Dragan Kiersted as he filled his lungs with the cold and dry air inside the bubble-shaped cockpit, savoring its chilling effect while flexing his gloved hands in anticipation.

Lying ahead were the last few miles of the large iceberg-dotted inlet before reaching Jakobshavn's tongue, the glacier's three-hundred-foot-tall seaward end floating on the waters of the fjord.

Like an icy Amazon River, the four-mile-wide Jakobshavn Isbræ flowed to the sea at a speed of 180 feet per day from the heart of Greenland--a dome of ice the size of the Gulf of Mexico--dumping nearly 20 cubic miles of ice each year into the North Atlantic.

Behind him, Dragan could barely see the distant lights of hundreds of merchant vessels making the now-routine journey along the North-West passage, the sea route running along the

Arctic coastline of North America previously clogged with thick ice.

Until five years ago, when global warming made it ice free through the entire summer, shortening the route from Europe or the Eastern Seaboard to Asia by nearly 4500 miles, drawing a lot of traffic away from the venerable Panama Canal.

Sitting in the copilot seat, Dragan shifted his gaze from the majestic sight to the slim profile of his pilot, Shin-Li, wearing a noise-cancellation headset. Her face was awash by the soft glow of the 12-inch Primary Flight Display directly in front of her.

A former top-notch captain in the People's Republic of China's Air Force, Shin-Li had abandoned her military career years ago lured by a smuggling business that promised wealth far beyond her government-issued Shanghai condominium and Audi sedan plus what amounted to five thousand dollars per month.

Dragan smiled to himself.

It had not been difficult to recruit her for this mission, nor had it been challenging to secure the equipment stored in the craft's modest cargo area behind the two rows of seats occupied by his team.

Shin-Li remained immobile, her features tight, her eyes focused on the PFD, the fingers of her right hand on the control column, left hand on the collective as she kept them steady and well below radar--not that Dragan expected any security in this remote corner of the world.

He sighed.

Most governments failed to recognize that this desolate spot along the North-West passage held the key to not only accelerating the rise in sea levels but also triggering a mini ice age across Europe.

The weather in the old continent was heavily influenced by the Greenland ice shelf as well as by the meltdown in the Arctic Sea, which pumped fresh water into the ocean, and over the course of a few decades would start diluting the salty sea enough to weaken the Gulf Stream, which carried warm water from the tropics to Europe. As the tropical water released its heat in the

North Atlantic, it sunk and flowed back to the equatorial regions along the ocean floor. This sinking effect formed the engine that powered the Gulf Stream. A massive and sudden meltwater gush into the North Atlantic from a catastrophic event in Greenland would exponentially accelerate the salt water dilution process to the point where within a matter of weeks the tropics-bounded current may not be dense enough to sink.

Such alluvial fresh water dump would kill the Gulf Stream, freezing Europe.

And this was a very desirable secondary effect of delivering his precious cargo to the heart of Jakobshavn's Isbræ.

First, I drown the world.

Then, I freeze Europe.

Dragan sighed, amazed at how easy the world scientific community and government officials made it for him to perform this noble act targeted at exterminating the cancer that was the human race, liberating the Earth from its ravaging societies.

The international security agencies called him a climate terrorist.

Dragan saw himself as a climate *liberator*.

The Earth had survived meteors, alluvial floods, massive volcanic eruptions, and countless ice ages. It would also survive the disaster he planned to induce.

But not man.

Not man.

He regarded his surroundings, still amazed at the lack of security.

If they realized just how critical Jakobshavn's tongue was to global climate, they would be protecting it like if it were the White House.

Idiots.

Those were the same incompetent scientists and politicians who had dismissed his father's theory on the relationship between solar activity and cloud coverage.

Henrik Kiersted, the once well-respected chief of the Danish National Space Center in Copenhagen, had spent years collecting solar activity and mapping it to decreasing cloud coverage, which resulted in a warmer Earth. Unfortunately, he had been ostracized for suggesting that solar energy could share the global warming stage with greenhouse gases.

Dragan tightened his fists in anger.

The politically-driven world scientific community ridiculed his father to the point that he had taken his own life in shame.

But they will pay for what they did to him, Dragan thought while observing the nearing Jakobshavn's tongue. *Just like they will pay for what they are all doing to our Earth.*

Dragan, an amateur climate researcher but also a former star in the *Fromandskorpset*, the Danish Navy Seals, had sworn then to dedicate his life and his family's fortune to punish a world who had not only ravaged the Earth but who had so maliciously wronged his father.

As they approached the soaring headwall of Jakobshavn's tongue, Shin-Li steadily increased altitude to clear it. This end of the glacier rose almost vertically three hundred feet above the fjord, thickening to one thousand feet as it reached land.

Shin-Li cleared the headwall by a slim margin as the helicopter reached the edge of the floating ice sheet.

Dragan pressed a button on the console, illuminating a red light in the main cabin to give his team the ten-minute signal.

She frowned. The operatives moving about while getting the cargo ready for deployment had upset the careful trim of the helicopter, taxing her flight skills, especially with only twenty feet of buffer in the twilight of an Arctic summer night.

Performing the duties of a navigator, Dragan double-checked the GPS coordinates on the 12-inch HD Multi-Function Display, which showed their position over Jakobshavn's tongue and a purple line towards their destination twelve miles away: a narrow cleft in the ice--a moulin--positioned close to the glacier's grounding line.

Dragan's data, which came from research conducted by a group of graduate students from the University of Colorado four months ago, indicated that this moulin reached halfway down the thousand-foot-thick tongue.

He watched as Shin-Li kept the aircraft locked on the navigation route while holding altitude even as the racket in the rear increased.

The outside air temperature reading on the MFD indicated minus seven degrees Centigrade. The satellite weather overlay on the GPS showed a light snow shower forecasted over their target zone. There was also a blizzard in the forecast but not for another hour, providing Dragan and his crew with ample time to deliver their nuclear package and head out before detonation.

"All set back there?" he asked, speaking into the mike of his noise-cancellation headset.

"Ready when you are, *boss*," came the deep and thickly-accented voice of his team's point, Mathias, a Nigerian operative who, like Dragan, had also spent time with his own country's special forces some years back.

"The team is ready," added Hans-Jorgen, a former colleague in the *Fromandskorpset*.

"Five miles," Shin-Li reported. "Snowflakes ahead."

Dragan began to check his gear, including the Heckler & Koch MP5 submachine gun strapped to his right thigh and the Sig Sauer .45-caliber pistol on his utility belt, which also held a half-dozen smoke grenades, clips for the Sig, a utility knife, and an ice hammer.

"Two miles."

As the snow intensified, Dragan checked the Velcro straps on his ice boots, which were integrated to a battery-powered body suit designed to keep him warm in sub-zero temperatures without the excessive bulk of passive thermal suits.

"I'm setting it down fifty feet from the target," she reported as the helicopter entered a hover while Dragan increased the resolution of the MFD, which depicted the start of the fissure with an accuracy of three feet. Three rivers of meltwater fed the crevice. Shin-Li would place the helicopter in between two of the rivers, on a dry area roughly one-hundred feet square flanked to the north and south by the gushing water and to the west by the abyss, their target.

"One minute," Dragan announced before removing his headset, briefly wincing as the loud rotor noise blasted against his eardrums, and donning a thermal mask with a built-in mike and ear piece to remain connected with the team.

The noise in the rear intensified as the team went through final preparations and shifted around the cabin, sabotaging Shin-Li's otherwise smooth decent, forcing her to constantly change pitch and bank while slowly lowering the collective, progressively decreasing lift until settling the helicopter on the ice sheet.

"Time!" Dragan shouted, pushing open the side door and jumping onto the ice, bending his knees as the serrated sole of his boots bit into the ice, locking him in place.

Mathias and the others joined him an instant later, six in total, as snow peppered their grey thermal suits. The large African with arms as wide as Dragan's thighs hoisted a waterproof case the size of a large footlocker from the rear of the craft and gently set it on the ice. It rested on a pair of built-in skis to make it easy to handle. The rest of the men hauled a mix of ropes, ice hammers, pitons, and other gear.

"Let's go!" Dragan screamed over the noise of the decelerating rotor as Shin-Li deployed the security pikes, anchoring the chopper to keep it from sliding. Hans-Jorgen remained with her to protect their getaway vessel and its pilot.

The team moved swiftly, with purpose.

Dragan led the way with Mathias, pushing the case towards the moulin a few dozen feet away under a rapidly darkening sky as the snow clouds thickened, blocking the burnt-orange glow from a sun looming just above the stark horizon.

The multiple fingers of meltwater rushed into the wide fissure with a roar that increased in pitch as the helicopter turbine decelerated.

Dragan stopped five feet from the edge of the dark chasm devouring massive amounts of grit-laden water in what reminded him of a miniature Niagara Falls as surface water gushed to the bottom of the melting glacier.

While Dragan and Mathias kept watch, scanning the snowy surroundings, the rest of the team operated with ease, securing the heavy case to a pair of long ropes devised to lower the cargo half way down the cleft, where the detonation would achieve maximum impact.

"Ready, boss!" Mathias shouted.

Dragan set his MP5 on the ice and took a knee while removing a key from a Velcro-secured pocket, which he used to open the case, exposing the nuclear device.

He entered a ten-digit code on a keypad, and a 5-inch screen came alive with a menu of options. Dragan selected the timer and programmed it to fifteen minutes. Five minutes to lower it into position and ten minutes to escape the blast zone. He entered a second code to activate the blasting sequence of the implosion-type nuclear device. Finally, he activated the tamper mechanism for immediate detonation should anyone try to open the case again after he closed it.

He started the timer on the device and on a digital chronograph strapped to his right wrist, before closing and locking the case, an action that made it impossible to deactivate the device.

"We're committed now! Let's do it!"

They had practiced this many times before. While two operatives hauled the case to the edge, two others anchored themselves to pitons fired into the ice and clutched the ropes connected to the top of the metallic housing. In unison they began to lower it.

The light breeze turned into a steady wind, blowing snow into his eyes, stinging them, forcing Dragan to don a pair of ski goggles as he watched the device disappear in the darkness.

"All good, yes?" Shin-Li asked through the built-in ear piece in her heavily accented English, the common language of his multi-national team.

"So far," he replied as Mathias stepped up to him. "Is the chopper ready to head back out in four minutes?"

"Yes. The rotor is at quarter speed."

"Good," Dragan replied. "We also need to--"

The gunshot cracked across the barren glacier. The head of one of his operatives exploded in a crimson cloud, collapsing unceremoniously on the ice.

Dragan and Mathias reacted in unison, dropping to the snow-filmed ice while scanning the horizon.

"See the shooter?" he asked.

"No, but it came from that direction!" the African replied, pointing beyond the wide river fifty feet south of them.

Dragan squinted, probing beyond the falling snow. "Can't see a thing," he replied.

"Someone double-crossed us!" the African shouted.

Dragan frowned as he pulled two smoke grenades from his utility belt and threw them in the direction of the shooter. Mathias did the same.

The African was right, of course. Canadian Command, chartered with patrolling the crowded North-West passage this time of the year never ventured up the fjord. In addition, very few people knew about his mission as Dragan had taken care of personally executing all of the researchers who had assisted him in identifying the weak link in Greenland.

All but Payden, he thought, recalling his former research colleague who worked under his father. It was James Payden who had pointed out this location on the map, the delicate pivot point where the glacier's tongue touched land.

Did he wrong me?

Survive this first. Then analyze . . . and get even.

Blue smoke immediately spewed from the grenades, mixing with the falling snow, forming a curtain, but not before additional reports echoed in the distance and three of his men fell on their backs while losing body parts to the explosive rounds, including one of the operatives lowering the cargo.

In the same instant, the second figure holding a rope collapsed under a fusillade that nearly tore his head off, letting go.

Remaining low, Mathias jumped on one of the ropes, clutching it with one hand while sliding towards the crevice, swinging an ice hammer wildly with the other, stabbing the ice twice before arresting the slide a few feet from the edge.

"Shin-Li get that chopper going! Hans-Jorgen, keep a close watch around the craft!" screamed Dragan into his mike while tugging two more smoke grenades from his utility belt and throwing them in the direction of the shots.

"I'm on it!" she replied through his ear piece.

"I'm watching," answered Hans-Jorgen.

Momentarily shielded by the gas and by the blizzard, Dragan reached down for the second rope, gripping it with both hands while sitting on the ice and anchoring the spikes lining the bottom of his boots against the ice.

"We need to get out of here, boss!" Mathias screamed as they started to release the rope in unison, but at a faster rate than Dragan would have preferred, feeling the heat building up in his thick gloves.

"We need depth, Mathi!" Dragan replied. "Or it won't work!"

"Two hundred feet!" Mathias shouted as a yellow rope marker rushed by in between his hands.

More Gun fire erupted from beyond the protective curtain, peppering the ice a few feet from them. It became obvious to them that they were dealing not only with multiple shooters but who also were armed with large-caliber weapons.

The blizzard and the smoke bought them precious time as they continued to lower the case, his hands beginning to burn through the thick gloves.

Three hundred feet.

The rotor noise increased, but along with it came the downwash that started to blow the smoke and the snow away.

Four hundred fifty feet.

Dragan could now see the opposite end of the river and spotted movement on the ice, seeing figures camouflaged in white crisscrossing each other clutching automatic weapons, muzzles flashing.

Dragan checked the chronometer. Four minutes had elapsed, but now the--

Mathias fell back as a burst of gunfire ripped through his chest and face, through his arms, the explosive rounds ripping them off his body as he released the rope.

Watching in horror the dismembered body of his comrade-in-arms, the resulting forward tug yanked Dragan to his feet while holding on to the remaining rope. In the same instant, stabbing pains jabbed his side and legs. Blood erupted through his thermal suit.

His grip weakening from the extreme pain arresting his body, Dragan reached for the ice hammer and drove the spike into the ice, hard, before looping the rope around it, securing it, keeping the crate from dropping to the bottom of the moulin and destroying its content before detona--

A round exploded through his right arm below the elbow, leaving only exposed bone, torn cartilage, and jetting blood.

The blizzard gathered strength, pounding his face as he watched his gloved hand and the bottom half of his forearm slide away, momentarily disorienting him as he tried to stand to go after it, cringing when placing any weight on his legs, watching as--

An invisible force punched him in the face, yanking off the goggles as his world turned red--as excruciating pain broadcasted from the right side of his face made him lose control of his bladder. He had been shot through the right cheek, and he suddenly could only see out of his left eye.

Feeling light headed, dizzy, nauseated, Dragan gained control and used his surviving hand to push himself in the direction of the rotor noise.

The blizzard intensified, turning everything around him blinding white.

Gunshots peppered the ice by his feet as the termination team lost line of sight, as he felt the end coming, as he grew weaker, as he stained the pristine ice crimson while dragging his maimed body in the direction of the--

Another colossal force tore into his lower legs, tossing him across the frozen hell with animal force as he lost sensation below the waist.

The extreme cold numbing the pain, Dragan Kiersted glided over the ice wishing for death, seeking closure and craving solace for his intense suffering.

His thoughts became distant, unfocused, propelled to the periphery of his mind as the blood-loss and the extreme cold took their toll on him, as he went into shock, trembling, shaking violently, the--

Something stopped his momentum--something that also began to tug him steadily by his left arm

He tried to mumble, tried to see, to hear, to beg his captor for a bullet in the head to put him out of his misery. But his wish went unheard as he continued to be dragged over the ice, the rotor noise and the howling blizzard blocking everything.

With pain reaching maddening levels, Dragan forced his good eye open, blinking rapidly, struggling to see through the whiteout, through the snowstorm, and for an instant recognizing the slim figure of Shin-Li back-dropped by the roaring helicopter.

A moment later the wind vanished as he landed on something hard before he felt hands undressing him. He cringed when the bitter cold tore into his exposed skin, heard the clanging of the emergency stretcher, felt hands propping him on it, and welcomed its cushioned surface.

Dragan heard the ripping of Velcro and the tearing of paper mixed with shouts from Shin-Li and Hans-Jorgen, muffled by the rotor noise outside and the bellowing wind. He winced at the sudden pressure of multiple field dressings on his legs and right arm, against his torso and face, and he tensed at the stabbing jabs of hypodermics and IVs. But he relished in the ensuing intoxicating warmth of the sedatives searing through his veins, washing away the pain.

The helicopter noise rose to an ear-piercing crescendo and he sensed upward motion, quivered against the stretcher's restrains as the helicopter soared in the blinding turbulence.

He closed his good eye, the chemicals relaxing him, signaling that he just might survive this.

But survive how? Crippled like this?

The craft pushed its way through the storm with intense vibration, its structure starting to come apart as Shin-Li revved up the turbine, accelerating the machine, ignoring the turbulence, the pounding wall of snow, violating the helicopter's design specifications.

Dragan suddenly realized why.

The bomb.

The countdown timer.

As he heard Shin-Li scream something about being followed by American gunships, Dragan tried to see his chronograph but he had worn it on his right wrist.

Surrendering to the enveloping chemical haze and the thickening fog clouding his thoughts, Dragan let it all go, the pain, the maimed limbs, the loss of his team as Shin-Li pushed the design envelope of the machine, widening the gap, getting them away from ground zero, from the kill zone of a device packing the power of one thousand Hiroshimas.

The whirling cyclone consuming his mind rushed him away from the reality of his situation, shrouding his world, dropping a dark curtain around him, shunting all sound, all sight, all thought. But not before a blinding flash pierced Dragan's substance-rich, dream-like state with the force of an apocalyptic bolt of lightning.

The shockwave that followed pushed him beyond the brink, and everything went dark.

❄

"Don't lose them, Captain!" shouted Erika Baxter as she sat behind Air Force Captain Harvey Lee, pilot of the A-10NG Warthog Next Generation—or NG—close support fighter in pursuit of the climate terrorists.

A senior officer of the CIA's Global Climate Counterterrorist Unit, Erika had been tracking Dragan Kiersted halfway around the world, and she had monitored the attack by the team of Navy SEALs from the navigator's seat of the Warthog-NG at a respectful distance for the past five minutes, as they nearly obliterated Dragan Kiersted's forces.

But it appeared that despite their best efforts, the terrorists, including Dragan, who had been wounded in the process, had managed to get into a helicopter and were now trying to depart the area.

Even after taking so many rounds!
Incredible!

As the SEAL team attempted to recover the cargo that the terrorists had lowered into a moulin, Erika ordered the Warthog-NG pilot to go in pursuit of the helicopter and blow it off the map.

"Range four miles," reported the Lee, whose voice came through clearly in the headset built into the helmet Erika wore as she squinted to see beyond the blizzard peppering the windshield. "Armed sidewinder. Seeking lock."

Although the A-10C's dual turbines were classified as stealth, they had remained several miles back to provide full silence to the SEAL team as they approached the terrorists.

Turbulence pushed her into her restraining harness as the storm intensified.

"Can't get a lock. It's going to get very rough very soon in this storm," the pilot announced.

"Don't worry about me, Captain! Just get the bastards!" she replied, having been in far worse situations than this one. And besides, the mighty Warthog-NG, a worthy successor to the venerable Warthog, was designed to take far more abuse than an Arctic blizzard.

"Yes, ma'am," Captain Lee replied.

She returned her attention to the screens dominating her navigation console, depicting a real-time image of the SEAL team reaching the Moulin and beginning to--

Alarms and warning lights filling the cockpit, Erika Baxter brought both hands to her visor, shielding her eyes as the night turned into day from the brightest flash she'd seen in her life.

Jesus! What in the world--

Then the thought slapped her, and the realization made her shiver with fear: the blinding flash had resulted from a nuclear explosion.

"My screens are toast!" screamed Captain Lee. "I'm losing control! We need to head inland!"

The initial flash ended before Erika could reply.

As the entire world spun out of control while the pilot struggled to keep the Warthog-NG flying, Erika managed to get a glimpse of the rapidly developing column of fire rising up to the sky just a few miles away.

"Mother of God," she whispered.

❄

The fireball's initial thermal energy of 100,000 degrees Centigrade ablated 25 cubic miles of ice--nearly half as much as all of Greenland had lost in the past year--along the glacier's grounding line.

A column of incandescent air rose to the heavens, reaching ten thousand feet as temperatures dropped to 7,700 degrees in an fireball that expanded outward in all directions at an initial velocity greater than the speed of sound and pressures exceeding a thousand tons per square foot, breaking off the four-mile-wide Jakobshavn's tongue while also obliterating the flotilla of icebergs crowding the fjord, forcing the sublimation of an additional 15 cubic miles of ice and melting twice as much.

A massive wave of ice and water propagated outward from the fjord at two hundred miles per hour. Nearly one hundred feet tall, the wave rushed towards Baffin Bay, across the crowded North-West passage, rapidly approaching the northern coast of Baffin Island, lying between Greenland and the Canadian mainland.

As the tidal wave propagated in a southwesterly direction, cool air rushed back towards ground zero to fill the partial vacuum created by the explosion. A surge of heated ocean collided against the thousand-foot-high headwall, jetting several cubic miles of water deep beneath the dying glacier, prying it off its bed.

Uncorking Jakobshavn Isbræ.

Lacking the buttress effect of its tongue, the glacier accelerated into the ocean to one thousand feet per day, nearly ten times its previous rate.

❄

The A-10NG was dropping fast.

The screens were blank from the nuclear blast, forcing Erika to shift her stare to the back-up analog altimeter as it rushed below seven thousand feet.

"We need to eject, Captain!" she barked.

"Not . . . yet . . . ma'am!" shouted Lee in a very strained voice as he struggled to keep the jet's nose pointed inland while diving away from the blast.

Six thousand feet.

She sighed, waiting, realizing the pilot's plan.

With Ground Zero only a few miles away, the pilot made the risky call to delay ejection in order to survive the rocketing exterior temperatures and shock wave that would soon follow.

The heat flash gave way to a powerful wind that shoved the A-10NG to the right, almost as if Lee were executing a maximum-G turn.

Erika felt light headed from the pressure as the windblast engulfing her--a mere fraction of the pressure that had pounded the region surrounding GZ--stressed the armored skin of the

Warthog, threatening to rip the wings off. But the rugged A-10NG held together as they dropped below three thousand feet.

"We need to eject Captain!" she shouted, recalling the minimum ejection altitude.

Silence.

Two thousand feet.

"You with me, Captain? . . . Captain? . . . shit!"

One thousand feet.

With the mushroom still visible in the distance and outside temperature readings dropping below 130 degrees, Erika saw the shiny surface of the vast glacier come up to meet her. At an altitude of five hundred feet, she ejected Captain Lee first and then herself.

The world seemed to catch fire around her as the clear canopy blew upward and she followed it under the power of the Martin-Baker ejection seat's solid rocket booster, which shot her up to two thousand feet as the Warthog-NG burst in a ball of flames that reached out for her.

Erika felt the intense heat as her ejection seat's rocket pushed her away through the heated air.

God, it's hot! her mind screamed, but her body couldn't do anything about it while strapped to the life-saving seat propelling her upward like a cannon ball.

Nearly crushing her chest, the windblast turned her upside down and to the side as she darted across the sky in a parabolic trajectory.

Visions of flames, mushroom clouds, icescapes, and stars flashed in front of her, but the images barely registered as a deep sense of isolation drowned her, a feeling of total helplessness . . . of raw fear.

A hard tug and the canopy blossomed.

The brutal windblast turned into a soft breeze that seemed to caress away the pain, the anger, the shock of what she had just witnessed; the terrible vision of fire and destruction unlike anything she'd seen before.

The ultimate nightmare had unfolded itself in front of Erika's very own pale-green eyes. Yellow fires billowed up in the distance. Explosions, like lightning flashes, illuminated the shaft of the dark mushroom menacing over what had been the massive tongue of Greenland's largest glacier.

Through the inferno, Erika could make out white vapor boiling up as massive amounts of ice were ablated in the aftermath of a nuclear blast.

But for Erika Baxter, senior member of the CIA's elite GCCU, and former global climate scientist, the worst was yet to come.

At that moment she was being bombarded by an invisible force: gamma rays.

Although she could not see it, smell it, or feel it, the radioactivity that filled the air entered her 115-pound body every time she inhaled. Her flight suit offered some protection by temporarily shielding her skin from the plutonium isotopes attacking all living cells, but even though she was now several miles away from the epicenter, in the few minutes it took her to reach the ground, Erika was still exposed to a radiation equivalent of two hundred chest X-rays.

The radar altimeter built into the ejection seat activated the retro booster the moment she reached an altitude of ten feet, cushioning her landing while briefly illuminating a large and flat surface of ice.

I'm on Jakobshavn Isbræ, she thought, realizing she had landed in the middle of Greenland's largest glacier.

Removing the safety harness, Erika checked her body for damage but found nothing, except for general soreness due to the ejection. She knew that adrenaline lessened the effects of the windblast and the spinal compression from being shot out of the Warthog-NG like a bullet.

She removed her helmet and brushed back her soaked, short auburn hair with a gloved hand. A five-foot-ten woman, Erika gave the impression of someone who worked out regularly, and she did. Her firm stomach, and slim but muscular arms and legs were the result of ten years of CIA operations tracking terrorists like Dragan Kiersted. Her reflection on the green visor of the helmet she held in her hands showed slim brows crowning a pair of alert and penetrating slanted eyes, a fine and straight nose, full lips always compressed as though with habitual resolve, and a somewhat bony, slopping face ending in a small chin.

Remembering her briefing prior to this flight, she unstrapped her seat survival kit, the removable section of the ejection seat that she had automatically attached herself to when strapping in and had remained with her through ejection and parachute landing. She then reached inside the seat survival kit and disabled the URT-33 beacon. She did this because the system broadcast an emergency signal at 121.5 MHz, the Guard emergency frequency, which would be monitored by all flights and rescue crews.

From another pouch, Erika pulled out a portable GPS and quickly determined that she was indeed the middle of nowhere, with the nearest town over a hundred miles away.

Swell, Erika thought as she looked about her, wondering where Captain Lee had landed, suddenly spotting his parachute swirling a short distance away in the twilight of the region's night.

She tried to walk but realized that her Army-issued boots lacked the required traction to walk on ice. So she opted for sliding in his direction, taking her well over five minutes to cover a few hundred feet, and falling several times in the process.

Kneeling by the helmeted pilot still attached to his ejection seat, Erika checked for a pulse and felt none.

Her eyes drifted to the helmet. As she stared into her own reflection on Lee's lowered green visor, Erika reached over to pull it up, and quickly realized that is was very hot to the touch.

Blinking twice, she pulled away, struggling to remain calm, her heart pounding again, her mouth dry.

Hot?

Then her logical side pieced it together, and the revelation made her breath in deeply, eyes closed, fists tightened.

Slowly, she exhaled through her clenched jaw, forcing her mind to remain focused, logical, professional.

It was the angle, Erika. The fucking angle!

Nodding, Erika Baxter realized how lucky she had been, and how *unlucky* Captain Harvey Lee had been.

The heat flash had occurred as the Warthog-NG spun out of control toward Earth, scorching all exposed surfaces, including those inside the cockpit. Unfortunately for Captain Harvey Lee, because of the angle of the plane with respect to the heat flash during that crucial fraction of a second, his helmet had been exposed directly to the incinerating blast.

That had been the reason why he had not responded right before ejection: he was already dead, or well on his way as his helmet suddenly turned into a high temperature oven, roasting his brain.

And for a moment, she wondered if Lee had been the lucky one. If they had been this close to the heat flash, it also meant that she had been exposed to a heavy dose of radiation.

Dear God.

Taking a deep breath, cursing Dragan Kiersted and his kind for what they had done, Erika rubbed her temples as she stared at the distant billowing cloud, as another realization pierced her mind.

The blast, if placed just deep enough, would have not only dislodged the glacier, which meant an acceleration in the melting of Greenland, the rise in sea levels, and the deceleration of the Gulf Stream, but more immediate, its proximity to shore also meant a tidal wave.

❄

Captain Alberto Massi stood on the bridge of the Carnival Cruise *Polar Voyager*, one of three pleasure mega ships recently built by the large cruise line for the new and increasingly popular North-West Passage route, treating tens of thousands of passengers each year with the unique beauty of the Arctic in summer time.

Tonight Captain Massi was relaxed. The forecast for the southwest channel of Baffin Bay was calm, and that meant that the 2657 passengers under his watch would enjoy a smooth evening beneath the soft orange glow of another Arctic sunset. There were blizzards over Greenland to their far east, but they were not expected to come his way.

Above, the moon hung high in the sky surrounded by a sea of stars.

They had left the port of New York two days ago, and he expected to reach the Alaska coastline in another two, where passengers would enjoy glacier tours, whale watching, and many other polar activities, including smaller excursions into Glacier Bay. The *Polar Voyager* would continue south from Alaska, following the Canadian coast, finally taking in at Seattle to drop off one-way passengers and pick up another replacement load for their return trip to New York. The New York-Seattle North-West passage cruise had become one of the premier summer vacation spots since global warming opened the route five years ago.

Massi scanned the array of color displays casting a dim glow on his crew. He found the effect almost--

A distant explosion on the starboard side made everyone on the bridge whip their heads to the panoramic windows along the right side of the bridge.

"What in the hell was *that?*" Massi asked his First Mate, Lieutenant Bruno Salvador.

Salvador, a tall and thin Spaniard with twenty years of experience at various cruise lines, including three years with the *Polar Voyager* working as second in command under Massi, rushed over to a set of multifunction displays linked to an assortment of satellites.

After a few seconds looking over the shoulders of a pair of operators, Salvador looked up and reported, "Captain, the infrared satellites indicate a nuclear detonation over the southwest coast of Greenland eleven minutes ago."

"Nuclear? How far away?"

"Looks like one hundred and fifty miles, sir."

"You're telling me we heard a nuclear detonation all the way from Greenland? That would mean . . ."

"Yes, sir," Salvador replied, understanding. Hearing it from such a distance meant it had to be in the megaton range.

"Did it happen over land?" Massi asked, also looking at the screen next to Salvador's.

"It was right at the coast line in the fjord of Greenland's largest glacier."

"Give me Canadian Command immediately," Massi replied, referring to the Canadian forces that had jurisdiction over most of the navigable North-West passage. "And turn to starboard."

"Starboard . . ." Salvador repeated while staring into his superior's eyes, suddenly realizing the danger they were in.

"Turn starboard! Full right rudder!" Salvador shouted, relaying Massi's command.

The 145-ton megaship, the largest of its class, began a long and slow turn to the east.

Massi grabbed a pair of binoculars and scanned the ocean in the direction of Greenland. Thirty second later he saw it.

"Dear God," he mumbled at the monster tidal wave moving towards them at incredible speed, before lowering the binoculars and closing his eyes.

The wave, as tall as the ship, struck broadside at 150 miles per hour in an explosion of foam, glass, and twisted metal. At that speed, the wall of water felt like a wall of reinforced concrete as it collided with the *Polar Voyager*'s superstructure. Millions of rivets popped like apocalyptic machine guns as the hull bent, twisted, and cracked in multiple places. The wave's colossal momentum transferred to the vessel, causing it to roll three times in its powerful wake.

A third of the souls on board perished during the seconds following initial impact, included everyone on the bridge, as the starboard side decks above water gave to the tidal wave, buckling in nearly fifty feet, crushing cabins, corridors, and stairs.

Freezing water burst through the hull into the core of the crushed vessel, cascading down to the lower decks, flooding packed movie theaters, dance halls, and restaurants, drowning all surviving passengers and crew, before leaving the vessel broken into four sections. Three of them sank right away. The stern, which bobbed in the water with its massive screws pointed at the stars, also disappeared from view ten minutes later.

The fast-moving surge continued its deadly path, sinking every vessel along with the *Polar Voyager*, including additional cruise ships, merchant vessels, fishing rigs, and even mega box ships, sending tens of thousands of passengers and crew--plus over a trillion dollars in cargo--to an icy grave at the bottom of the Baffin Bay.

The tidal wave finally reached the cliffs, coastal plains, and glacier outlets of Baffin Island, drowning dozens of thriving ports built in the past five years to cater to the increased summer commerce in the region, and drowning an additional fifteen thousand souls in minutes while continuing inland for several miles, flattening every structure, before retreating to the ocean.

As the once-fabled and now thriving North-West passage, the silver lining of global warming, became the worst disaster of the twenty-first century, dozens of cubic miles of sublimated ice, released as water vapor into the atmosphere by the detonation, returned in the form of alluvial rains across the region in the following days, hampering relief operations.

This massive meltdown of freshwater, combined with the cubic miles of thawed icebergs in the fjord and the accelerated flow of Jakobshavn into the Baffin Bay, exponentially diluted the salt water content of the North Atlantic.

As the world mourned the consequences of a despicable climate terrorist act, the Gulf Stream slowed down, causing temperatures across Europe to drop by a seasonal average of ten degrees Fahrenheit, throwing the continent into an early winter.

By the end of October, as Europe endured the coldest blizzard on record, global sea levels rose by almost two feet, striking havoc into the heart of the Gulf Coast, Bangladesh, Singapore, the Netherlands, Shanghai, and a host of other sea-level territories, resulting in the deaths of hundreds of thousands, the displacement of tens of millions, and the loss of hundreds of thousands of square miles and trillions of dollars.

And the worst was yet to come.

R. J. Pineiro

1 Surprises

"Greenhouse warming and other human alterations of the earth system may increase the possibility of large, abrupt, and unwelcome regional or global climatic events. Future abrupt changes cannot be predicted with confidence, and climate surprises are to be expected."
-- *U.S. National Academy of Science.*

NORTH SLOPE BOROUGH. ALASKA.

July 6, 2019.

They flew in from the south, high above craggy mountain ridges that abruptly turned into a sea of thawing ice and tundra, a massive expanse of meltwater lakes and rivers disappearing into a horizon dotted by glacier-carved cirques surrounding monumental walls capped with snow.

Glaciers, ice on slanted terrain set into motion by the earth's gravity, streamed out of high mountains, pushing aside all which stood in its way, spreading vast blankets of white that slowly turned into meandering fingers of thawed ice as it reached the distant coastal plains.

Sitting directly behind the pilot of the two-seater amphibious Piper Cub, and wearing a noise-cancellation headset and dark sunglasses, Dr. Natasha Shakhiva followed the shadow cast by the single-engine plane over dozens of glassy lagoons of icy water stained with vivid hues by the day's first shades of sunrise orange, creating dazzling mirrors of infinite shapes and sizes surrounded by distant sleepy volcanoes dotted with snowy forests.

From a distance the land looked peaceful, tranquil, in harmony, seemingly immune from the global warming acceleration triggered by that infamous Greenland terrorist strike that had spread so much chaos around the world in the past year.

But even before the Greenland event drowned the world and froze Europe, global warming fueled by greenhouse gases had steadily eroded the quality of life on the planet. African countries had suffered the most. The spread of disease--malaria, dengue fever, cholera--as a result of cycles of droughts followed by Biblical floods, had triggered massive migrations north, to Europe, taxing the continent's infrastructure.

Closer to home, the United States struggled to contain the largest wave of refugees from Latin America in history as food sources declined south of the border. But America was also coping with its own natural disasters. Monster tornadoes, wildfires, heat waves, and hurricanes continued to plague a dozen states.

And yet, the world's super powers, the politicians, the policy makers, the lobbyists, the CEOs of the world's largest corporations--all continued to give plenty of lip service to global warming but little else to the disasters staring them in the face, to the repeated warnings from the scientific community.

But that's why you are here, Natasha thought. *To continue to raise awareness of the danger we are in.*

The fifty-year-old global climate specialist leading one of this year's International Arctic Research Center teams--sponsored by the University of Alaska, Fairbanks--looked beyond the cosmetics of the magical sight, ignoring the dawn-streaked ice. Her veteran eyes surveyed the lake levels and compared them to the graphical information displayed on the FlexScreen she unrolled on her lap like a scroll.

The IARC logo momentarily filled the screen, prompting her for a password, which she entered by tapping the on-screen keypad. The logo vanished and the screen filled with the real-time satellite data linking her paper-thin system to hundreds of GPS sensors deployed across this melting land.

She frowned.

The images confirmed her observations--and those reported by the IARC team stationed near the shores of Shirukak Lake twenty miles away: record-low lake levels correlated with the increased loss of ice mass from the many glaciers that fed them during the summer months.

And that also correlates to the three degrees Centigrade average higher temperature than just ten years ago, thought the Ukrainian-born climate researcher, pushing out her lower lip. Unfortunately, the observation didn't align with the IARC's most recent computer modeling predicting the rate of ice melting in the region.

A flock of northern fulmars hunted in patches of bluish water bruising the thawing ice sheet. The native birds picked prey just beneath the surface while making their way to their roosting nests high in the cliffs of the Brooks Mountain Range, where Natasha had spent the past three days hiking to clear her head from IARC work.

Her legs sore from the long climbs, Natasha momentarily enjoyed the sight, watching the slick fulmars drop to the water like fighter jets, stabbing the surface, plunging through, disappearing from sight before surging back up, winging skyward with their writhing prize clamped in their black beaks.

She returned to her analysis.

Computer modeling at the turn of the century had assumed that glaciers and ice sheets would melt steadily with rising temperatures over the next centuries, which meant a minor increase in sea levels by 2100. But scientists had discovered a decade ago that large ice masses were prone to feedback loops. As ice thawed into darker blue water, it stopped reflecting sunlight and started to absorb it, accelerating the melting process, causing the ice to shrink at a rate faster than any scientist could have predicted.

In response, scientists adjusted models to comprehend this new feedback observation.

But the feedback loop itself has also been accelerating, Natasha noted, resulting in even higher temperatures and deeper ice shrinkages than the revised models projected.

The light aircraft banked to the right and began a shallow decent towards the west shore of Shirukak Lake.

Natasha stared into the northern horizon, her mind going just a little farther, to Arctic sea ice that had shrunk steadily 7% per decade for the past three decades, to an ice sheet that had lost 60% of its thickness since the 1990s.

Dropping her gaze to the FlexScreen, she tapped the upper left corner and accessed the British Arctic Survey site through the drop down menu, bringing up the latest images of the Arctic Sea ice cover, and comparing them to still shots of this time of the year in prior decades back to 1979. Running her forefinger on the left side of the FlexScreen's surface, Natasha adjusted the range.

Incredible, she thought, staring at the significant ice cover retreat in the past forty years.

That, of course, had some effect on sea levels, but most of the recent rise, which had triggered evacuations all around the world and had also mortally wounded the Gulf Stream, was caused by the exponentially increased loss of the ice blanketing Greenland in the past year.

"We'll reach the base in five minutes, Doctor," the pilot announced over the intercom.

"Thanks, Mario," she replied, in English lightly tainted with a Slavic accent. She pulled up a graph on the sea level rise potential from the British Antarctic Survey site, which ranked global ice masses according to their potential contribution to sea-level rise. A complete meltdown of the ice on the earth's surface would result in a sea level rise of around 207 feet. Antarctica alone contributed nearly 88% or 182 feet. The Greenland ice sheet soaked up 22 feet, or 10.5%, leaving just 1.5% or around 2.5 feet for all of the world's glaciers, polar caps, and sea ice.

And since the Greenland event last year, sea levels have risen almost two feet, she thought, her mind recalling the images of the massive evacuations along the Gulf Coast as Florida, Louisiana, and Mississippi lost over 30% of their land. New Orleans had all but vanished, as well as Biloxi, Pensacola and many cities along the eastern coast of Florida. Miami had survived temporarily and was being connected to the mainland by a series of long bridges. The Caribbean had lost nearly 30% of its islands. Even the Texas coastline suffered marked losses, mandating the emergency build up of higher levees to contain the rising ocean from erasing Houston off the map. Shanghai had nearly vanished from the map, triggering a recession in China which was felt around the globe. The Netherlands had almost become a gulf in the evolving geography of Europe, which was now in a permanent winter.

Natasha heard the engine's reduced RPM as Mario Escobar started his descent. The young Bolivian-born bush pilot and glacier researcher had joined her IARC team a year ago, soon after she first arrived in Fairbanks as a transfer professor from the University of Kiev.

Escobar used to study the tropical Andes glaciers of his home country until a relentless series of El Niños devastated them over the course of twenty years, forcing him to head north in pursuit of ice. Taller than her own five-foot-nine stature and sporting the fair skin and green eyes of European decent, Mario Escobar had seen his beloved glaciers shrink as El Niños diverted the moisture away from the tropical Andes, starving the glaciers of their sun-blocking snow and triggering rapid meltdowns. But Natasha had not recruited Escobar because of his thorough knowledge of glaciers, global warming, or aviation--very handy skills in these regions. Natasha had selected the Bolivian glacier researcher because of his passion, because of the fire burning in his belly, and because of the anger etched in his lined face after spending two decades watching his country's ice melt away in the wake of global warming.

Passion.

You have to have passion for this, my dear Natasha.

As they continued their descent, Natasha Shakhiva remembered her late husband, Doctor Sergei Shakhiva, a world renowned glacier scientist who had lost a battle to an aggressive strain of malaria in New Zealand on his way back from an Antarctic expedition three years ago.

Without passion you will not endure the hard battle ahead, the politics, the criticism for the work we do by the large corporations--and the governments--responsible for global warming.

Ten years her senior, Sergei Shakhiva had died while living life by his own rules, which was precisely how Natasha had sworn to live hers: at the outer reaches of a warming world doing the work few could endure, many criticized, some misunderstood, and most had ignored until just over a decade ago, when the level of disasters--natural and terrorist induced-- had finally awakened a formerly indifferent world.

But Natasha had not come to Alaska to study retreating glaciers or to measure the thickness of the ice shelf. Neither was she being sponsored by the University of Alaska, Fairbanks, to investigate sea-levels, melt rates, lake levels, or regional temperatures. That work was carried out by hordes of traditional global climatologists through multi-million-dollar grants from conglomerates seeking endorsements for renewable energy sources, the British Antarctic Survey, the World Meteorological Organization, and even the Department of Defense, who became a believer that climate change was a threat multiplier to international terrorism after Greenland.

Doctor Natasha Shakhiva had been lured to this part of the world by renegade scientist and long-time colleague and close friend Dr. Konrad Malone, the controversial dean of the department of geology of the University of Alaska, Fairbanks, to spearhead a non-traditional study of the Alaska permafrost. The frozen soil formed 11,000 years ago, at the end of the last ice age, covered over 85% of Alaska and most of northern Canada--in addition to the Northern Eurasia permafrost domain spanning an area equivalent to the United States.

Malone was known as the "Ice Man" for having spent most of his adult life studying ice somewhere around the world while running research projects for UAF that eventually earned him the appointment as dean of geology. Malone had taken part in her husband's final Antarctica expedition three years ago and he too had contracted malaria in New Zealand. But Malone, forty years old at the time and in superb physical shape, had managed to survive the malaria strain which consumed her sixty-year-old husband.

Malone had eventually caught up with Natasha two years later at a joint U.S.-Russian East Siberian Sea cruise, where he convinced her to come to Alaska for a change of scenery.

The change will do you good, Tasha. Sergei would have wanted you to move on, to live life by your own rules.

Natasha sighed.

To live life by your own rules.

Although their relationship had always been strictly professional, there was something about Konrad Malone that made Natasha feel different, alive--even young. Perhaps it was because Malone was nearly a decade younger than her, or maybe it was his energy, his determination, the passion he had for his work, a passion that equaled--if not surpassed--that of her late husband. Graduate students at UAF often joked that Konrad Malone wasn't human, that he seldom slept, and that he had espresso running through his veins. There was even a rumor at UAF that Malone had a secret pact with the devil for having survived numerous accidents in his decades-long adventures on the ice shelves of the world.

Natasha wasn't sure, but she did know that somehow Konrad Malone had managed to pull her out of a two-year-long state of depression on that ESS cruise a year ago. So when he had asked her to join him at UAF, it had only taken her a few days to finally agree.

Natasha stared at her reflection on the Piper Cub's side window. The damage from years of exposure to extreme elements were certainly taken a toll on her once smooth skin, and those lines of age had deepened during her mourning years, when she stopped taking care of herself.

She frowned. Her aging image reminded her of the cruel passage of time, something that had stopped mattering when her husband died.

Until Koni came along.

She sighed, a part of her still feeling guilty for the hope that Malone had brought back into her life. She had loved her husband dearly, but he was gone, and she still had some life before her.

Which I plan to live just as you did, my beloved Sergei.

Natasha looked beyond her image on the Plexiglas, her stare fixed on the distant Brooks Mountain Range. Malone had brought her up the mountains during her first week here, while she was still mourning her husband. Alaska's cool breeze, clean air, and clear skies had kicked off the healing process, the beginning of a new life.

Hiking in the mountains was her escape from this crazy world. It was her brief but frequent lone hikes, when Escobar would drop them off by the shores of lagoons at the foot of the range, that allowed her to add perspective to her life. There was something about being alone for a few days every couple of weeks, just Koni and her, their backpacks, and Alaska's beautiful yet rugged scenery, that gave her an appreciation for the gift of life, for the time she was being granted on this Earth, and for the opportunity to live again.

And although Malone had gone to Africa for a few months, Natasha had continued this tradition of hiking in the mountains at least twice a month to clear her head, and to put things in perspective, before heading back to the realities of a world spinning into self destruction.

Hiking time is over for now, she thought, watching the distant shores of Shirukak Lake materializing in the distance.

Back to work.

Her mission in this remote section of Alaska, however, was not to assess the thawing permafrost's risk to buildings' foundations, roads, or infrastructure on this unstable soil, or the increasing number of the so-called drunken trees in forests rooted in softening soil. In the eyes of Malone, those unfortunate but largely regional results of the thawing of the surface-level permafrost were inconsequential compared to the global implications of the thawing of the deeper permafrost, the frozen shield protecting the world from Gigatons of trapped methane gas.

A year ago Malone had convinced a reluctant UAF to allow him to conduct a deeper permafrost study in spite of the pressure the university had received in prior years from corporate sponsors to focus grant money on the infrastructure effects of surface-level frozen soil--in the destruction of roads, railroads, buildings, airports--not in the research that Malone believed to be more important to the world.

Malone had also been successful a year ago convincing the Pentagon to direct the Army Corps of Engineers to dig a new permafrost tunnel near the shores of Shirukak Lake.

Just as he convinced me into leading the tunnel project with the Army Corps of Engineers while he went to Africa to document the final months of that continent's dying tropical glaciers.

The Piper Cub dropped to three hundred feet over the lake's smooth surface and Escobar pointed the plane's nose into the wind while lowering the flaps and further retarding the throttle.

As the IARC base camp loomed into view, reminding her of the ten long months she had spent here working on Malone's controversial project in the shadows of better funded and staffed IARC initiatives, Natasha's mind drifted to another time and place, to the overarching reason Konrad Malone was so obsessed in probing deep beneath the surface.

To understand just how close we are to another Permian-Triassic extinction event.

To the unthinkable.

"Doctor, it looks like Koni's military friends have arrived," Escobar said in his thick accent, pointing to a pair of dark-green military transport helicopters tied down at the west end of the base.

"Well, he talked them into building the damned thing for us," she replied in the Americanized English she had mastered during her years teaching at UAF way back when. "It's about time they showed up to see what they got for their taxpayer's dollars."

The thought of the months invested by the Army Corps of Engineers to build a new permafrost tunnel for the IARC team--a deeper and longer version than the one they dug in the 1960s in nearby Barstow--inexorably let her mind to a Permian-Triassic extinction event. Two-thirds of the world's species were wiped out 250 million years ago, an event whose cause had been long argued by the best scientific minds of the world for the past century--an event that just recently had caught the attention of the Department of Defense due to its potential global implications.

An event that made last year's terrorist strike in Greenland-- and its devastating effects on the world--seem like child's play.

2 Bad Air

"A child dying from malaria every 30 seconds is completely unacceptable when we have effective and affordable ways to help children and adults avoid infection. Incredibly, one out of four child deaths in Africa are due to malaria."
--Dr. Carol Bellamy, Executive Director, UNICEF.

FURTWÄNGLER GLACIER. NEAR THE SUMMIT OF MOUNT KILIMANJARO. TANZANIA.

July 7, 2019.

Dawn.

A stabbing pain in his stomach awoke him.

Dr. Konrad Malone stirred and sat up in his cot in the half-light stillness of a tent pitched near the downhill edge of the shrinking ice sheet blanketing the sloping rock, several hundred yards from the main camp.

Malone had come here three months ago to record the final moments of one of the world's last tropical glaciers. Malone, UAF sponsor of Natasha's team on the shores of Shirukak Lake, believed that the death of these tropical glaciers coincided with the thawing permafrost as they were both formed 11,000 years ago, at the end of the last Ice Age. His data suggested that the glaciers near the equator were the Earth's early warning system for the release of the tens of thousands of Gigatons of methane trapped beneath the permafrost in the northern hemis--

Another pain stung his gut, and he cringed.

What's wrong with me?

Altitude sickness?

His mouth dry and pasty, Malone parted the mosquito net draped over his cot and stood, stretching, collecting his three-month-old long blond hair behind his neck and sliding a rubber band, turning it into a pony tail to keep it out of his way.

Perhaps last night's meal didn't agree with me, he thought, before glancing over to his desk opposite the cot, where a large FlexScreen housed the color images from the cores he had collected since arriving here.

Slipping into a pair of tight jeans, a sweatshirt, and snow boots, he stumbled towards the desk, feeling nauseated and a bit sore.

But sore from what? He thought. Not only was he in superb shape from a lifetime of hiking and living outdoors, but after three months of daily treks on the ice hauling heavy gear to drill for samples, his forty-three-year-old body was slim, hard.

Maybe I have food poisoning, he decided, going over last night's meal, which had consisted of a can of tuna, dry toast, and canned peaches.

He powered up the 30-inch polymer FlexScreen lying flat on the desk's surface. The system came alive, displaying the IARC logo and prompting him for a password, which he entered. A collection of color images from recent core samples filled the display. He noticed a small image of Natasha on the top right hand side of the screen, signaling that she had sent him a v-mail from the shores of Shirukak Lake. The hazel eyes on a narrow and pale face with fine lines across her forehead and around her eyes stared back at him beneath dark hair pulled back in a pony tail, much like his own.

He opened v-mail and the media stream stored in the flash drive of the FlexScreen came alive.

"Dear Koni," she began in her very unique Bostonian-Ukrainian accent from her years living in Massachusetts, where she earned her bachelor's and master's in climatology from MIT before heading back to the University of Kiev for her PhD, where she fell in love and married one of her professors, Dr. Sergei Shakhiva. Malone had first met the climatology couple at the turn of the millennium at a British Arctic Survey dinner in London, immediately making a connection with the passionate scientists and forging a life-long friendship. "The Pentagon arrived early this morning, *finally*, to get an update on our tunnel project in preparation for an update prior to the president's address to the nation on global warming next month. I will be taking them down tomorrow morning as they missed the window for today. Methane readings continue to increase in frequency. I'm afraid there is a correlation to your work in Africa, which means your glacier must be growing more and more unstable. Be careful Koni, Furtwängler can go at any moment with you on it drilling for core samples. Please drink lots of fluids, keep taking your malaria medicine, and get enough sleep. I just returned from three days hiking in Brooks. I missed you terribly and hope to see you soon. With all my love. Your Tasha."

The transmission ended and was replaced by the IARC logo.

Malone looked away while frowning. He had been the one who broke the news to her about her husband's death. Sergei Shakhiva had died in his arms in a remote clinic in New Zealand and Malone had brought his body home for her to bury. He had left her to mourn but continued to check in from time to time. During the ESS cruise last year, he had talked her into leaving her teaching position in Kiev to join him at UAF to study the region's thawing permafrost, which led her to the shores of Shirukak Lake to guide the U.S. Army Corps of Engineers digging a new permafrost tunnel.

The Ukrainian scientist had begged him not to go to Africa, but Malone had convinced her.

The tropical glaciers in South America have already disappeared, Tasha, he had told her. *Once the ones atop Mount Kilimanjaro vanish, I fear the thawing soil will not be able to contain the monster. I must go and monitor them and take the final samples.*

So Doctor Konrad Malone had left the IARC base camp at Shirukak Lake--and the side of a woman he had grown quite fond of--to hop on jetliners and travel a half world away to witness the death of the last tropical glacier on the planet.

His job consisted primarily of collecting ice cores using automatic ice-drilling equipment flown here via helicopter, scanning the cores before packaging them for their long trip to UAF, and loading his data into the network to complement the satellite imagery from GLIMS, or Global Land Ice Measurement from Space, the consortium of 24 countries that monitored the world's glaciers from orbit. But satellites could not measure thicknesses or collect core samples like Malone could, preserving ice which had been formed 11,000 years ago in special containers shipped each week via the same helicopter that brought them their supplies. The chopper took the samples directly to a refrigerated plane that brought them to the basement freezers of UAF's department of geology.

In the process, Malone also had to deal with local authorities and pay for endless permits and handlers to be allowed to camp near the unstable ice sheet in this closed section of Kilimanjaro National Park to remove the final samples from a glacier doomed into extinction. The fate of all tropical ice formations had been sealed years before by a global warming trend accelerated by mankind.

And there was nothing anyone could do.

Even if all greenhouse gas emissions stopped overnight, the global inertia from decades of excessive consumption of fossil fuels would maintain the rise in temperatures for centuries.

Of all the ice sheets that had once crowned this mountain, only Furtwängler remained at this altitude. Named after Walter Furtwängler, the fourth person to ascend to the summit on Kilimanjaro in 1912, the glacier had lost over 80% of its ice by the year 2000. In 2006, scientists discovered a large hole in the middle of the glacier, which continued to grow over the course of several months, finally splitting the glacier in two, accelerating the shrinking process. More meltwater continued to sip beneath the ice, acting as a lubricant over the inclined bedrock, creating a glacier hazard that Natasha believed could send the final section of ice--a half square mile and nearly twenty feet thick--tumbling down the side of Mount Kilimanjaro in another month or two. Similar events had already taken place around the planet as the ice thawed, like the 2002 headwall collapse and slide of Kolka Glacier in Russia, which killed 120 people in the village of Karmadon; or the sliding glaciers in Peru in 2017 that nearly killed their colleague, Mario Escobar, and which resulted in over a thousand deaths and tens of thousands homeless in downhill towns.

I have to go, Tasha. Furtwängler is an indicator of things to come. It is the canary in the coalmine.

Be careful, Koni. Furtwängler can go at any moment with you on it drilling for core samples.

Malone rubbed his aching belly while tapping the side of his FlexScreen to browse through a vast collection of high-resolution images of core samples. The green system was powered by an array of rechargeable batteries interfaced to a bank of solar cells that also powered the satellite dish linking him to UAF.

At least while they keep funding me, he thought, aware of the questions being raised at UAF regarding the value of his Kilimanjaro expedition at a time when budgets were tight and pressure was being applied to the university by a conglomerate of corporations to shift the research dollars to practical global climate projects in the northern hemisphere, such as surface-level permafrost studies, the slowing Gulf Stream and the resulting lower temperatures in Europe, and the rising sea levels.

Malone reached for the small espresso maker next to the FlexScreen, powered by the same solar energy. He filled the water dispenser with crushed 5000-year-old ice from an ice chest beneath the table and waited a minute for the system to warm up and melt the ice before placing his stained coffee mug beneath the dispenser. He pressed the red button in front of the machine three times, giving himself a triple dose of finely-ground Kenyan coffee, which he drank without any cream or sugar slowly, letting the brew do its magical work.

Although Malone had shared with Natasha the mounting pressure UAF was getting from its corporate sponsors about the Kilimanjaro expedition, he had not told her about the v-mail he'd received two weeks ago from UAF chancellor. Continued funding for his African excursion was up for review, and there was a chance it may be eliminated from next month's budget.

And for Malone that meant he had to accelerate the core-collection operation before the money ran out to pay for the exorbitant weekly fees to camp here, plus handlers, guides, porters, helicopter services, drilling equipment, fuel, transatlantic flights for his cores in refrigerated compartments, supplies, satellite links, and a host of other expenses.

Even if the chancellor and his financial staff get their heads out of their asses next month, this glacier may be long gone by then.

That had pushed Malone two weeks ago to make a bold move in order to accelerate drilling: he moved his operation right in front of the sliding glacier instead of keeping it at the main camp off to the side of an ice sheet sliding downhill at the rate of three inches per hour. This allowed him far more time each day collecting samples instead of having to spend so many hours moving, setting up, and dismantling the gear to keep it out of the way at night. All personnel, who by now amounted to Malone and two remaining local guides, slept in the main camp a few hundred yards away, just outside of the hazard zone.

Tasha would kill me if she knew I was doing this.

So Malone had kept this one to himself, carefully monitoring the sliding rate because glacier databases warned that the chance of an avalanche increased proportionally to the slide rate. The monitors included pressure stakes deployed in front of the ice sheet to trigger an evacuation alarm should the ice decided to accelerate.

And to make matters even riskier, last night a beautiful full moon had allowed him to stay up very late drilling, and he did not have the energy to walk back to the safety zone, opting to spend the night in the operations tent.

He sighed, knowing very well the risk he took. If his calculations were wrong, an avalanching wall of prehistoric ice would crush him with little warning as even his alarms might not give him enough time to rush to the safety camp several hundred yards to the east.

And, his so-called safety zone could be endangered should the ice sheet shift while breaking up, placing his local guides in jeopardy. Malone had an honest discussion with them two weeks ago concerning the higher risk of the safety camp's new location closer to the unstable glacier. Only two decided to remain with him. The rest had headed back down to take their chances with the civil strife that had plagued Tanzania in recent years, which Malone believed was triggered in part by the same environmental causes that had afflicted Darfur, Somalia, Angola, Ethiopia, and other drought-struck and malaria-ridden nations of the Dark Continent.

Many Africans--along with millions of refugees from an equally climate-afflicted Middle-East--had sought shelter in an increasingly crowded Europe, pushing most countries already struggling from relentless heat waves, floods, drugs, and crime to the very brink of economic collapse.

Which plays right into the hands of terrorists, he thought, rubbing his aching stomach while eyeing the top-left corner of the FlexScreen, where CNN reported the latest bout of disasters from around the world. The list included droughts in Indonesia that had fueled a new civil war, the famine in North Africa that allowed rebels to gain the upper hand, the sandstorms swallowing Beijing, and the tornadoes tearing the American Midwest. There was even a mention of a recent hail storm in Alaska, which were becoming commonplace in the summer months for reasons no one could explain. Sighing, remembering a couple of times when Natasha and him had to seek refuge in caves during hiking trips in Brooks to escape incoming walls of falling ice, Malone read about the devastated Netherlands, where the small regions that had survived the floods were now under ten feet of snow as Europe endured a seemingly endless winter as well as waves of northern Africa immigrants crowding Italy, France, and--

He tensed as another cramp raked his intestines like a hot claw.

Pressing a hand against the offending spot, he breathed in, exhaling slowly, and breathing in again as the sting slowly passed. His current state of misery for a moment made him question his commitment for being here, in the middle of a dying continent as the clock ticked down on funding he view as mission critical to seek answers he hoped would be trapped in the thawing glacier.

Africa was considered the cradle of civilization and this glacier contained atmospheric history spanning many thousands of years of humankind.

In spite of the pain, he knew he had to stick it out.

When we lose the ice, we lose the history.

But that still doesn't justify putting those local guides in danger by keeping them so close to the unstable glacier.

He sighed, momentarily thinking of Gideon and Lashi, the two guides who had remained with him during his final weeks here. They both had families.

But I have no choice.

In addition to his belief that the timing of this melting glacier was connected to the potential global release of methane, Malone needed to collect as much surface area from ice formed 4000 years ago to search for clues trapped by the frozen layer that might help prepare the world very likely upcoming global events. The ice in question resided ten feet above the bottom of the sliding ice sheet, which he drilled horizontally to collect as much of it as he possibly could.

Frozen in time in Furtwängler Glacier was an inch-thick dust band that captured a dramatic climate event across Africa when millions of square miles of fertile ground turned into what was now the Sahara desert. The samples that Malone collected foretold a story of extreme drought that plagued ancient Egypt and threatened the rule of the pharaohs, and which coincided with a drastic shift in weather patterns that lasted around 300 years.

Like the weather shift the world has been experiencing for the past--

A cramp doubled him over, and Malone dropped the soda, collapsing on the floor in a fetal position holding his abdomen.

Dear God! My stomach . . . my--

His vision blurring, Malone reached for the two-way radio to alert his guides sleeping in the safety zone, but hardly a sound left his throat when a massive seizure gripped his body with savage force.

Hanging on to the radio, he thumbed the transmitter button three times fast, three slow, and three fast, telegraphing an SOS, and repeating the sequence until he could no longer hold it.

Trembling uncontrollably, he hugged himself--his body feeling on fire, a headache flaring, his vision tunneling, his ears ringing as a fever spiked.

Malone wasn't sure how much time elapsed as the convulsions intensified, as the headache pounded his mind, as cold shivers rushed through his system followed by hot flashes. But somewhere in the distance, he finally heard voices, saw shadows shifting in the dim orange glow.

"Koni-man?" said Gideon, one of this guides as he entered the tent followed by Lashi, Gideon's younger assistant. "Are you all right?"

"I . . . my head . . . my stomach," Malone whispered as Gideon leaned down, placing a palm on his sweaty forehead.

"You are running a fever, my friend," Gideon said in his thick accent, which made it sound as if he was singing his words.

"No . . . no shit," Malone replied, his convulsions intensifying. "Tell me something . . . I don't know."

"Koni-man, you have malaria," Gideon replied, before adding, "Lashi, get the medicine kit."

Malaria?

"No . . . I can't . . . not again . . ." he mumbled.

"Yes, my friend," Gideon insisted. "You have the symptoms. You need medicine immediately or you will die. There is no time to lose."

Impossible, Malone thought. The extreme trembling prevented him from speaking, from explaining to them that for the past months, at the insistence of Natasha, he had been taking antimalarial medicine even though the altitude alone should have been enough to keep the anopheles mosquitoes plaguing the plains below from reaching him.

She even made me . . . promise I would sleep . . . inside mosquito nets . . .

In fact, since this was a UAF-funded expedition, everyone had to use the nets, even the local guides, handlers, and porters.

Malone suddenly got very cold, then hot again--boiling hot--his ears ringing, his eyes feeling like they would burn off his face, reminding him of New Zealand, of the week-long bout he fought with the deadly disease three years ago.

He closed his eyes, shutting everything out, praying he would pass out.

Someone peeled one of his arms away from his quivering body, and Malone felt the jab of a hypodermic as his guides hooked him up to an IV to feed him the newest malaria cure that Natasha had forced him to take along on his trip. Based on an old Chinese herbal medicine, the cocktail called artemisinin, as powerful as quinine, should kill the parasites that had ambushed his body--if Gideon was correct and Malone had indeed once more caught the pandemic disease that was responsible for one in every two deaths since the beginning of civilization.

He had to play it safe when it came to malaria. He had to assume he had the disease and get immediate treatment. If he didn't have malaria, then he would have just wasted a small amount of medicine. But if he did have it and didn't get treatment, the parasites would migrate to his brain, turning the infection into cerebral malaria, which if it didn't kill him would likely cripple him for life.

That's what happened to Sergei, he thought, remembering how the stubborn Ukrainian scientist refused to believe he had malaria. By then even the strongest injections of antimalarial medicine were not able to save him. Plus he was sixty. His aging body had collapsed. Malone had played it safe and got the injections early, as soon as the initial symptoms showed up. That, plus his younger and fit body, allowed him to survive.

But how in the hell did I catch it?

He understood why he had caught the disease in hot and humid New Zealand.

But here?

At this altitude?

He had arrived to the Kilimanjaro International Airport and immediately transferred to a helicopter that took him to an altitude traditionally high enough to keep him above the mosquito layer.

Meaning, there was only one answer.

Tasha was right.

He felt a stab in his other arm, followed by warmth spreading up his forearm. Almost immediately, the pain started to recede. Gideon had just administered a sedative to take the edge off.

"This should help you rest, Koni-man," he heard Gideon say. "We will get you help, my friend. We will get you help soon."

"The ice . . . Gideon," Malone mumbled. "Monitor the slide . . . rate . . ."

A fog soon enveloped him, pulling him away from the burning fever, from the pounding headaches, from the cramps and convulsions of a disease he should not have gotten so close to the summit.

Tasha was right.

The same warming trend that devastated the vast icecap that had once crowned Mount Kilimanjaro was also allowing mosquitoes to colonize previously inhospitable highlands.

As he felt his guides carrying him back to the cot and draping the mosquito net over him, the fever propelled his thoughts to the periphery of his consciousness.

Malone began to drift away, departing the misery of his situation, floating far away from Mount Kilimanjaro, from Tanzania, from Africa. In his chemically-induced dream, Malone headed northeast, across the Atlantic, to the place he suddenly longed to be, to his home state.

To Alaska.

To Natasha Shakhiva.

Konrad Malone continued to tremble, but he no longer felt the stabbing pains, the fever, the aches. The powerful sedative rescued him from this reality while the artemisinin cocktail worked its magic, tackling the reproductive ability of the parasites while also methodically exterminating them.

He kept his eyes closed but in his mind he saw the glaciers, saw the fingers of meltwater staining the pristine ice sheet. The Arctic climatologist saw the shores of Shirukak Lake.

Malone saw the hazel eyes of Natasha Shakhiva staring back at him as he boarded the flight in Fairbanks to head here.

Be careful, Koni. Furtwängler can go at any moment with you on it drilling for core samples.

The ice, Gideon . . . monitor the slide rate . . .

3 Threat Multiplier

"Climate change will provide the conditions that will extend the war on terror."
--Admiral T. Joseph Lopez, USN (Ret.)
Former Commander-in-Chief Naval Forces Europe and of Allied Forces, Southern Europe

PARIS, FRANCE.

July 7, 2019.

Erika Baxter hated this town.

No one could be trusted; neither the Muslim taxi driver zigzagging through thinning Parisian traffic this bitterly cold evening nor the cyberjunkies wearing SmartShades shooting up with nanohallucinogen cocktails huddled by the neon-washed wireless portal of a sidewalk Internet bordello on the Boulevard de Clichy, in the heart of Montmartre.

It amused and saddened Erika, watching them through the side window of a weathered Toyota sedan as they caught a red light. Beyond the snow-pelted glass they injected themselves with concoctions designed to maximize the wireless, sexual high downloaded directly to the SmartShades from the cyberpimp tending the glimmering lavender access port.

Summer in Paris.

With snow on the ground.

Erika sighed at the way in which the world had turned to shit, especially since Greenland.

And to make matters worse, today she turned forty.

At some point in her life, she would not have minded spending that often dreaded day in a place like this, partying heavily to help her forget not just the fact that she was forty but that the past two decades had rushed by before she could get her personal life started.

Not only had the City of Lights lost its luster long ago as a desirable place to celebrate such milestones, she was also on assignment tracking down a critical informant.

And there was the cold weather, of course, which continued to plague the continent after terrorists just about killed the Gulf Stream a year ago.

And to top it all off, this past year she had also fought and survived a bout of radiation sickness including reduced salivary gland activity, thinner and more brittle hair, paler skin, and of course, the full hysterectomy she had to undergo as the gamma rays destroyed her ability to reproduce.

But the real effects would take five to ten years to show up, she thought, remembering what the Agency doctors had told her. Her future was bright with possibilities, from breast, lung, and kidney cancer to lymphoma, melanoma, and leukemia.

Happy fucking birthday to me.

Erika sighed, leaned back, and forced the poker face already painted on Case Montana, the CIA officer sitting in the back of the Toyota next to her--the same expression that had kept her alive at a host of exotic destinations she had the pleasure of visiting during her decade working for the Global Climate Counterterrorism Unit of the Department of Defense.

Albeit from very different backgrounds, Erika considered Case and her professionals, a reality not shared by the Muslim, whose hungry eyes undressed her through the rearview mirror on the other side of the thick glass pane protecting him from the rough clientele in this part of town.

Or is it repulsion that he feels because my face isn't veiled, like those subjugated women in Arab Town, the new name for Paris' Latin Quarter after the Muslim influx of 2016?

Erika immediately looked away, ignoring the pervert's stare, though not out of fear of unwanted access of the wireless interface coating her recently-installed SmartLenses. Her firewall was always enabled, preventing anyone with the latest OcuWare from wirelessly probing beneath the surface of her computerized lenses and sucking her into an unwanted fantasy.

Funny how perverts turned high tech into another weapon to prey on women and children.

The Toyota jerked forward under the power of hydrogen batteries, its electric motor humming as it revved up, leaving behind the sidewalk cybersex party.

She shot the government escort she had met just this morning at the embassy a sideways glance.

Case Montana, the CIA operative from Langley assigned to escort her, stared out of his window, which sported a picture-perfect view of the lower section of the Eiffel Tower in the distance beyond the light snow flurries dancing in the stale air. The tower's top third had been missing since Islamic extremists blew it off back in 2014, the year that Europe started to slip away from the Europeans.

Erika Baxter frowned at the unfortunate sequence of events triggered by a significant decrease in cloud coverage, which led to a rapid decrease in precipitation over the course of 2013 and 2014, which further led to reduced flows of the Jordan and Yarmuk rivers, triggering severe water shortages in Israel and Jordan. Combined with shortages in Iraq, Oman, Iran, and Egypt--plus a rise in sea levels from melting glaciers and ice sheets--the drought exacerbated saltwater intrusion into coastal fresh aquifers destroying not only vast supplies of fresh water but also entire crops, triggering famine and disease.

And that's when the wave of immigrants began, she thought. Unfortunate, the number of extremists amidst the hordes of Middle Eastern and African immigrants was such that within a year, Europe--France in particular--became the new Mecca for Islamic clashing factions, for terrorist training grounds, and the promised land of suicidal fanatics.

The Beirut of the twenty-first century.

"Almost there," Case said, stretching the index finger of his gloved right hand towards one of a dozen bars lining his side of what had once been a vibrant, light-filled boulevard. Now a breed of cyberbordellos mixed with traditional ones--for those who still preferred carnal pleasures--dominated the semi-dark streets.

A cluster of UN soldiers, mostly Pakistani, Russian, and Latin American--dressed in their now year-round winter uniforms-- patrolled this sector of red-light district, where most buildings depicted varying degrees of damage from the wave of car bombings that razed the city six months ago.

Erika glared at the soldiers through the glass. They were armed with enough weapons to start a small revolution, but in classic UN tradition, their presence was largely cosmetic. They couldn't use any of their advanced hardware unless directly approved by the Secretary General--even when under attack.

Useless bastards.

She frowned again.

She considered these security forces as powerless as the World Health Organization, who were still struggling with the rapid spread of malaria across not just Africa and Latin America, but now Europe, North America, and Asia as global warming allowed the deadly anopheles mosquitoes to populate new regions of the planet.

Following the on-board navigator that Case had programmed via remote when boarding thirty minutes ago by the Place the la Concorde, near the American Embassy, the Muslim stopped in front of *La Scène*, a strip club on Boulevard de Clichy less than a block from the *Moulin Rouge*, the former world-famous nightclub and now a run-of-the-mill whorehouse packed with Asian, African and Middle Eastern women catering to lonely UN enlisted men.

Peeling back the thumb of his skin-tight glove to tap the fingerprint scanner on the side of his credit card, Case wired the fare to the cab's meter, whose 5-inch screen flashed a green MERCI sign a moment later, signaling the posting of the payment.

The magnetic locks disengaged, releasing the curb-side door. A hydraulic arm swung it open over a puddle of dark water surrounded by stained concrete.

Case slipped on a pair of custom SmartShades, the black FlexFrame conforming to his face, creating a perfect fit. The mirror-tint film of the SmartShades was nanorized, shielding him from all known forms of retinal intrusions.

He stepped out first, boots splashing water as he surveyed the bustling crowd--mostly off-duty UN personnel looking to trade their hard-earned Euros for sex, even if the majority of the surrounding hookers used SmartLenses and chemical blockers to keep their minds from remembering the experience.

That was another unexpected but interesting twist of high technology: selectively jamming unwanted experiences through black-market SmartLenses software, hardware, and injections, making it too easy for women to sell their bodies in the evenings without any mental scarring.

Erika mused. *With the right blocking software, proper vaccinations, and a good pimp, they could, in theory, go on with their daily lives while making quite the income at shit holes like this a couple of nights per week.*
In theory.

The reality was that the blocking software and chemicals had their quirks, resulting in the most unpleasant--and oftentimes shocking--awakenings of part-time hookers halfway through a trick.

And the realization of the limitations of today's software and hardware was precisely why Erika, although in possession of powerful protection in her SmartLenses, reached for a pair of SmartShades in a side pocket, holding them in her left hand as they exited the taxi.

Stepping over the snow accumulated by the curb, she settled next to Case in time to catch a glimpse of the Muslim checking her out through the large side mirror before the door shut and the Toyota sped off.

"I think you made a friend there," Case said. He was slightly taller than Erika and quite muscular but on the slim side, with dark-olive skin, and very short brown hair. A powerful chin and chiseled features beneath the mirror tint of his SmartShades glared back at her as the right end of his lips lifted almost imperceptibly, in a way she found attractive. Case seemed CIA through and through, and before that he had spent time with the SEALs--at least according to the dossier she had read on the flight over from Washington last night, before meeting him at the embassy.

"This body isn't for sale," she said, breathing in the cold air, briefly removing the shades while staring at the departing pervert.

"Sure it is. Why else would you be in this lovely place tonight?"

Erika stared at him and smiled without humor before glancing at the freezing, gray, and basically utterly depressing surroundings, where Uncle Sam was forcing her to spend her fortieth.

Happy birthday to me.

For an instant, she caught her reflection on his glasses. Her short auburn hair hugged the sides of her triangular face. Very dark eye shadow enhanced her cat-like eyes and matched her lipstick as well as the dark polish of her fingernails.

"Where's Payden?" he asked.

"Inside," she replied slipping on the SmartShades, in essence double-bagging her eyes.

Case's hard-etched features tightened as he frowned while regarding the surrounding decadence. "Your boyfriend sure loves shit holes."

"For the record, Jimmy's *not* my boyfriend."

"I don't really care either way," Case replied, with a slight grin. "But since you're not hitched, I'm sure you won't mind if I nail his balls to his forehead if he decides not to cooperate."

Erika raised a fine brow on her pale face before running a hand through the thinning hair she was still getting used to as she remembered James Payden back in college in Colorado. They had dated for about a year before Erika, who funded her college through the GI bill, had to pay back Uncle Sam upon graduation by using her degree in glaciology and climatology to assist the U.S. Navy in a variety of expeditions to Antarctica before getting an honorable discharge and getting hired back by the CIA's emerging Global Climate Counterterrorism Unit.

He shrugged at her silence and added, "Yeah, I figured you couldn't argue that he had it coming to him. The bastard's been giving the Agency headaches for over a decade."

"First things first," Erika said, shoving the memory of the James Payden she once knew aside. "We need intel. And if the information we obtain is useful, he gets a full pardon."

"Pretty fucking ironic, isn't it?"

"What is?" she asked.

"That a petty crook gets ten to twenty for holding up a liquor store but this bastard, who is responsible for so much harm gets to walk?"

The dossier had warned Erika that Case, like so many CIA operatives with strong military backgrounds, tended to see the world in fewer shades of gray than the average born and raised CIA officer. But the dossier also suggested that what the man lacked in moral flexibility he more than made up in operative skills.

"I don't make up the rules," she replied. "But we get paid to follow them, and the bosses in Langley say he goes free if he cooperates."

Lifting his shoulders a trifle again, Case held one of the smoked-glass double doors open, letting a pair of Pakistani soldiers in the company of petite Mongolian whores wearing fake minks exit the dark establishment before extending a gloved palm towards the murky entryway.

"Quite the gentleman I see," Erika said, grinning.

Case winked. "You have no idea."

Erika smiled. The dossier had indicated that Case married very young, had two kids, and got divorced over seven years ago, very likely due to his profession. Spies and families never mixed well, which at the end of the day was probably the best explanation for her still being single. In a way she felt a bit jealous of Case Montana. Albeit divorced, he had children. She, on the other hand, was completely alone--deceased parents, no husband or boyfriend, certainly no kids in the future, and a bleak health outlook.

She stepped inside. An air of whiskey, cheap perfume, cigarette smoke, and body odor washed over her.

Under the mauve and emerald glow of neon lights, a long bar stretched down the left side of a warehouse-like room, where patrons sat in stools surrounded by scantily-clad women of varying ethnic origins while bar tenders in dark uniforms busily moved about serving drinks. Behind them, 3D holograms of whores and ridiculously-endowed men performed sexual acts in every conceivable position on a raised stage backed by high-definition natural scenes, from rain forests and tropical beaches to snowy mountain peaks.

Erika eyed the natural scenes, the glaciers bringing back memories of her years with the Navy. She had actually been happy then, working outdoors at the far and remote reaches of the planet. The air had been fresh and invigorating; the scenery clean, pure, and unspoiled by humans.

Definitely in sharp contrast with the filth and decadence filling this bar--and this city.

Why did I ever leave that world?

The answer was always the same: the glaciologist in Erika Baxter had fallen in love with the hypnotizing beauty of Antarctica to the point that she became obsessed with protecting it from the global warming trend that had steadily shrunk the

Antarctic Peninsula and many surrounding glaciers during her years stationed in the area.

And that obsession had led her to the Global Climate Counterterrorism Unit of the CIA, chartered with fighting terrorism tied to the exploitation or augmentation of climate events, such as the devastating strike in Greenland last August.

And here you are, my dear.

Erika frowned while surveying the room.

The second-generation holograms lacked atmospheric-particle-balancing software and became partially distorted when cigarette smoke coiled through them, altering their effect to something almost comical rather than sexual.

A mix of whistles and howls from the bar and tables, the clattering of glasses and bottles, plus the surround-sound moans and screams from the cybershow mixed with a Cuban tune flowing out of unseen speakers, its steady Salsa beat reverberating across the packed room.

"Classy joint," Case observed. "Maybe I'll reserve it for my next birthday party."

Erika dropped her gaze to the floor while frowning, not knowing how to reply to that.

Case took notice and asked, "Are you alright?"

"I'm just dandy, Case," she replied. "Just *fucking* dandy. Stop worrying about me. We've got intel to gather."

"Indeed," he said, dropping his eyebrows at her before continuing to survey the place, finally stretching a gloved index finger at the rear of the establishment while saying, "Payden."

Erika peered through the thick haze not certain how Case could see anyone in the back. But then her SmartLenses worked in combination with her SmartShades to resolve the image by averaging out the smoke, giving her a better view of the lone figure wearing a brown suede jersey and a cowboy hat sitting at a table sipping from a longneck Kirin.

Erika filled her lungs with re-circulated air, remembering.

James Payden had been a superstar global climate student at the University of Colorado when she met him. Upon completion of their graduate work, she left to join the U.S. Navy research program in Antarctica to pay back Uncle Sam while Payden became inspired by the research of Doctor Henrik Kiersted from the Danish National Space Center in Copenhagen. There, Payden joined the highly controversial climatologist in his theory that the sun played a major role in global warming. The theory proposed that solar activity turned cloudiness up and down, which had an effect on the warming or cooling of the Earth's surface temperature. Kiersted, a scientist and a philanthropist who self-funded his contentious research, believed that energy particles from interstellar media, mainly from supernova explosions, entered the magnetic field that is streaming nonstop from the sun, to create clouds in our atmosphere. If solar activity was high, as had been the case for some time, less of these cosmic rays would enter the magnetic field, and therefore that would lead to fewer clouds, which would result in global warming.

And this, of course, was considered heresy by the world's scientific community as it implied that global warming was not primarily due to greenhouse gases.

Overnight, Kiersted was ostracized by the scientific community. With his life's work ridiculed by his colleagues, Henrik Kiersted took his own life that same year.

Payden became tainted by his association with Kiersted and his job opportunities dried up, forcing him to become a shadowy consultant for oil and chemical conglomerates, making a fortune helping corporations loophole their way through environmental policy. When the EPA tried to crucify him, Payden went underground, assisting the Chinese get around the agreements from the Kyoto Protocol and later from the Bangladesh Accords of 2012. In addition, rumor had it that he even developed--or maybe stole--global climate computer models to help anticipate droughts and floods for the benefit of corrupt insurance companies and shadowy financial institutions that the Global Climate Counterterrorism Unit believed were ultimately tied to climate terrorist groups.

"Are you ready for this?" Case asked.

Erika nodded. "Let's do it."

They proceeded towards the back of the club, zigzagging their way through a sea of tables packed with off-duty soldiers and whores, beyond dozens of bouncers and pimps keeping a watchful eye, ready to evict anyone abusing the merchandise.

They approached Payden's table, past a group of Pakistani soldiers in the company of African prostitutes. Behind him doors led to the restrooms adjacent to a large metal door, the rear emergency exit. A neon <u>SORTIE</u> sign hung above it, its crimson glow pulsating from the club's stroboscopic lights slaved to the Salsa beat.

"Hey Jimmy."

Payden looked up slowly, his brown eyes under the brim of his Stetson squinting for a moment, before glinting recognition. He didn't wear any SmartShades, which meant he was either in the possession of the latest generation of SmartLenses or he was abysmally stupid, especially in a place like this.

Payden briefly sized up Case before looking back at Erika, his eyes still narrowed, obviously taking in her new look. For an instant Erika thought she saw a twinkle of affection.

He broke the eye lock abruptly, took a sip of beer, and stared at the distant sex show before saying, "What's with the shades, guys? Afraid someone's going to fuck your minds?"

Erika frowned at the thought that she had actually dated this man back in Colorado; though at the time James Payden had been a clean-cut, kind, and bright student with a promising future. Unfortunately, he had gone off the deep with Kiersted's solar theory.

Ignoring his remark, Case and Erika sat across from Payden as he took a swig, set the Kirin on the seamless alloy surface, and added, "If you don't trust me enough to look me in the eye, I suggest you go back to whatever shit hole you came from."

Erika sighed at the irony of the comment considering where they were, but she slowly removed her SmartShades--though her retinal shields were up and ready to tackle anything Payden or anyone else might want to throw her way. Case continued wearing his eye protection.

"Good enough," Payden said, peering into her eyes, though he didn't attempt any wireless probe; just a basic natural stare. Grinning, exposing his shiny platinum dental work, which Payden had gotten somewhere in China after losing his bottom jaw to frostbite in Tibet years ago--at least according to the dossier the CIA kept on him--he added, "Nice change. I sure missed those green eyes."

"These green eyes wouldn't mind locking your ass in hell and throwing away the key."

"Ah, but you see. We already _are_ in hell--a cold hell--and there isn't a damn thing anyone can do about it. You shouldn't have dismissed Kiersted's work so quickly. Now deal with the consequences of pissing off his son through your political actions."

Erika made a face. "For the record, Jimmy. Europe being cold has nothing to do with Kiersted's theory but with the actions of his terrorist son. But put that aside for a moment. After all these years, are you still thinking that global warming is due to solar activity and the formation of clouds?"

"I don't _think_ there is a relationship, my dear Erika. We _proved_ it with good, solid science. But the eminent scientists of the world refused to accept a new idea because it upset the established orthodoxy. Believe me. Solar energy modulates cloud coverage, which in turn modules surface temperatures. We never said that solar energy was fully responsible, only that it was a contributing factor in the warming trend, which the politics within the global climate scientific community could not accept, choosing instead to ridicule our work."

"That theory didn't make sense when it was first proposed, and it doesn't make sense now," she said.

"And yet, you willingly crossed into this European netherworld seeking my assistance. That alone tells me that--"

"Let's cut through the bullshit, Payden," Case interjected. "Your funds have dried up and you are no longer viewed in the best light by your former employers, especially Dragan Kiersted. We are your best option. You'll be getting funds and a presidential pardon by cooperating. Now what do you know about Dragan's whereabouts?"

Payden's eyes remained locked with Erika's as he said, "Keep your pit bull on a leash, my dear Erika, or this meeting is over."

Case leaned forward and was about to stand when Erika put a hand on his forearm. He paused in mid stride, exhaled heavily, and slowly settled back in his seat.

"Good cop bad cop? I'm going to enjoy this," Payden said, grinning again, the lavender overheads reflecting off the smooth platinum beneath his lips.

"You of all people should know I'm no good cop, Jimmy, but he's my back-up, and I wouldn't antagonize him. He can crush you before any of those bouncers can react."

"Assuming, of course, that I was stupid enough to agree to this meeting without bringing some protection of my own. Just because you can't see it doesn't mean it isn't here."

"So," Erika said after a moment of silence and staring. "How about it, Jimmy? We are here in good faith, and we can really help each other out. Are you going to tell us what you've heard?"

"Sure. That the good people of the GCCU failed to prevent my old research buddy from detonating a suitcase nuke at Jakobshavn's tongue. Way to go there, girls."

"You fucking bastard," Case hissed, almost getting up again. "I knew most of those SEALs you help killed on that glacier."

"Like I said, my dear Erika," Payden replied while looking straight at her. "Keep him on a leash."

Erika kept a hand on Case's forearm. CIA intelligence indicated that Dragan had used Payden's extensive knowledge of glaciology to detonate a single 10-megaton thermonuclear device beneath the glacier's most vulnerable point, where the tongue met the bedrock. The intelligence gathered by the Global Climate Counterterrorism Unit was used by a Navy SEAL team, who came close to terminating the terrorists but in the end failed to prevent detonation, perishing in the process. To make matters worse, Dragan had escaped during the ensuing fight thanks to a sudden blizzard sweeping across the ice sheet and a daredevil take-off in zero visibility by his pilot, who managed to evade everyone, including Erika aboard that ill-fated Warthog-NG.

"Good ol' Dragan," Payden said. "Why bother nuking a couple of cities when you can drown the world?"

"Bastard escaped," said Erika with a heavy sigh, to this day still unsure how Dragan could have survived the onslaught of explosive rounds the Navy SEAL team had scored on him before the blizzard struck. "It won't happen again."

Payden shrugged. "Dragan was always nuts, even before his dad killed himself. And after Greenland, word I got was that the man's now only half human, madder than hell and more paranoid than ever. You should never let a wounded animal escape."

"Yeah, too bad he blamed you for the mistake," Case said. "Wounded animal's coming after your ass."

Payden's eyes glinted with anger. "Like I told you people when you first contacted me, I just highlighted to Dragan the weak point in the glacier, which any glaciologist could have done," he said. "I wasn't a part of any operation, but I got the blame as the only outsider to his network."

"And now he wants you dead," said Case. "And that makes us your new best friend."

"Fucking half-human nut job," Payden hissed. "He should have died in Greenland."

"We can help you, Jimmy, but you need to help us first. Where is Dragan now?" Erika asked.

"First the letter," he replied, touching the brim of his hat with a forefinger. "It's going to take much more than your pretty eyes, fuck-me lips, perky c-cups, and cute ass for me to tell you what I know. Though I have to say you're still packing it quite well considering you got nuked, got gutted out, and are turning the big four oh today."

"You're an asshole, Jimmy," Erika said, looking away.

Case reacted swiftly, reaching across the table and grabbing Payden by the neck with his right hand and pulling half his body over the table towards him. The informant placed both hands on Payden's muscular forearm but it was evident he would not be able to break the CIA officer's vice-like grip.

"Apologize to the lady," Case ordered.

"What . . . lady?" Payden mumbled.

Case tightened the grip. Payden's eyes bulged as he turned red.

In the same instant, the bathroom doors swung open and two large Asians in business suits stepped out and moved towards them.

"Let him go," Erika said.

"First he apologizes," Case said, keeping his clutch on the cowboy, turning Payden's face purple now, eyes bulging, tongue flapping between parted lips.

The bodyguards were almost on top of them.

Erika put a hand on Case's shoulder and squeezed gently. "Case, please. We need the intel, and he needs our help even though he's too proud to admit it. He needs the pardon to get back in the U.S. to get away from Dragan and others who are now after him."

Case sighed and complied, in the process shoving Payden back in his chair.

The informant coughed and swallowed while raising his right hand and staring at Case, an action that made his bodyguards halt their advance, settling behind their principal, their dark eyes burning the CIA officer, who sat back and crossed his legs.

"I would not do that again if I were you," said Payden, adjusting his hat, inhaling deeply.

"I would not insult her again if I were you," replied Case.

"Fair enough," said Payden. "Now, are we going to do business or not?"

Erika and Case exchanged another glance, before he produced a letter from a coat pocket, tossing it across the table.

Payden tore through the presidential seal and unfolded a single sheet of paper, reading it before producing a small

FlexScreen, which he used to scan the holographic presidential seal at the bottom of the sheet.

"All right," he said. "It's real. Now the money."

Case looked at Erika, who nodded, before tapping a finger against the side of a CIA card, transferring the agreed-upon funds.

"You get half now and half if the intel leads us to him," said Case. "If you lie to us, the deal is off and we come after you."

"My information is solid," said Payden.

Case placed both forearms on the table. "I just want you to know that if you fuck with us, we will hunt you down."

Salsa music continued to reverberate across the dark establishment, along with the howls from the customers and the moans of the holographs.

Payden nodded as he verified the transaction in his FlexScreen. He handed the letter to one of his bodyguards and the FlexScreen to another.

"Where, Jimmy," asked Erika. Where in the hell is he?"

"Siberia," replied Payden with a grin, the platinum dental work gleaming.

"What's he doing there?" asked Case, leaning forward.

"He's going after the permafrost," he replied. "He wants to set the world on fire."

"How, Jimmy? How is he going to do that?"

As Payden was about to reply, a fireball expanded behind his bodyguards, who instinctively jumped over their principal, shielding Payden.

Before she could react, Case threw himself over her, embracing her while pulling her down to the floor just as her ears registered a massive explosion.

In slow motion, she watched as a sheet of fire projected above them, before everything went black.

4 Acts of Man

"As parliamentarians, we have to stand on platforms around the planet and explain to electors why the forest is burning, the cattle are dying, why there is surf in the High Street. To explain ...that these are not Acts of God, but Acts of Man."
--Tom Spencer, Member of the European Parliament

NORTH SLOPE BOROUGH. ALASKA.

July 7, 2019.

The circular tunnel, thirty feet in diameter, projected at a shallow angle deep into the permafrost, where the U.S. Army Corps of Engineers had built tracks upon which Natasha Shakhiva rode inside a battery-powered vehicle accompanied by US Army Colonel Marcus Stone, the newly appointed chief of the National Climate Defense Alliance, a recent and much-overdue partnership between environmental scientists and the defense and intelligence communities.

Sitting on the left-front seat of the 6-person, air-tight tunnel transport system, referred to as "The Pod" by the IARC team, Natasha reached for the control lever, which resembled a jetliner's throttle mounted in the center console separating her from her single passenger.

Wearing a tight pair of jeans, hiking boots, and gray UAF sweatshirt, her shoulder-length hair pulled back in a pony tail to get it off her face while she worked, Natasha curled her long and thin fingers around the lever and inched it forward.

The Pod started its slow descent into the permafrost shaft in a silence broken only by the steady hum of the refrigeration units on the surface keeping the tunnel's entrance below freezing to protect the permafrost down the mile-long pipe.

Daylight receded behind them, replaced by glowing Xeon lights evenly spaced on dark-grey walls made of wind-blown silt mixed with ice that filled up this valley during the last ice age. Above and below them, glass wedges, formed when surface water drained below and froze, reflected the Xeon's steady white glow.

It didn't matter how many times she made this trip, Natasha always felt as if the Pod was transporting her through a journey back in time, down glistening walls of ice and soil from another era, through layers of history dating back to prehistoric times, to the end of the last ice age.

But her scientific eyes saw beyond pristine crystal formations sculpted by nature's formidable hand, by millennia of pressure and cold that preceded human life on this planet, spanning the beginning of intelligence to the modern marvels of today.

The vehicle carried them deeper into the layer of permafrost at a forward speed of thirty miles per hour, reaching a depth of one-hundred meters in minutes.

Natasha retarded the throttle, gently slowing them down to a halt.

She read the shaft's air quality data on the ten-inch color screen in front of the center console, confirming the absence of methane. As added insurance, she glanced at the methane-detectors located every fifty feet and hanging from the roof of the tunnel. They were all green.

"No methane today, Colonel," she replied. "Air's good."

"So we do have bad air quality days down here?" Stone asked, frowning, the freckles on his square face shifting beneath a full head of closely-cropped orange hair. The colonel wore the new generation Army Combat Uniform, or ACU-NG, sporting a digital camouflage pattern that suggested shapes and colors without actually being shapes and colors, resembling more like visual green-black-and-grey noise. Even the U.S. flag emblem on his shoulder had been digitized into mutated greens and blacks. The tightly-fitting ACU suggested a body as hard as Stone's cold-blue stare.

For an instant Natasha wondered if the good colonel, who appeared to be in his mid forties, ate stones in his morning cereal.

She nodded while pressing a button on the side of the control lever, and the glass canopy slid back, an action that automatically shut off the Pod's compressed-air system. "Eleven days so far this summer with a reading above five percent, enough to ignite the air--and we're only in the middle of July. But most of the activity has taken place in the middle of the afternoon, when the surface permafrost is at its warmest."

She glanced at her watch as she stepped onto an observation platform that ran for a hundred yards down the right side of the shaft. Stone followed her.

"It's only nine am," she said. We're okay for at least a couple of hours."

"Then what?"

"Then we leave and seal the entrance to extract any methane through the ventilation system and into a surface storage tank."

"What do you do with the methane?"

"We use it to power the camp's generators. The IARC base is environmentally friendly."

Stone nodded. "Doctor, do you have any data to compare this year to prior years?"

She frowned. "We lack a pure baseline because this tunnel didn't exist last summer," she replied. "But we do have the data from the Barstow tunnel and from the hundreds of bore holes drilled by prior IARC teams over the years across this region. Our best estimate is that ten years ago there were zero methane readings this deep at ignition concentrations. Historical IARC data shows the first reading above five percent four years ago, at the beginning of August. Last year we had three ignition-level events the entire summer. Today the number is eleven, six of which have occurred in the last ten days, and we still have another six weeks of heat. None of the events resulted in measurable surface-level methane release."

"So . . . it's exponential," Stone said.

"I'm afraid it is worse, Colonel" she replied before compressing the full lips on her pale face.

Stone blinked, before saying, "Please explain."

"The problem is the feedback loop," she replied, taking a laser pointer and directing the red dot towards a soil and ice formation just above them. It glistened more than others in this section.

"Looks wet," Stone observed, a hand on his chin, lips pursed.

"It's *thawing*," Natasha corrected. "Mind you that we are one hundred feet below the surface, and by our estimates around five hundred feet above a massive pocket of trapped methane."

"But, I thought that at this depth the temperature remained well below freezing all year around, Doctor," Stone replied. "How can it be thawing? Is it the tunnel lights, or maybe because this tunnel is connected to the outside world?"

"The tunnel, unfortunately, has nothing to do with it. At the moment, surface temperatures are close to sixty degrees, which is around eight degrees warmer than ten years ago. Back in those days, the temperature dropped very fast during the first three feet to just below freezing, and dropped maybe another degree by this depth. So most of the temperature change occurred near the surface. Today, that constant temperature level starts deeper, closer to fifteen feet, and it remains at or just above freezing all the way down here. That's why the walls are starting to bleed."

Colonel Marcus Stone, a civil engineer who worked for the Army Corp of Engineers for many years before being appointed by the president to lead the National Climate Defense Alliance a month ago, stared at the tunnel's inner walls for a moment and asked, "Will that be a problem for the structure of this shaft?"

Natasha shook her head. "Not for a while. What is of more immediate concern is the effect that the rise in temperature has on the permafrost's CH_4 transport ability--or what we call the permafrost's *methane flux*--to the atmosphere. An increase in five degrees at a depth of just two feet increases the methane flux by nearly 120 percent. And today at that depth we are over eight degrees warmer than ten years ago, which increases the methane flux by over 200 percent, because the rate is also exponential. Said another way, global warming is rapidly decreasing the permafrost's ability to contain the methane deposits trapped below us since the end of the last ice age."

"And that correlates to the increased number of methane events," said Colonel Stone with a heavy sigh, arms crossed while staring at the glistening ice outcrop.

Natasha solemnly nodded, glad that this military man was getting a good perspective of the magnitude of the problem facing them. Perhaps with the help of the National Climate Defense Alliance the White House would--

"Now," Stone said, interrupting her thought, "The permafrost region covers most of the upper portion of the northern hemisphere, right?"

Natasha nodded while smiling politely. Colonel Stone apparently had read some of the literature she had forwarded to him when he took office a month ago. "It basically covers most of Canada and Alaska as well as Siberia. By our calculations, the amount of methane stored in gas-hydrates beneath the permafrost and the onshore permafrost reservoir is roughly estimated to be around thirty-two thousand Gigatons. To put it in perspective, this amounts to one million times more methane than what has been released in the atmosphere by all northern ecosystems in the past fifty years. This is why a small disturbance of trapped gas hydrates could cause catastrophic consequences in a very short time."

The freckles on his face shifted again as his face tightened.

"And this is where the positive cycles increase the risk," she continued, letting him take the full effect of the problem. "As methane is released through the permafrost, it will get trapped in the atmosphere, bootstrapping the greenhouse effect and resulting in warmer temperatures, which will increase the rate of polar ice melting, which will release methane gas trapped in ice--in addition to the rise in sea levels. On top of the resulting floods, the rise in sea level will cause warmer ocean water to extend over existing permafrost regions, disturbing methane pockets formed before the Holocene flooding 10,000 years ago. We saw these methane plumes erupt in the waters of the East Siberian Sea last year during the fifth Russian-U.S. joint cruise. These are some of the ways ancient methane enters the modern chemical cycle. By the way, the event in Greenland last year has elevated sea levels by almost two feet, accelerating the methane-release process."

The thought of the ESS cruise made her think of Konrad Malone.

They returned to the Pod and continued in silence down the shaft to its maximum depth of 200 feet, which was designed by Natasha to allow them not just to study the permafrost but also create the ultimate early-warning system. The moment the pockets of methane gas four hundred feet below pierced the coldest portion of the region's permafrost shield, invading the tunnel in large quantities, Natasha knew it would be time to pull the fire alarm with the National Climate Protection Alliance.

"So this is in essence our canary in the coalmine," observed Stone.

"Yes, Colonel, with the exception that when the coal miners saw the dead birds they immediately left the mine. We live in the mine, Planet Earth. There is no place to run."

Standing on a spot that made them the closest humans to the flammable gas in Biblical quantities, large enough to incinerate entire societies, Natasha checked her watch.

Ten o'clock.

Another hour and they would have to--

The high-pitch of a methane detector echoed inside the tunnel, its sound amplified by the enclosure. The methane detectors hanging from the tunnel's ceiling had all turned yellow.

"Methane event," she said, returning to the Pod and inspecting the screen above the center console. "Two point eight percent. Not enough to ignite, but unprecedented at this time of the day nevertheless."

She looked up from inside the Pod at the colonel standing tall and strong on the platform, arms crossed. "That would be our cue to leave, Colonel."

"I don't smell anything," Stone said, getting in the Pod before the canopy slid forward.

"Methane, like carbon dioxide, is odorless to us, Colonel, and in these concentrations not harmful to humans in short exposures."

She placed the control lever in reverse and the Pod began its ascent to the surface.

"Methane is now reaching the tunnel four hours before any previous recorded time of the day, Colonel, adding to the exponential nature of the positive cycle."

"I'm calling the Pentagon, Doctor," said Colonel Stone.

She nodded, feeling as if she were sitting atop a time bomb the size of which the civilized world had never known; sensing the beginning of a very different era for the Earth.

Doctor Natasha Shakhiva stared at the walls of trapped time surrounding her as her mind once more traveled back to the Permian-Triassic Extinction Event which evidence at hand suggested could become reality again.

An event that the powers of the world had not yet come to terms could just happen again.

5 The Enemy of My Enemy

"There is nothing so likely to produce peace as to be well prepared to meet the enemy."
--George Washington

PARIS, FRANCE.

July 7, 2019.

The smell of cordite assaulted her nostrils.

Erika Baxter opened her eyes and watched the glow from emergency lights diffusing through the smoke, dancing in the thickening haze that veiled the cries and screams mixing with the ringing in her ears.

Case Montana lay nearby caked in white dust, no longer wearing the SmartShades, his face wincing in obvious pain as he also came around.

Behind them blue flames crawled up the walls and across the ceiling of the club, flickering through the smoke.

She remembered now.

The blast; the pressure against her chest; Case using his body to shield her, taking the brunt of the impact.

On clambering hands and knees, feeling the heat on the back of her neck, the roar of whooshing flames drowning all other sounds, Erika remained low, shoving debris aside, reaching Case's side, checking for wounds, finding none.

"Case!" she shouted above the bellowing fire and the cries of patrons, as shadows stumbled in the descending inky cloud, scrambling towards the front of the building away from the inferno sealing the rear emergency exit. "Can you hear me?"

The CIA operative blinked, coming around as she screamed again while shaking him. "We need to get out of here!"

"Payden," Case said with effort, pressing an elbow against the floor to prop himself up while his other hand reached for the SIG-Sauer P220 .45 caliber semiautomatic tucked in his pants, against his spine. "Find him."

Relieved that Case was not badly injured, Erika turned around and started searching for the informant.

Squinting, the smoke stinging her even with the protection of her SmartLenses, Erika gazed around the bar, pressing the sleeve of her shirt against her mouth, breathing through it.

The ocular software kicked in, filtering the inky particles obscuring the place, cleaning the scene as she probed her darkening surroundings, searching for the shape of--

There.

Payden shifted under the weight of his inert bodyguards a dozen feet away, blood oozing from their noses and ears, their backs charred, smoke coiling to join the boiling layer accumulating on the ceiling. They had shielded their principal, absorbing the brunt of the blast, just as Case had done; only they had been closer to the explosion. In addition, Erika realized that the bodyguards had also shielded Case and her with their bulky bodies by standing behind Payden when the bomb detonated.

Lucky for her.

Not so for Payden.

But your luck won't last long if you can't get out of here soon, she thought, the blaring inferno swallowing the rear of the building leaping towards them, hungry, seeking fuel, reaching the bodyguards who lay on top of Payden.

"Jimmy!" she screamed, crawling over to him, grabbing his wrists, tugging hard to free him beneath the heavy bodyguards, to get him away from the rumbling fire.

Payden cringed, coughing blood, moaning in pain as she pulled hard, her skin burning from the intense heat.

She remained as low as she could, dragging the renegade scientist out from under his dead bodyguards and towards where Case knelt.

Through the smoke, Erika saw the burns across Payden's legs, on his chest, the smell of charred skin and singed hair filling her nostrils, nauseating her, blending with the swirling cloud threatening to swallow--

The blaring reports of gunfire thundered inside the structure. Sparks exploded to her right as rounds struck the stained concrete floor, the sound mixing with the swelling flames as she released Payden while reaching for her own weapon, a 9mm Beretta, the same gun she had learned to shoot in the Navy.

Case grabbed the table where they had sat and forced it on its side with his free hand, momentarily shielding them from their quarry.

Erika laid sideways on the floor, exposing her upper torso around her side of the heavy table, her Beretta clutched in both hands, her SmartLenses probing deep, resolving two figures shifting in the smoke clutching automatic weapons.

"See them?" Case asked, mimicking her posture on the other side.

"Yep," she replied, aligning the incoming threat in the sights of her weapon. "Ready when you are."

They fired in unison, the reports cracking above the inferno.

One assassin arched back on impact while trying to return the fire, ripping through the scorched ceiling; red-hot cinders and smoking debris rained on Erika and Case.

They instinctively rolled to shake off the smoldering chunks of ceiling while firing again; the second assassin abruptly stepped sideways before diving out of sight.

"Did we get him?" she asked, dropping behind the table alongside Case while also kicking the smoking plaster away from them and from Payden, who continue to moan while coughing up more blood.

"Don't think so," Case replied, his weapon trained on the spot where the mark had vanished.

Adrenaline searing through her system, Erika looked beyond them, scanning for more threats, her mind going in a dozen directions as the operative in her took over.

Who sent the termination team?

Was Jimmy the target, or Case and me?

Did Dragan make us? If so, how?

Analyze later!

The heat continued to rise as the flames behind them threatened to set their backs ablaze. Erika's eyes began to burn even with the protection of the SmartLenses.

"He's waiting for the fire to flush us out," Erika finally said, realizing the assassin's tactic.

"Yep," said Case. "Then he will pick us one by one."

"Time's on his side," she said over the rumbling fire, looking at him and slowly nodding.

"Did you see anyone else?"

"Nope," she replied, her SmartLenses resolving only patrons stumbling through the smoke towards the front exit.

"Same here," Case said. "Meaning it's just him against us."

"What do you have in mind?"

"The assassin who died," Case replied, narrowing his eyes. "He gave me an idea. Be ready to shoot the moment he gets up."

Erika suddenly understood as Case pointed his weapon at the smoldering ceiling exactly above where the assassin had vanished and opened fire, discharging his entire load in ear-shattering crescendo, before reloading and firing again in circles at the ceiling, tearing through it.

Fire rained a dozen feet from them, like a meteor shower, followed by a scream and a dark silhouette rising through the smoldering debris and charging to his left.

Sweating profusely and feeling lightheaded from the debilitating heat, Erika forced savage focus, firing again and again, spent casings flying off to the right. She ignored the heat, the near-blinding smoke, and the tongues of flames converging on them, her SmartLenses tracking the shadow leaping across her field of view.

The assassin clutched his chest, dropping from sight as he fired at nothing, the brief reports from his weapon vanishing just as he did.

"Now!" Case said, surging to his feet while grabbing Payden by the right shoulder. Half conscious, the informant moaned as Erika ran her free arm under the other shoulder, hoisting him to his feet.

They moved swiftly towards the exit in a deep crouch, dragging Payden as the fire consumed the bar.

Her skin protested the heat just as her lungs rebelled from the scorching wind she sucked in while shielding her mouth with the sleeve of her shooting hand, trying to breathe through it.

Sirens in the distance signaled nearing emergency vehicles, their sound mixing with their clicking footsteps, with the grumbling fire, with the flaring headache pounding her temples.

Help was on its way.

But not for them.

They were CIA.

They were supposed to be invisible and could not afford to be questioned by local authorities.

Tears veiled the exit thirty feet away, her throat seared by hot smoke, choking her as a huge burning beam broke loose from the ceiling above the bar to their left, crashing over the stage with a deafening sound that shook the entire structure. The impact kicked up a scorching cloud of sparks and flaming debris, dancing in front of them like a million fireflies.

Shielding their faces while dashing through it and across the final dozen feet, they reached the exit, the street, safety.

Erika took a deep breath as the dark smoke began to clear, revealing a night stained by the red and yellow lights of arriving emergency vehicles, by a large crowd of onlookers forming a semicircle a respectful distance from the entrance.

Following professional habits, Case and Erika concealed their weapons and cut left with Payden in tow, remaining at the edge where the smoke thinned, using it to shroud them from a potential second team positioned at a vantage point across the street or from converging U.N. Security forces.

They reached the crowd and pressed on, going through a cordon of onlookers more interested in watching the burning building than in the departing trio.

"He won't last long," said Erika, her short hair soaked with perspiration and stuck to the sides of her head as they continued dragging Payden, turning right at the corner, and left at the next one, reaching a dark alley away from the chaos on Boulevard de Clichy.

They hid in between two dumpsters and carefully set Payden down. Erika knelt on one side and Case on the other.

"Jimmy. Can you hear me?"

Breathing in short raspy gasps, Payden slowly opened his eyes, coughing blood, before nodding.

"Who did this, Jimmy? Who tried to kill us?"

"It has to be . . . Dragan . . ." he replied. "Bastard . . . tracked me . . . down . . . somehow . . ."

Erika glanced at Case, who motioned her to continue.

"How do I find Dragan, Jimmy?"

Payden coughed more blood, his eyes losing focus. He was going into shock.

Erika leaned closer, cupping his face with his hands, forcing him to stare at her.

"Tell me, Jimmy. Tell me how to find him."

Payden's stare locked with hers. Breathing deeply, he said, "Vorota . . ." his breath pungent with beer, his mouth a mess of shiny platinum and blood. In a strange way he looked almost robotic. "Andrei . . . Vorota."

"Who is he?"

"Russian . . . arms dealer . . ."

Case was already checking his handheld FlexScreen, producing a moment later a photo of the dealer taken a year ago according to the CIA online dossier.

He showed the 3-inch-square screen to Payden. "Is this him?"

Payden's breathing became more erratic, with the gurgling sob that signaled internal bleeding. He was slowly drowning in his own blood. Still, the informant managed to stare at the digital image for long enough to nod ever so slightly before going into spasms.

Erika held him for a final minute, until all movement ceased.

"Come," said Case, already standing, offering a hand. "We need to reach the embassy and get over to the airport ASAP. I'm going to request an Agency jet."

Erika nodded slightly and took his hand.

They walked to the opposite end of the alley in a silence broken by the sound of fire engines and police vehicles rattling in the background.

She looked back just as they turned the corner; for one final instant she stared at the still figure of someone whom she had once cared for deeply. As much as he hated James Payden for the choices he had made in his life, for betraying her as well as the global climate community, for selling his intellect to the dark side--for showing the monster Dragan Kiersted where to plant his suitcase nuke, and nuking her in the process--he had been the only person on the planet who remembered that today was her birthday. Her parents had died long ago and she was an only child. All of her adult relations had been short-lived due to the demands of her job, requiring her to travel the world in search of potential climate threat. Even the place she called her home, the Global Climate Counterterrorism Unit, amounted to little more than a handful of acquaintances plus an impersonal cubicle lost in a sea of government offices in Washington, D.C.

So Erika Baxter, forty years old, had no one to share this milestone in her life, no one to celebrate her birthday because no one knew or cared.

Except for James Payden, and he too was now dead, though in Erika's mind he had died long ago. And the thought of death made her think of her very dark medical prognosis.

Happy birthday to me.

She walked next to Case Montana towards the American Embassy on the Champs-Elysées, near the Place the la Concorde. She walked in silence.

6 Climate Dissidents

"Those who are absolutely certain that the rise in temperatures is due solely to carbon dioxide have no scientific justification. It's pure guesswork."
--Henrik Svensmark, Director of the Centre for Sun-Climate Research, Danish National Space Centre

SOUTH OF KANGERLUSSUAQ.
GREENLAND'S NORTHWEST COAST.

July 8, 2019.

The distant gunshot cracked across the vast expanse of tundra, echoing against the rocky hills surrounding it.

Standing at the edge of an overhang above a coastal valley once permanently covered with ice, Dragan Kiersted observed the carnage below.

Villagers had gathered most of their sled dogs and were shooting them.

Dogs in Arctic communities such as the one below were working animals, used to travel to other villages or to hunt the whales and seals that often got trapped in frozen bays. The retreating Greenland ice shelf had robbed them of their work, and lacking any seal scraps to feed them, their owners had no choice but to put them down.

Mosquitoes buzzing about him--another result of the warming trend--Dragan frowned at the four-by-four trucks parked along the east end of the sea-side village, the local's new mode of transportation through the thawed tundra and the trails and unpaved roads leading nearby towns and seaports.

Another shot whipped across the valley, followed by a high-pitched yelp as a villager's bullet failed to kill a large grey and white Alaskan husky, who thrashed and yelped on the grassy meadow amidst the barks and howls from other condemned dogs and the cries of the villagers.

These people love their dogs, Dragan thought as another armed villager put the animal out of its misery with a well-placed round to the head.

The yelping ceased, but the barking continued from a dozen chained huskies as two men picked up the carcass by its legs and carried it to a nearby pile, which they doused with kerosene before setting it ablaze.

Dragan stared at the inky smoke coiling to the blue skies as more shots echoed across the field, before walking away from the edge and towards the large Cessna Caravan turboprop being refueled at the tiny hilltop airstrip.

Once used heavily by glacier-tour groups, the strip remained in operation primarily to serve general aviation aircraft traveling between America and Europe for a variety of reasons, including ferry pilots performing aircraft deliveries, corporate jets on business trips, and Arctic research teams such as the one Dragan and his small team pretended to be.

He stared at the red and blue emblem painted on the sides of the 12-passenger Caravan from the European Arctic Research Agency, a front company Dragan had founded to allow him easy access to most Arctic-region countries. His credentials had been good enough to fool the two part-time customs officials smoking by the terminal across the tarmac--at least enough for them not to question the strange machinery stored in the plane's rear cargo compartment.

Or to realize the weapons we're carrying in a secret compartment beneath the floor.

The massive Caravan stood tall atop a pair of Wipline 8000 amphibian floats that sported retractable wheels beneath them, turning the venerable Cessna turboprop into a truly versatile machine. And making it the largest plane on floats commercially available today.

As more reports reached the airstrip, Dragan paused to admire the tall and slim silhouette of Shin-Li supervising the fueling process.

Two mechanics on ladders huddled over the open turboprop engine cowling while a ground attendant, also on a ladder, finished fueling the tank in the Cessna's left wing before shifting over to the right one.

After discussing something with the mechanics, who headed back to the terminal, Shin-Li used the ground crew's twenty-foot-tall fueling ladder to inspect the level of the tank with a dip stick, satisfying herself that she had received the correct amount, before walking beneath the wing and taking fuel samples from the multiple drain points with a clear plastic sampler cup, checking for water and other contaminants.

Dragan admired the fluidity, grace, and precision in her movements as she performed a preflight check, making her way around the plane. She was a pro and an asset to his mission. Shin-Li could fly the heavy Caravan at tree-top level for hours and take-off and land on any body of water or virtually anywhere on land flat enough and in pretty much any weather. She had incredible physical and mental endurance, spoke Mandarin, English, Russian, and Spanish, and also could handle any firearm with expert ease.

Dragan had recruited her during a drug run in Kazakhstan three years ago, and she had been with him ever since. It was Shin-Li who had dragged him half-dead after taking multiple bullets and shoved him into their getaway plane when the American commandoes surrounded his team in Jakobshavn's tongue. It was Shin-Li's superb flying skills that had allowed her to take-off in zero visibility just minutes before the Americans overran their position. It was Shin-Li who had tricked a dozen aircraft dispatched to intercept their escape, flying in a blizzard through mountainous terrain. It was Shin-Li who had kept him alive in a remote hospital north of Beijing in the midst of the world's largest manhunt. And it was Shin-Li who had secured the services of world's best surgeons to reconstruct his maimed body and made him whole again.

Wearing skin-tight blue jeans and a black sweater, Shin-Li looked up to inspect the underside of the Caravan's nose, beneath the engine, aiming the beam of the flashlight she held in her right hand.

Dragan approached her from the rear as she reached down to inspect something on the ground.

The ends of his lips curving upward when spotting the tiny red dragon tattooed on an exposed inch of bronze skin between her jeans and sweater, just above her buttocks.

"All set?"

She continued to inspect what looked like a small puddle of oil as she said, "Enjoying the view, yes?"

Dragan smiled. And top it all off, Shin-Li was an insatiable partner, wanting him for who he was, not what he looked like.

She straightened and turned around, her long hair swirling in the light breeze, framing the smooth skin of her narrow face, her fine features tightening. She looked more Indonesian than Chinese, her light olive skin glistening in the morning sun.

She put a hand on her child-thin waistline while compressing her crimson lips into a frown.

"What?" he asked.

"Minor leak." He trained the beam of her flashlight on a dark circle on the tarmac directly under the engine.

Dragan shrugged. "Fine. Fix it."

"Need to show them how. They went to get tools. Ten more minutes."

Dragan nodded. Like all top-notch military pilots, Shin-Li knew her aircraft's systems well.

He returned to the edge of the field and regarded the sea beyond the abyss, comfortable that she had her end of this mission covered.

The strip stretched for nearly a mile on this wide plateau, once blanketed with ice except for the air field. But the ice no longer returned to these coastal regions during the winter months. In its place a rising sea in the past year had swallowed many of the coastal villages, and those which survived, like the one below, were doomed into a very different form of existence.

Dragan lost track of time as he stared at the product of his handy work on the glacier's tongue, drowning the world and triggering a soft ice age across Europe by slowing the Gulf Stream.

They should have listened to my father, he thought. They should have treated him with the respect he deserved.

And now they will pay again for what they did to him.

They will pay for what they did to me.

The world will die in two days.

By fire!

"Talking to yourself again?"

Dragan turned around and stared at Shin-Li, arms crossed and head cocked to the right, a shrewd smile on her face while regarding him with dark amusement.

As he was about to reply, another gunshot cracked in the coastal valley as the column of smoke continued to rise, pushed inland by the sea breeze.

"Finished?" he asked, ignoring her question. For better or for worse, Shin-Li knew him far deeper than any other soul on the planet, and he owed her his life.

"Of course," she replied.

He grinned at the confidence exuding from this woman.

They walked side by side to the Caravan, entering through the retractable step ladder, which Dragan pulled up behind him, locking the hatch.

She blew him a kiss before heading towards the cockpit while Dragan turned aft, beyond the sleeping figure of Hans-Jorgen, the only other surviving member of the Greenland strike along with Shin-Li and him, and who had been instrumental in staunching the bleeding while Shin-Li few the helicopter in the blizzard. Hans-Jorgen was now his most-trusted operative aside from Shin-Li. Behind Hans-Jorgen sat Doctor Yuri Gerchenko, the elder Russian mechanical engineer in charge of their precious equipment safely secured in the cargo area behind the lavatory.

And that formed this team, this cell of his global climate terrorist organization--small, nimble, and operating completely independent from his other cells.

Dragan took his seat next to the snoring Danish warrior, whose bulk dwarfed even the wide leather seat of the executive seating configuration of his Cessna Caravan, which Dragan had received as payment for successfully handling an arms deal for Al Qaeda two years ago. Shin-Li had personally chosen the options on the brand new aircraft normally configured to carry 12 to 15 passengers. Instead, she customized it as a long-range cruiser with four executive seats in the main cabin, a generous lavatory, and plenty of utility capability for the various cargoes they would be hauling.

The single turboprop came alive and Shin-Li taxied to the end of the runway before turning into the wind.

As expected, the former Chinese military pilot treated them to a smooth takeoff before pointing the nose west, to northern Canada.

This time they will not hurt me, he thought, flexing his right forearm muscles, which nerve endings controlled the micro pneumatic servos of the third generation iLimb prosthetic hand and wrist that surgeons in Beijing had surgically fitted to his maimed limb. To interface it, Dragan's forearm had been injected with hundreds of myoelectric sensors, which detected the muscle activity before wirelessly transmitting commands to the artificial hand. Power came from a hydrogen peroxide pneumatic system that had replaced the bulky and slow electric motors of prior generation units. The hydrogen peroxide reacted with an iridium catalyst to drive the hand's movements. Dragan simply replaced replace a small capsule of hydrogen peroxide every month in a compartment just below the thumb and he changed the even smaller iridium catalyst unit next to it once per year to keep his hand fully operational.

The climate terrorist watched as his fingers stretched before slowly curling into a tight fist. It had taken three frustrating months of therapy to control finger movement with enough dexterity to tie his own shoe laces, type on a computer, and even handle a knife or firearm as expertly as he could with his right hand. Plus the iLimb included a rotating thumb, which allowed him more freedom of movement than his real hand and a stronger grip. And to top it all off, the iLimb looked as real as his biological hand, down to the flesh color, veins, hair, and fingernails.

But it was the fingers of his right hand that Dragan used to feel the scar tissue on his abdomen, just below the sternum, where four American bullets had ripped it open filling his stomach and intestines with molten lead. Dragan no longer could eat like a normal human being after Chinese surgeons removed his damaged digestive system, leaving him with very little of his stomach and the ability to process most foods. Nourishment now came in the form of liquids he took orally or intravenously.

Dragan lowered his only natural limb to touch his artificial legs, amputated above the knees after gangrene set in before Shin-Li could reach the hospital in China. The third generation prosthetics, also from iLimb, operated on the same principle as his artificial hand, detecting the movement of his remaining thigh muscles for control and also powered by hydrogen peroxide capsules and iridium catalysts.

But it was his face that bothered him the most. He had lost the right side to an explosive round, forcing him to get fitted with a flesh-colored carbon fiber mask, fake hair, and a third-generation lens that wasn't quite as sharp as his undamaged eye, but provided him with the peripheral vision and depth perception he had lost on that dreaded day on Jakobshavn's Isbræ.

Dragan looked at his reflection on the Cessna's oval side window, cringing in an anger he seldom showed. Plastic surgeons had done what they could to mold the carbon fiber and transplanted tissues to match the left side of his face, but the overall effect was more android-like than human.

Dragan closed his eyes in fury at the world for robbing his father of his due credit, for ridiculing him, for pushing him to the edge, to commit suicide.

And for robbing me of my humanity.

As Shin-Li reached their cruising altitude high above a layer of broken clouds, Dragan Kiersted opened his eyes and stared into the distant horizon.

This time it will be different.

This time the Americans will not hurt me.

But I will hurt them, again.

And again.

And the fifty-year-old Soviet technology safely strapped in the rear compartment may just provide him with the means to scorch the world, to eradicate the disease that was the human race and give the Earth a fresh beginning.

This one is for you, father.

This one is for you and for the Earth!

7 The Fist of God

"And there were lightning, and voices, and thundering, and an earthquake, and great hail."
--Revelation 8:12

FURTWÄNGLER GLACIER. NEAR THE SUMMIT OF MOUNT KILIMANJARO. TANZANIA.

July 9, 2019.

It happened suddenly.

The crystal lattice formed 11,000 years ago cracked along the eastern rim of the towering headwall.

Multiple fissures channeled surface meltwater down to the base of the ice sheet, lubricating its contact with the bedrock, allowing the gravitational pull to exceed the opposing surface friction.

The moulin--the widening cleft in the ice--swallowed blue streams of grit-laden water in a cascading rush at the heart of Furtwängler's rapidly expanding ablation zone.

Decades of relentless warming and decreased sun-blocking snow tore through the heart of the last ice sheet in Africa, the final pocket of white on Mount Kilimanjaro as molecular bonds disintegrated by the trillions, deforming the crystal lattice, turning ice into slush; turning slush into rivers gushing out from beneath the hydroplaning glacier.

And the moulin widened.

Resembling a bolt of lightning in slow motion, the rift propagated across the ice like a ravenous cancer, devouring foaming torrents of deep-blue water across the icescape while spreading its jagged tentacles in all directions, fracturing the surface like a collapsing windshield; and going deeper, to the base of the glacier.

Yielding to heat and gravity, Furtwängler trembled, struggling to remain whole, resisting the forces pulling it apart, rapidly losing its grip on the inclined bedrock as the deluge percolating from the surface released its brakes.

❄

The soul-numbing crash rattled Dr. Konrad Malone from his malaria-induced sleep.

The ice Gideon . . . monitor the--

The loud explosion that followed tipped his cot, the sound reverberating inside his tent, pounding his eardrums.

Malone tumbled to the ground, skinning both palms as he broke the fall. He tried to stand but fell again as another explosion shook the rocky terrain beneath him.

Sweet Mother of--

The ensuing shockwave ripped through the canvas, exposing the surreal sight outside while pushing him back with animal strength, as if the Fist of God had punched him squarely on the chest, knocking the wind out of him, striking him down, leaving him gasping for air curled up on the gravel floor.

Beyond the shredded canvas a thick column of ice three stories high broke away from the collapsing headwall, striking a rock formation a fifty feet from him, roaring while breaking up on impact in a deadly avalanche of car-size blocks careening down the steep mountainside, accelerated by a deafening wave of icy water shooting out from beneath the glacier, shattering into smaller chunks amidst clouds of white foam, disappearing from view.

Stumbling to his feet, Konrad Malone struggled to clear his mind. He needed to get out, had to exit the tent, gain perspective, define an escape path.

He looked about him, realizing he wasn't in the operations tent in front of the glacier anymore.

Gideon and Lashi must have carried me to--

Gideon and Lashi! Where are--

A massive sheet of ice tore away from the glacier's sidewall with a high-pitch shriek, almost as if crying out to the heavens in a final moment of agony, briefly looming over him just as Furtwängler shifted.

Malone stared at it with frozen terror, the sheer magnitude and proximity of the tilting wall of ice gripping his senses, savagely humbling him as he momentarily recognized his tiny reflection standing in the middle of the collapsed tent facing this glistening monster.

Instead of leaning downhill, the colliding forces of the glacier pushed the seceding ice wall towards the safety camp.

Towards a stunned Konrad Malone.

The glaciologist dashed away from the doomed tent, from the massive blast shaking the bedrock beneath his bare feet as the exploding frozen barrage swallowed his tent seconds later in a cloud of glacial shrapnel.

Malone ran, ignoring the gravel stinging his feet, the shards of ice slashing him with the power of a hundred whips. He had to get away; had to--

The shockwave kicked him in the back, bending him like a bow, lifting him off his feet, tossing him into the larger dining tent, which collapsed on impact.

More ice separated from the headwall as it gathered speed, breaking up in motion while following the steep contour of Mount Kilimanjaro, its sheer mass setting off a gust of wind that lifted the canvas where he lay dazed, confused, tossing him up several feet in the air.

Malone looked about him as the exploding glacier, the sky, and the flapping canvas below him changed places again and again in a nauseating whirl until he struck something soft, briefly cushioning his fall.

Fighting the sudden urge to vomit, Malone staggered once more to his feet in the middle of the dining tent, scrambling away from the wintry onslaught behind him.

The incessant Arctic volleys from the collapsing ice sheet, like a bombardment of hand grenades detonating in uncontrolled fashion all around him, pounded his eardrums as he kicked harder against the terrain grinding the bottoms of his feet.

But he persisted, ignoring it all--the blasts, the avalanches, the scraping gravel, the roaring glacier, his growing dizziness, the thought that Natasha had been right in her repeated warnings about operating so close to the doomed glacier.

Be careful, Koni. Furtwängler can go at any moment with you on it drilling for--

More explosions rumbled across the safety camp, shredding tents and destroying equipment; the blinding-white hail-laden salvos battered him, smacked him, and pushed him into a small communications tent at the farthest edge of the camp.

Malone braced himself for impact as he flew sideways for a dozen feet, hands on his face to protect it from the flesh-ripping ice, sinking his right torso into the canvas, which wrapped around him, momentarily lessening the blow before a hard object rammed into his gut, bending him in half.

Coiled in a fetal position, quivering, gasping for air, his arms, chest, and back slashed and bruised by the ice, Konrad Malone watched through tears the doomed glacier rushing downhill in a death spiral amidst ground-trembling bursts of silver and white beneath the African sky.

Scourged, his weakened body whipped raw, no longer capable of running, Malone surrendered to nature and simply lay there as the avalanche lurched towards the valley thousands of feet below, its ear-piercing roar steadily dwindling, receding into a distant low rumble, before vanishing altogether, replaced by the whistling wind sweeping over the rocky ledge where the glacier had lived since the end of the last Ice Age.

Malone stared at the naked bedrock in silence, breathing in and out, swallowing, the realization of what he had just witnessed overshadowed by the sheer disbelief that he had actually survived this.

But where are Gideon and Lashi?

Malone did not recall hearing them in the past two minutes, though the roaring ice would have drowned their cries.

We will get you help, Koni-man. We will get you help soon.

Malone remembered now.

Gideon had indicated they would get help, meaning they must have left him alone.

He checked his watch, realizing he had been sleeping for nearly 24 hours.

Maybe they did leave to get help for me and will be back soon?

Maybe they did survive this.

Konrad Malone could only hope that they had, but whatever the answer, he recognized that although he had survived this, for the time being he was alone, and it was not clear when help would arrive.

But through the shock and the pain, through his throbbing abdomen and lacerated body, through the terrifying near-death experience, Malone had another realization: The secrets trapped in Furtwängler were safe; they were alive in the core samples he had taken for the past months.

And in them, forever frozen in time, lay the proof he needed to warn the world of the upcoming nightmare.

But first you need to get to the proof, to the core samples.

Malone needed to reach the basement labs of the University of Alaska, Fairbanks, where the bulk of the ice he extracted from the vanished glacier resided.

Hidden in the layers of dust trapped by millennia of glacial activity was the proof he needed to convince and prepare the world for the apocalyptic events the planet would face very soon.

The climate problems plaguing the world today would be child's play compared to the terrifying events that would unfold over the next few years, the same Biblical nightmare Egypt experienced four thousand years ago.

8 Divine Kingship

"Have the wisdom to abandon the values of a time that has passed and pick out the constituents of the future. An environment must be suited to the age and men to their environment."
--Ancient Egyptian proverb found in the temples of Luxor.

MEMPHIS, EGYPT
(CAPITAL OF THE OLD KINGDOM, 12 MILES SOUTH OF
MODERN-DAY CAIRO).

2210 B.C.

He had never seen so much spilled blood in his forty years as pharaoh of Egypt.

Pepi II Neferkare stared at the crimson pool surrounding the altar coagulating in the mid-morning sun.

The sacrifices began shortly before dawn, the coolest time of the day, before the scorching heat forced most to seek the shelter offered by the thick limestone walls of pyramids and temples.

One by one young slave women furnished with fine linen, lapis beads, gold necklaces, and ivory and turquoise bracelets had been escorted in complete secrecy by his personal guards up the steps of the Temple of Ptah, the creator god of Memphis' holy triad.

One by one the slaves' backs had been forced onto the smooth granite surface of the altar and held down while the chief priest and his entourage standing behind him carved out their beating hearts, which he offered to Ptah.

The middle-age pharaoh inhaled deeply.

It was here, at the terraced summit of the Djoser Complex of the necropolis of Saqqara, on the outskirts of Memphis, out of sight from his decimated people, where Neferkare carried on this extreme ritual.

The desperate measures of a desperate man.

He looked out into the distance at the meeting point of the Nile Valley and the Delta, as well as at the capital of the most powerful empire on Earth, erected hundreds of years ago by Min, the legendary first king of Egypt who unified the north and south kingdoms.

Now a force not from man but from the angered gods threatened to destroy centuries of prosperity.

But he couldn't understand their anger as he returned his stare at the slaughter before him. None of his priests, his scribes, his scientists--even his closest advisors--could conjure an explanation.

Neferkare sighed.

Three of his wives had accompanied him this morning, and so far two had left in shame. Iput II, his youngest consort and also his niece, had started vomiting and had to be escorted out. Neith, his half-sister wife had fainted at the sight of so much blood and was carried back to her chambers. Only Udjebten remained, the oldest of his wives, but still ten years her junior, sitting still and quite pale, her crimson lips trembling, her eyes filled with tears.

They are all weak, he thought, *and their offspring are weak.*

Neferkare ruled by divine kingship, seen by all in Egypt as the mediator between the gods and the people, who held him accountable for controlling the yearly floods of the Nile, enabling the agriculture that fed his nation.

The pharaoh and his family had to be strong for Egypt, especially in present times when the Nile's yearly floods had shrunk significantly as clouds thinned and rainfall decreased, resulting in less and less arable land, diminishing produce, triggering hunger--famine in some regions--and civil unrest.

The very source of life for Egypt was vanishing in front of his frustrated eyes, and all of his spells, all of his offerings, and all of his sacrifices would not appease Ptah.

The Nile floods would not stop receding season after season.

The rainfall would not increase.

The relentless heat would not stop, even in the winter.

Former fertile grounds were rapidly turning into arid tundra and desert, spreading famine and disease.

And he was surrounded by a family of weaklings, royals who had grown fat and complacent and lacked the stomach to do what needed to be done.

It was at times like this that Pepi II Neferkare wished for his mother, the legendary Ankhesenpepi II, who upon the death of her husband, Pharaoh Merenre, when Neferkare had just been born, kept Egypt together by force and ruled as regent until Neferkare turned six years old. She then continued to advice him until her death twenty years later.

I miss you, mother, he thought, having spent most of his adult life searching for a worthy queen among his many beautiful but inadequate wives, who in turn birthed and reared feeble offspring.

Holding the crook and the flail as icons of royalty, Neferkare dropped his gaze to the thick bracelets hugging his wrists. They were made of gold from Nubia and sported lapis falcons symbolizing the god Horus inlaid with precious stones from the deserts of Egypt and neighboring countries. The crook in his left hand, a cane with a hooked handle, gold-plated and reinforced with blue copper bands, represented his control over Egypt, his right to rule. The flail in his right hand, a solid gold rod with three attached beaded strands of precious stones, represented his benevolence and wisdom. The crook and flail and the bracelets, along with an equally ornate and heavy necklace in the shape of a falcon with its wings spread, and his gold and copper headdress sporting a blue Horus above his forehead, telegraphed him as pharaoh of Egypt wherever he went.

And Neferkare had used this divine power his entire life to enforce the law in the name of Maat, the goddess of truth, morality, and justice.

Just as his mother had taught him.

He briefly closed his eyes.

Truth, Morality, and Justice for the benefit of the citizens of Egypt.

And that's precisely what he did today, lifting the crook at each female slave brought forth before him, sentencing them to death for the greater good of his people He needed to appease Ptah and return the floods of the Nile for the benefit of his loyal subjects. The army of male slaves dying by the thousands each month building ever-greater temples and pyramids was not enough, forcing him to resort to this dark ritual.

Truth, Morality, and Justice.

By his feet lay a young cheetah, a gift from Harkhuf, governor of the city of Aswan and one of his most trusted generals and advisors, during one of his many expeditions into Nubia this past year. In fact, Harkhuf was charioting down to Nubia once again in search of more slaves.

The cheetah had been one of several brought back by Harkfuf and raised by Neferkare's personal handlers, who turned the wild beast into one of his favorite exotic pets accompanying him this steamy morning along with the two falcons perched on either side of his large throne.

The cheetah, the only female in the litter, stared at her master for a moment before growling at Udjebten, who, like the rest of his wives, were frightened of the beast, to the delight of Neferkare, who despised them all for failing to produce a suitable successor to the throne.

Neferkare raised his eyes as the guards escorted the next female slave onto the terrace. Unlike those preceding her, this one did not attempt to fight back, holding her head high. Her stance was proud, royal-like, and her strides elegant. She bowed gracefully when presented to him.

Neferkare hesitated a moment, sensing he had seen her before but failing to remember, finally raising the crook, condemning her just as he had every other female slave this morning.

The guards dragged her away, lifting her light frame and slamming her against the flat surface of the altar.

And unlike the other slaves, she didn't utter a scream, a complaint, a plea, further intriguing the pharaoh.

As the guards held her by the ankles and wrists, the high priest ripped open her linen garment, exposing her young breasts. Her dark-olive chest heaved as he loomed over her clutching a serrated copper blade.

She was beautiful indeed, probably not older than sixteen or seventeen but already a woman, with fine Nubian features, captivating light-green eyes, and lips the color of rubies.

Truth, morality, and justice, my son.

The words echoed in his mind as the young woman's eyes, encased in heavy dark makeup, widened when the tip of the blade touched the smooth flesh just below her left nipple. It was indeed a shame that such beauty had to perish by the sword, but Neferkare had to sacrifice the slaves for the benefit of the citizens, of the royals, of his armies.

At that moment, just as the chief cleric raised the blade to make the initial cut, Neferkare recognized the skin paint on her exposed right shoulder. It was the seated figure of the goddess Hathor, placed only on Nubian royalty.

She made eye contact with Neferkare, who suddenly remembered her from Harkhuf's last campaign in northern Nubia a month ago. She had been the only daughter of the noble chief ruling the region.

A Nubian princess.

Royalty!

Neferkare raise the flail in his right hand, an action that immediately stopped the priest just as he nicked the skin, making her twitch on the stone.

His beliefs in truth, morality, and justice could not allow him to slaughter royalty, irrespective of it being Egyptian, Nubian, Syrian, or Arabian.

Slaves were dispensable, to be sacrificed in any way imaginable to appease angered gods.

But royalty was royalty.

They did not die by the sword unless in battle defending Egypt or if guilty of high crime or treason.

The pharaoh gestured for her to lie by his feet, next to the cheetah, and action that earned him a curious glance from Udjebten sitting by his side. But the lavishly-dressed woman didn't dare utter a single word.

Udjebten, in her thirty-fifth year of age, had birthed him four useless children; three insolent daughters whom Neferkare had finally gotten married by forcing three of his captains to do so or face castration, and a son who was too weak to serve in the military, too stupid to study the sciences, and lacking the sense and wisdom required to be king.

The guards complied immediately, lifting her light frame off the altar and depositing her gently in front of the godking.

A single drop of blood trickling down the right side of her chest, the Nubian princess hugged his feet and kissed them, before raising her appreciative gaze to him while placing a hand on the cheetah's head, stroking it gently, pleasantly surprising the pharaoh--and shocking Udjebten, who released a barely audible gasp.

The high priest was momentarily confused, before understanding his terrible mistake and immediately dropping to his knees seeking forgiveness.

"My lord, my god," the Nubian princess said with a deep and sensuous voice that belonged to a goddess. "I am prepared to die for you if my death can bring rain and prosperity to Egypt."

Albeit impressed, and immensely delighted for annoying Udjebten, Neferkare simply nodded. The Nubian wasn't afraid of death, and she certainly didn't fear the large cat and the massive fangs that could disembowel her in an instant.

Strength.

Neferkare saw courage in her eyes, in her pose as she sat not like a slave, but like royalty.

Harkfuf had reported that her father had fought courageously during the two-week siege of the border city of Buhen, resisting with an intensity he had not seen in years. But the Buhen militia had been no match for Egypt's superior war machine, Harkhuf's trained army. Her father and his militia had perished in the end, resulting in the capture of many slaves, which Neferkare used to build his monuments, to augment Memphis' power and beauty.

Power and beauty.

The Nubian princess, mistaken by the clergy as a slave--a crime carrying the punishment of death by dismemberment--certainly possessed both, and that meant that in addition to providing him with pleasure following days like today, she could also birth him strong and beautiful children, mixed royals who, albeit may never become pharaohs, could still ascend to positions of leadership in his government, in his armies, and whom his country would need to lead Egypt after his death. Such Nubian-Egyptian children could also prove valuable in future negotiations with Egypt's large neighbor to the south.

The high priest, still prostrated by Neferkare, Udjebten, and the princess, awaited his fate.

Neferkare decided to test the Nubian's royal acumen by pointing at the high priest while locking eyes with her. She immediately placed a hand over his right bracelet, which hand clutched the flail.

Motioning the relieved cleric to continue, Neferkare gestured the brave and merciful princess to watch as the guards dragged the next slave, also Nubian, onto the terrace.

This one was a bit older than the princess and quite feisty, like the ones he had ordered slaughtered through the morning, tugging and shoving to free herself from her captors.

Neferkare lifted the crook.

The guards slammed her onto the altar, her back and head crashing against the rock, blood immediately spurting from a gash on her skull, soaking her hair, stunning her as the priest tore off her tunic, exposing breasts larger than the princess', who had already draped the torn garment over her exposed skin, protecting her regency.

Still in a daze, the Nubian slave slowly moved her bleeding head from side to side lethargically as the cleric brought the knife slowly over her bronze skin, pressing its serrated tip against her smooth skin but without piercing it, locating the exact spot for the incision.

He quickly sank the blade, blood jetting, arresting her from the head-crash-induced stupor.

Remembering where she was, realizing what was being done to her, the slave kicked and screamed, refusing to accept her fate, fingers tense as she tugged at the vice-like grips of the muscular guards, trying to resist as the priest cut deeper into her chest, blood gushing, staining her frayed garment.

Neferkare checked on the princess, who maintained her poise, chin up, gaze steady on the altar just as she had been commanded by her lord, a hand slowly rubbing his feet while the other tenderly stroked the cheetah, who was now resting its large head on her lap, eyes closed.

Incredible, he thought. Not once in his life had he witnessed such display of sensuous courage by another woman besides his beautiful and powerful mother, Ankhesenpepi II.

The priest cut deeper, pressing her waist against the rock as blood and foam exploded through her mouth, through her nostrils, drowning her cries as she writhed and coughed, spraying his white tunic crimson.

Udjebten leaned forward and vomited before collapsing on her side sobbing and shaking. A pair of chamber maids rushed to her side.

Neferkare rolled his eyes before shifting his gaze to the princess, who stoically continued to watch the carnage while the maids took Udjebten away.

The slave jerked a hand free, stretching it towards the princess. "Nitocris! My princess! Please have mercy! Please help--"

A guard slapped her twice, grabbing her wrist, regaining control as the cleric hacked across her chest.

She coughed, crimson froth bursting through her lips.

Neferkare once more looked at the Nubian royal whom the slave had called Nitocris. He admired her poise, her graceful strength as she continued petting the cat; the control she exhibited in the face of the butchering of someone she apparently knew.

Her face smeared in blood, the dying slave screamed her name again and again, fingers stretched at Nitocris, until the guard punched her across the temple, silencing her.

Memphis' chief cleric continued, beads of sweat filming his face as he carved, sawing through bone and cartilage in a semi circle, blood soaking the torn fabric, dripping to the limestone floor.

The Nubian coughed more blood in between guttural grunts, convulsing, her eyes briefly losing focus before staring directly at Nitocris, who remained impassive.

The slave tensed, tugged at the strong hold of the guards, tried to twist herself free, for an instant managing to pull her chest back, away from the blade.

But the priest regained control, digging deeper but with care. It was important not to damage the heart during the procedure. It had to be pulsating when offered to Ptah.

The slave tried to escape her fate one final time to no avail, chest heaving, taking in slurry breaths as she drowned in her own blood, as she became sluggish, surrendering to the sharp metal.

The priest released her pelvis and sunk his free hand in the chest cavity while working the copper tool with the other, ignoring her dying moans, her gasping sobs, the whites of her eyes, the tongue hanging out of her mouth as if possessed by a demon.

Her back bent like a bow and her lungs wheezed out a final shriek, calling out for the Nubian princess, as he made the final cut, severing the heart, plucking it out still pulsating from the serrated void, holding it over her as she collapsed back on the altar already a corpse, dead eyes staring into the distance.

He first offered the throbbing organ to Neferkare before setting it by the foot of Ptah's marble statue, where it beat for a few silent moments.

As the guards dragged the body away, another girl slave was escorted onto the terraced summit.

Truth, morality, and justice.

The pharaoh hated being forced to reenact such terrifying practice for the first time in hundreds of years that he had forbidden its recording, dismissing the scribes and sculptors that always followed him to capture his daily ruling on papyrus and in stone for all posterity. Neferkare had decreed the worse form of death to anyone who ever spoke or recorded the events that had taken place this past week, the slaughter of hundreds of young female slaves--virgins--from Nubia, Syria, Libya, and Arabia to appease an unappeasable Ptah.

Sitting on a throne of carved wood inlaid with silver, gold, and an assortment of stones--amethysts, lapis lazuli, garnets and jaspers--beneath the shade of a bright-green linen canopy and fanned by petrified Syrian female slaves, the godking contemplated the statue of Ptah, standing tall next to that of Ptah's wife, Sekhmet, goddess of war.

War.

Ptah was lucky to have by his side such zealous and beautiful wife. Sekhmet was the icon of strength in a country that urgently needed firm and decisive leadership.

Neferkare stood, an action that forced many to their knees, heads against the stone floor, including the Nubian princess. His personal guards--ten of them--and the Syrian slaves holding large fans made of colorful peacock feathers remained standing by royal decree.

The heavily armed guards always shadowed Neferkare, ready to sacrifice their lives for the godking. The female slaves followed Neferkare with orders to never stop cooling him. A breeze should always caress the skin of the chosen one.

Neferkare leaned down and touched the hand of the Nubian princess. "Come," he said. "Stand by my side."

"My lord," Nitocris replied, standing with grace, a hand keeping her tunic closed, the other held by Neferkare. She was as tall as him, with a swan-like neck, a triangular face, high cheekbones and a fine nose over moist lips that awakened something in the forty-six-year-old pharaoh.

He snapped his fingers once and two maids produced fresh linen garments and a carved-wood bowl filled with jewelry. Every soul on that terrace except for the two chamber maids looked away and froze as they removed Nitocris' shredded tunic, exposing her recently waxed body to him, devoid of any hair except for the lush black waves framing her dark-olive face.

Neferkare held up a hand, prompting the maids to pause and also look away.

The pharaoh and the Nubian princess faced each other in the late-morning breeze, the world around them temporarily immobilized, forbidden from gazing at them, and completely immobilized, as if time had stopped by his hand.

He touched the tip of his tongue with his index finger, wetting it before softly rubbing off the trickle of blood below her left breast.

She shuddered at his divine touch, for the first time displayed an emotion, her eyes filling as she said, "Thank you, my lord."

Neferkare would have her tonight, and the night after that, and the night after that, until she birthed him a worthy successor.

Satisfied, he gave his command to the maids, who dressed her in a beautiful gold gown and matching sandals, bracelets, rings, and necklaces.

The effect magnified her regent presence, her bronze skin radiating a glow that challenged the sun, her emerald, cat-like eyes narrowing as she offered him a brief smile.

Satisfied, Neferkare ordered time to continue on the terrace.

The priest began to slaughter the slave on the altar, the sawing and slicing of bones and muscle, the harrowing screams fading as he lost himself in Nitocris' captivating eyes, in her parted lips.

Could this be the one, mother?

The godking took a deep breath and held her hand as they walked towards two warriors kneeling by the edge of the terrace, messengers from Harkfuf, whom Neferkare had dispatched last week on another Nubian expedition to seize more slaves.

The warriors wore dark wrap-around kilts and reed sandals. Their chariot and weapons--copper swords, spears, daggers, bows and arrows--were parked in the Great Courtyard under the sizzling sun by the foot of the steps leading to the terrace. No one could approach Neferkare armed, except for his personal guards, whose loyalty was guaranteed through their families, their mothers, fathers, wives, and kids. Neferkare would have all his guards' families tortured and slaughtered should any one of them harm him in any way.

"Rise," Neferkare commanded, flanked by his guards while the Syrian slaves kept up their incessant fanning. It wasn't even noon and the heat had already grown unbearable in the shade.

The two warriors complied, standing.

"What news do you bring from Harkfuf?"

The oldest warrior produced a small papyrus scroll, which he unrolled and began to read.

Neferkare remained impassive as the messenger conveyed the general's report, which, to Neferkare's surprise didn't describe his Nubian slave-hunting campaign. Rather, the messenger described the severe drought in several regions north of Nubia which were forcing Nomarchs, regional representatives of Neferkare, to take control of their estates, assuming responsibility for maintaining order, and threatening to splinter Egypt into feudal states.

"General Harkfuf requests a reinforcement of chariots to quench the insurgency, my lord," the messenger concluded, rolling the scroll. "The Nomarchs are growing too strong in the south."

Neferkare maintained his stoic composure but internally he was enraged.

Memphis needs slaves!

The intense heat and lack of water was killing them faster than he could replenish them. And now Harkfuf was having difficulty reaching Nubia. His mission south had been interrupted by Neferkare's own Nomarchs--his own nobles whom he had personally empowered with lands, wealth, slaves, and militias to be his representatives in the outer reaches of the empire. Now those same Nomarchs were challenging his divine rule, slapping the very hand that had enabled them.

Such treachery, punishable by the worst kind of death for all perpetrators and their families, would be dealt with swiftly and publicly to set a much needed example for all Nomarchs in Egypt.

Neferkare ruled, dispatching a contingent of five hundred chariots and three thousand soldiers to the region to restore the peace and bring the offending Nomarchs and their families back to Memphis to face their nightmarish punishment.

But as he felt the infuriating heat against his tanned skin, as the high priest held up yet another beating heart to an unmerciful Ptah, as the fertile valleys bordering the Nile dwindled with each passing season, something told Neferkare that such punishment would not matter in the long run. Something told him such Nomarch insurgencies would become the norm.

The hands of his priests were crimson from the spilled blood of incessant human sacrifice. The backs of his slaves were raw from hauling the stones of massive structures rising up to the heavens to pacify the gods. His people were starving. His armies grew restless. The Nomarchs were increasing their stronghold and starting to rebel against Memphis.

His nation was slowly disintegrating.

But the clouds would not return.

The rain would not fall on his land.

His divine power would not return the floods.

The god-king of a dying world stared into the distance, growing angry at the gods, at the unfairness of his situation, before doing the only thing he could against an enemy that didn't fight with swords and chariots.

The final pharaoh of the Sixth Dynasty of Egypt's unified Old Kingdom signaled his priests to bring forth the next slave to the sacrificial altar.

9 Regrets

"Day doth daily draw my sorrows longer, and night doth nightly make grief's length seem stronger"
--Sir William Shakespeare.

31,000 FEET OVER NORTHERN GERMANY.

July 10, 2019

"How did you get into this business?"

Erika looked up from the FlexScreen on her lap, where she had been reviewing the latest incarnation of the CIA plan to capture arms dealer Andrei Vorota in Moscow.

She stared at Case Montana's dark eyes as he sat across from her in the club-style seating of the main cabin of one of the CIA jets. This particular one, a Citation X manufactured by Cessna, had been customized as an airborne operations center, complete with dedicated satellite links to connect it to the massive servers in the basement of the CIA headquarters in Langley, Virginia. Three CIA operators in the rear of the cabin sat at workstations linked to Langley via satellite working out the final preparations before landing at the Russian capital in one hour.

She considered his question a moment and said, "I couldn't afford college, so I got Uncle Sam to pay for it. Growing up in Denver, I'd loved the outdoors, the ice, so I picked glaciology at the University of Colorado. After graduation, the Navy sent me to Antarctica for ten years to pay my debt. I fell in love with the place, just as I had with winters in Colorado, and when I heard about the potential threat of global terrorism, I decided to do something about it. Through friends in the Pentagon I got connected with the CIA climate counterterrorism team, and the rest is history."

He nodded before staring out of his window at a magnificent dawn. They had reached the embassy just past midnight and by three in the morning they were at Charles de Gaulle International Airport, where the jet was waiting to take them to Moscow.

"So you're here to save the world? To make a difference?"

She shrugged. "You could say that."

"Would you do it over again?" he asked, eyes still on the indigo sky stained with orange and crimson.

She tilted her head. "What kind of question is that?"

"Back in that alley," he said, "you seemed very sad, and not just at the lost of your former colleague. I didn't sense much lost love there. It was something else, almost as if you regretted your life."

She stared at him, puzzled that he had been able to read her so well.

"My life's a package deal," she replied. "But it's for a good cause, though at times it does feel like a losing battle."

"How so? Don't you believe that at the end of the day your work makes a difference for the better?"

"Didn't seem that way after Greenland."

"You can't win them all, Erika."

"That's the thing. Those of us in climate counterterrorism must get lucky *every* time. The damned climate terrorists only need to get lucky one time . . . and we get Greenland.

He shrugged. "What's the alternative?"

"There isn't one. We need to keep hunting monsters like Dragan Kiersted to the end of the world."

"That is certainly words to live by, Erika," he replied, his gaze shifting from her back outside.

"You haven't asked me about the radiation sickness . . . it's okay, you know."

Case shrugged. "That seemed like a bit too much prying, and from I can tell it hasn't affected your ability to do your job. But, for what it's worth, I hope things haven't been to rough for you. This job is hard enough as it is."

She nodded. "I'm fine now. And thanks for taking up for me back in Paris with Payden."

Case crossed his arms and frowned while staring out the window. "Bastard had no right telling you that. In the end he got what he deserved."

Erika couldn't disagree with that, although a part of her still felt sorry for the way Payden's life had gone.

Deciding to change the subject, she asked, "How often do you get to see your kids?"

He turned back to her, arms still crossed, brows dropping, his features tightening as he narrowed his eyes. "How do you . . . never mind."

"I'm sure you read my dossier too," she said.

He nodded. "Mother died at childbirth. Father abandoned you. Raised by your grandparents in Denver. Then Colorado State, Antarctica, and the GCCU, and, of course, the stuff you went through after Greenland, before you asked to be reassigned to the Dragan case. Never been married, no kids, and no current personal relation . . . which is quite a waste if you ask me."

She smiled. "I thought you said you back in Paris that you didn't care either way."

A grin broke through his poker face and he winked. "I'm a spook. I lie for a living."

"Are you lying now?"

Case Montana suddenly turned serious. "If you weren't GCCU and I wasn't CIA, and we weren't in the middle of what could be the mission of the decade . . . and I would have walked into a bar and spotted you alone. I think I would have bought you a drink, Erika Baxter."

The comment caught her completely unprepared.

"But we are who we are," he said.

"And we are where we are," she added.

"For now anyway, and to answer your question, I don't get to see my kids very often, especially after my ex remarried a Rodeo Drive plastic surgeon and moved to LA."

She leaned forward and rested a hand on his knee, squeezing it softly. "I'm very sorry, Case."

He tilted his head. "It's all right. I wasn't a very good husband . . . or father for that matter. Hard to be there for them when you're always on some assignment around the world."

"How old are they?"

Case's face softened as he grinned while reaching into a hidden pocket in his slacks and producing two small pictures. "Cameron is fifteen and Ashley is seventeen. I was supposed to spend three weeks this summer with them but from the looks of it I doubt is going to happen."

Erika looked at the pictures. The boy looked like him, with well defined facial features, a strong chin, full lips, and dark hair to complement his dark-brown eyes and thick eyebrows. The girl was a drop-dead gorgeous blond with perfect hair, perfect skin, perfect features, and incredible blue eyes.

"Well, Cameron certainly looks like you, but not Ashley. She is quite the prom queen."

"Yep. That's her alright. Ashley looks just like Molly, my ex, who used to be a New York model. To Molly it's all about the looks, and unfortunately so it is for Ashley thanks to my wife's influence and all of the free procedures they get from the new head of the household."

She kept her hand on his knee and continued to pet him. "But they're still your babies," she said.

Case nodded with a sigh as he put the pictures away.

"When does your leave start?"

He smiled. "Tomorrow. I'm going to have to call them from Moscow and try to explain. It's not going to be pretty, and my ex doesn't really help either."

"For what is worth," she said. "I want you to know I'm here for you."

He smiled, placed a hand on top of hers and patted her gently while saying, "Well, Erika, for what is worth, happy belated birthday. And I will buy you a drink as soon as this is over."

"No, Case, I think I'm the one who needs to buy you a drink."

He narrowed his gaze at her, and for a moment she thought he saw tears welling in his eyes. The man obviously had sacrificed plenty for Uncle Sam, just like so many other unsung heroes of this war against terrorism.

"Promise?" he finally asked.

"Promise," she replied.

As they looked deeply into each other's eyes, the pilot came on the intercom announcing the start of their decent into Moscow. A contingent from the local CIA station would take them directly to the American Embassy for a brief on the intelligence gathered on Andrei Vorota.

"Ready to show the world that we still have what it takes?" she asked, pointing at her FlexScreen.

"Absolutely," he replied, his face turning back to business.

Erika squeezed his leg one last time before gently retrieving her hand. "Business before pleasure," she said, winking.

He winked back. "Business before pleasure."

10 Opposing Forces

"Climate change should be seen as the greatest challenge to face man and treated as a much bigger priority in the United Kingdom."
--Prince Charles

NORTH SLOPE BOROUGH. ALASKA.

July 10, 2019

"Loosely defined," Natasha Shakhiva said, sitting across from Colonel Marcus Stone in the mess tent of the IARC camp, "Radiative forcing is the net result between the incoming radiation energy from the sun and the outgoing radiation energy reflected back into space. These are the primary forces modulating global temperature change."

Stone bit into a turkey sandwich, chewing quickly, swallowing, before asking, "I read about that in your report. A sort of tug-of-war between positive and negative forces steering the direction of temperature change on the planet, right?"

Natasha had to give the man credit. There seemed to be a brain behind the camouflage fatigues.

"Correct," she said, tossing her salad with a plastic fork. They sat alone late in the evening trying to eat something even though neither felt like eating. The day had ended with so many methane events in the tunnel that their storage tanks were filled by noon, requiring the excess gas channeled to the burnoff vent, which, similar to those in oil refineries, released a roaring plume of orange fire atop a fifty-foot-tall chute. Even at this late hour the burnoff unit continued to consume the excess methane, casting a novel flickering glow across the camp, which Natasha saw as an omen of things to come.

Pointing at the fire beyond the screened window with her white fork, she added, "That's one of the positive forces, along with CO2 and Ozone, which absorbs some of the infrared energy emitted by the earth."

"I thought there were others."

She nodded. "But not as significant. There's nitrous oxide, halocarbons, jet contrails, and even an element of solar energy."

Stone's freckles shifted on his face beneath the orange hair while holding the sandwich with both hands. "Solar energy? I thought that was the theory of that Danish nut who was discredited by your scientific community some years ago, and whose terrorist son was responsible for Greenland."

"Henrik Kiersted," she replied, frowning. "There's actually an element of global warming tied to solar energy, but it is quite negligible compared to greenhouse gases. Kiersted claimed that solar activity significantly reduced cloud formations, which increased temperatures. And his work implied that this phenomenon shared the stage with greenhouse gases, which caused his work to be dismissed."

Stone chewed another mouthful before asking, "What are the negative radiative forces?"

"Primarily sulphate aerosols and white smoke, both of which reflect sunlight. And then there's the terrestrial albedo effect, whose total contribution to global warming is difficult to calculate with precision."

Stone lowered his sandwich and gave her a puzzled look. Since arriving here yesterday, the good colonel had been picking her brains, trying to absorb as much global climate intelligence as possible before heading back to Washington to brief the president and officially start his new job. But what amazed her was the fact that Stone didn't write anything down, yet he seemed to retain the relevant information, the elements driving global warming.

"Albedo effect?"

"The albedo of snow, for example, is 90%, meaning it reflects 90% of solar energy back into space while only absorbing 10%. At the other end of the spectrum is the albedo of fresh asphalt, the darkest surface on the planet, at 4%, meaning it absorbs 96% of the sun's heat and injects it straight into the Earth. Human activity has changed the Earth's albedo due to forest clearance, roads, and farming. On average the data suggests we are worse than we were a few decades ago, especially when you throw in the feedback loops created by the albedo effect."

Stone finished his sandwich and crumpled the plastic wrap and napkin into a tight little ball.

"What do you mean?"

"A classic example is the snow-temperature feedback loop. When an area covered with snow warms up, the snow naturally melts, decreasing that region's albedo, which causes more heat to be absorbed, and the temperature increases further, causing more snow to melt. This is also called a positive feedback loop, which is helping us understand why ice sheets and glaciers are melting at faster rates than modeled. Of course, it doesn't really help when a terrorist like Dragan Kiersted accelerates the process even more."

Stone sighed, before stretching a thumb at the column of fire burning high above the camp. "That," he said, "can't be a good thing, right Doctor?"

"No, Colonel. I'm afraid it isn't. At the moment, Carbon Dioxide has the crown for the largest positive radiating force in the atmosphere thanks to humans. The concentration of methane relative to CO_2 is quite small today, averaging less than 3%, but because it is such an effective greenhouse gas--far more effective than CO_2--its radiative force is about a third of that of CO_2. So even though methane today takes a second place to CO_2 with only a third of the radiative force even though, it does so with a very small amount of the gas present in the atmosphere relative to

CO2. And this is why the fire outside is the bearer of such terrible news. It is telling us that the permafrost shield is vaporizing in front of our eyes and no less than seventy thousand *Gigatons* of methane could be released into the atmosphere. That amount represents nearly a million times more methane than exists today, and given its massive efficiency as a greenhouse gas, it will represent a major inflection point in global warming."

"Meaning?"

"It will vastly accelerate the process. What our current models project taking decades or even centuries to happen, like sea-level rises, the melting of ice sheets, and the probable creation of new ecosystems--such as the mini ice age in Europe today--could take place in a matter of a few years. And that doesn't take into consideration the drastic reduction of oxygen in the atmosphere as it gets replaced by methane. We would be headed back to the Permian-Triassic extinction event should that happen. Initially, the worst affected areas would be where the methane gets actually released into the atmosphere, which could include massive fires if the gas is ignited by humans or by nature, like a lightning strike. Then, in the following weeks, as the fire and ashes and any methane not consumed spread down from the permafrost regions, other parts of the globe will be affected."

"I read in your brief that you and Malone believe that it was a massive methane release that triggered the Permian-Triassic extinction event?"

She slowly nodded. "We don't think it was a comet or asteroid, like what killed the dinosaurs over one hundred and fifty years later. The Permian period is marked by many clues pointing to a methane release."

She reached for her handheld FlexScreen, unfolded the screen, and tapped a few commands, bringing up the picture of a large tiger-like creature with massive cyber teeth fighting against a Dimetrodon, the famous reptile sporting a large sail-like dorsal fin. She showed it to Stone. "Here are a couple of the most memorable creatures from that time. Paleontologists have recovered many of their bones, as well as from other creatures of the same time period, and they all show high methane readings. These creatures as well as many others were exposed to high levels of methane in the atmosphere around 250 million years ago, at the end of the Permian period."

"I recognize the Dimetrodon from my kid's books," Stone said, peering at the 5-inch screen while chewing. "But that other one looks like a saber-tooth tiger. I thought they roamed the Earth much later, after the dinosaurs."

Natasha smiled. "That's correct. Saber-tooth tigers were warm-blooded mammals who lived from several years ago up to around nine thousand years ago, but certainly not hundreds of millions of years ago. The last species, called the Smilodon, is the one most people think about when they hear the words saber tooth tiger, and it shared the world with Neanderthals and Homo sapiens. This one here is called a Gorgonopsian, or Gorgo for short, and it was the top predator back in the Permian days, when the continents were all joined into a supercontinent called Pangaea. We believe Gorgos became extinct when the herbivores they preyed on died away as methane releases and subsequent fires consumed most of the Earth vegetation, killing their food supply."

"I never knew there were mammals creatures that far back."

Natasha leaned forward, planting her elbows on the table. "Technically Gorgos weren't mammals, but they were the predecessors who never got a chance to continue evolving because of the methane. Now, here is an interesting one to think about, Colonel. What would have happened to our world if the Permian-Triassic extinction event never occurred?"

Stone stopped chewing, swallowed, and made a face. "I don't follow."

"Two hundred and fifty million years ago, the first mammal-like creatures, like the Gorgos, began to roam the Earth, just like a few million years ago the early versions of the saber tooth showed up on Earth to be followed by more developed mammals, including early men. Unfortunately, life as it was developing on Earth back in the Permian period came to a crashing end, killing any possibility of further evolution, including men. The slate was wiped clean and the dinosaurs took over, until ninety million years ago, when it was wiped clean once more by an asteroid, kicking off the evolutionary process that resulted in the current species. Imagine the possibilities. What if the Permian period would have continued evolving? Mammal-like creatures would have continued to advance, perhaps into actual mammals, dominating the Earth, potentially giving the human race well over a hundred million years' head start. Imagine the possibilities. It took man just ten thousand years to develop modern civilization."

"If only," said Stone, narrowing his stare, before looking over his shoulder and asking, "And that fire outside is our early-warning signal that history is about to repeat itself?"

Natasha sighed and nodded. "It appears so, Colonel. It certainly appears so."

"Is this camp still safe, Doctor?"

Natasha looked away. She had discussed that question with Mario Escobar for most of the afternoon, soon after the burnoff started. They had arrived to the same conclusion.

"We think it is safe this year," she replied. "The permafrost's methane flux is low enough to keep most of the trapped gas contained . . . again, this year. But I can't say with certainty next year, or the year after that as the Earth gets progressively warmer. The sensors in the tunnel indicate that most of the flux into the tunnel is taking place at a depth of 140 feet or deeper with a concentration as high as 16%, which explains the steady burn, and we think it will continue to burn at least through September. After that the cold temperatures will shut off the flux until the following summer. But next year we will get just a dash warmer, meaning the permafrost will get incrementally softer and the flux will increase. The million-dollar question is when will it reach the surface, and also, will it do so evenly across the global permafrost regions?"

"That would depend on the actual depth of the pockets, right?"

"Yes, in part. But also it will depend on the corresponding rise in sea levels, which would cover some of the methane hydrates formed beneath the soil in coastal region. These are ice formations that encapsulate the gas molecules and are scattered several hundred meters deep and in fact are being mined today as a source of clean-burning energy. When sea levels rise and cover the soil, the water will warm it and melt the crystals, releasing the methane in unpredictable ways, compounding the problem."

"So the Greenland event certainly isn't helping, right?"

"Correct," she replied.

"Sounds like it's only a matter of time before . . ."

"Correct again," she said.

Stone nodded solemnly, crossed his arms, and just stared at the glowing fire casting a somewhat magical glow on the camp.

Natasha also stared at the blazing radiance outside. For reasons she could not explain, the soft glow carried with it an image of Konrad Malone, standing tall with his salt-and-pepper closely-cropped beard, pony tail, and mirror-tint sunglasses basking in the bright sun of an Alaskan summer.

She closed her eyes, wishing they were alone somewhere in the Brooks Mountain Range sharing a sleeping bag, holding her tight as the world slowly closed in on them.

Dammit, Koni. When will I see you again?

"You okay there, Doc?"

Before she could stop herself, she said, "Call me Natasha, Colonel. And no, I'm not okay. I'm missing someone." She regretted saying that the moment it came out.

Stone dropped his bushy orange brows over his eyes. "That explains the sadness I've noticed in those blue eyes since I got here yesterday, Natasha. Who's the lucky fellow?"

"Excuse me?"

For the first time since arriving there, a smile cracked the stoic face of Colonel Marcus Stone as he said, "Who is the lucky fellow who stole your heart?"

Annoyed at herself for allowing personal feelings to surface, she was considering her reply when agitated Mario Escobar, wearing a khaki cargo pants, an IARC pullover sweater, and sneakers, stormed into the mess tent hauling a black FlexScreen notebook computer.

"Mario? What's the matter?"

The middle-age Hispanic glaciologist and bush pilot, visibly agitated, set the unit on the table in between Natasha and Stone, and deployed the 19-inch screen, already depicting the still image of a bare mountain peak, which Natasha immediately recognized.

"Oh, no," she replied. "When did it happen?" she asked, her throat suddenly going dry at the thought of Konrad Malone.

"About six hours ago."

"What is it?" asked Stone, shifting his gaze between the high-resolution image and the Ukrainian scientist.

"It's Furtwängler, Colonel," she replied, controlling her emotions. "The last tropical glacier on the planet, located on Mount Kilimanjaro, has collapsed."

Natasha slowly turned to Escobar and asked, "Mario, what about, Koni?"

Instead of replying, the dark-skinned scientist shifted his gaze to the screen while tapping the REWIND button, which caused the image to come alive showing a video in fast reverse, depicting an avalanche of crumbling ice looming at the bottom of the screen while making its way up the peak, covering it while hardening. "That's what I wanted to show you," he finally said, stopping the image and hitting the PLAY button on the screen. "Here are the final moments of the glacier as recorded by our satellites."

Her vision tunneling, her heartbeat pounding against her temples, Natasha forced herself to watch as rifts streaked across the ice sheet, as its headwall collapsed in bursts of white before tumbling downhill.

Escobar panned to the right side of the screen while zooming in, nearly filling the display with an aerial view of the safety camp, a dozen tents and carts of equipment scattered across a bare rock clearing next to the right end of the ice sheet.

What followed was nearly impossible to believe: a lone figure racing away from the collapsing glacier, which shifted while breaking up, causing massive boulders to crash by the rocky slope on the outskirts of the camp, avalanching over tents and equipment. The single figure disappeared in the resulting haze before emerging again, scrambling in obvious frantic, getting tossed about by resulting shockwaves, only to get up again and again, until finally crashing into a tent on the opposite end of the camp as the ice sheet disappeared from view.

"That's Koni," Natasha said with certainty. "That's him. I can feel it in my--"

"Who is Koni?" interrupted Stone.

"Konrad Malone, Colonel," replied Escobar while Natasha felt as if she were having an out-of-body experience, the feeling reminiscent of getting the news about Sergei three years before.

This can't be happening to me! Not again!

"How can you be so certain?" asked Escobar while Stone watched her closely, his eyes mere slits of genuine concern.

Taking a deep breath, her voice beginning to crack, she said, "Only someone as experienced, hard-headed, and *damned lucky* as Koni Malone would have survived something like that."

"Whoever he is," replied Escobar, "satellite coverage shows that he hasn't moved in six hours. Perhaps--"

"Perhaps *my ass*, Mario!" she snapped, losing her patience. "That's him! He *is* alive, and we need to get him the hell out of there! Get it?"

Escobar blinked and quickly nodded. "Su--sure, Tasha. I will start making calls right away," he replied, closing the system.

She crossed her arms, fell back on her chair, and exhaled heavily before adding, "We need a chopper on that mountain cliff within the hour, Mario. It's already been six hours. We don't have time to spare!"

As Escobar scurried away, Stone regarded Natasha with intriguing eyes beneath his freckled forehead.

"What?" she asked, feeling color coming to her cheeks, her throat tight with feelings she found difficult to suppress.

Stone leaned forward and said, "Well, Natasha, that Konrad Malone is indeed one *lucky* fellow. Would you also like me to make some calls?"

Unable to prevent her eyes from filling, she replied, "I lost my husband three years ago. I can't lose him too."

He placed a hand over hers and said, "Call me Marcus, Natasha. We will find Konrad Malone and get him home."

11 Cold Heart

"Warm weather fosters growth: cold weather destroys it."
--Hung Tzu-Cheng.

MOSCOW, RUSSIA.

July 10, 2019

The heavy base echoing off the red-brick walls reverberated in Andrei Vorota's chest as he sipped a Bacardi mojito at a reserved corner booth next to the spacious dance floor at one of Moscow's first and most popular nightclubs, the Propaganda Café, located two blocks from Lubyanskaya Square and just five blocks from the legendary Red Square in the heart of the city.

For the past decade, as most cities in Europe, starting with Paris, declined in the quality of life due to the influx of African and Middle-Easter immigrants, Moscow flourished, in part because Russia had closed its borders to all refugees. And last year's event in Greenland, which dropped temperatures across Europe, had made Moscow even more desirable than ever because the weather patterns controlled by the Gulf Stream didn't impact Moscow much--or other northern Europe cities for that matter. To Muscovites like Vorota, a ten-degree drop in temperatures meant just another layer of clothing. This place was always cold, and therefore it was designed to handle it, meaning that life pretty much went unchanged while the most of southern Europe, in particular France, Spain, Portugal, and Italy froze to death.

It was expatriate night at the *Propaganda*, meaning a lot of single clubbers from the large international community who were doing business in the Russian capital gathered here to blow off steam and mix it up with the locals while dancing to an energetic and eclectic selection of Pop, Rap, and Salsa, tunes by the three DJs working behind the glass booth high above the illuminated floor.

On this lively night, English was the language of choice. Those who spoke it well had the best chance to get lucky. Those who didn't were typically frowned upon as local illiterate trash not worthy of mingling with the wave of affluent, well-dressed, and mostly lonely foreigners. But to get in you still had to get past the bulky doormen controlling access to the club from the long line already formed outside, which by now almost reached Lubyanskaya Square.

Just as Vorota finished his mojito one of his two armed bodyguards was cruising back from the bar with another one, which mixing he personally supervised to ensure the longevity of one of Russia's wealthiest black-market arms dealers.

Dressed in a gray double-breasted Armani suit, Berluti loafers, no tie, a diamond-studded Hammer and Sickle pendant hanging from a gold chain around his thick neck, and a Patek Philippe watch worth more than his armored Mercedes sedan, Vorota ignored the twin local whores giggling next to him while reaching for the fresh drink, which he sipped slowly as he watched a foreign woman, presumably American, dancing alone at the edge of the floor.

She wore a black cocktail dress which he recognized as classic Versace and black Manolo Blahnik high-heels at the end of shapely legs; a single strand of black pearls adorned her neck. Her shoulder-length auburn hair framed a soft face accented with fine dark make-up, including a pair of full lips she compressed while dancing with her eyes closed.

Vorota, tanned, moisturized, and groomed to metro-sexual levels, watched with growing interest as she pouted ever so slightly but in a way that aroused him far more than the clinically enhanced courtesan sisters he had hired for the evening, and who had long failed to warm his cold heart beyond brief carnal pleasures.

But the woman dancing seemed different, capable of taking him places the whores never would. And he decided it was her eyes, an angelic hazel, which gripped him as she slowly opened them, flapping her long lashes twice before closing them again, immersed in the music, moving her tight body with subtle grace. Even his bodyguards, stoically standing at each end of the booth ready to spring into action for their principal, seemed to be enjoying the show.

She wasn't young, like the twin Slavic beauties cuddling by his side, but appeared more in her mid thirties, though whatever she lacked in youth she more than made up with class. Everything seemed perfect with her, even the fine lines over her temples, radiating from the edges of her eyes as she enjoyed the Salsa beat.

The instant the music stopped, she briskly turned around and went straight for the bar, pulling out a cigarette, which the bartender immediately lit for her while she whispered something. A moment later, as she sat stood alone by the counter the bartender presented her with a mojito.

Vorota grinned.

His smile widened as she rejected three different men propositioning her within five minutes, and watched with interest as she checked her watch while frowning and looking towards the entrance, waiting for someone who was apparently late.

As he continued to enjoy the mojito while wondering what kind of idiot would stand her up, her eyes glinted in recognition before bringing a hand to her face to cover obvious surprise.

A tall and impeccably attired muscular man stopped by her in mid stride while in the company of a beautiful and much younger blonde who seemed confused.

An argument sparked between the man and the red head, surprising the blonde, before being whisked away by the well-dressed man, leaving the auburn beauty visibly upset and scrambling to pull a cigarette out of a pack she fished from her purse.

It all happened very quickly, but the same keen business sense that had made him rich--and had kept him alive in this unmerciful town for two decades--now focused on the incredible opportunity that had just materialized in front of his very eyes.

Vorota sprung to his feet, startling his bodyguards and the twin prostitutes, reaching into a pocket to produce a solid-gold lighter as she freed a cigarette and placed it with trembling fingers in between her lips.

Her magnificent hazel eyes, filmed with tears she fought to hold back, fell on him and the lighter for an instant, before closing them as he thumbed a flame and placed it under the tip of the cigarette.

She took a long drag, exhaling though fine nostrils before mumbling, "*Balshoye Spasiba,*" with a heavy American accent.

"You are most welcomed," Vorota replied, smiling, exposing two perfectly straight rows of gleaming teeth, softly inhaling her perfume. "May I offer a more comfortable option to sit in this crowded place?"

She regarded him for a moment, before saying, "Your English . . . it is very polished for a Russian."

"I split my time between Moscow and New York with my business," he replied.

She considered that for a moment before extending a hand with five scarlet fingernails. "I'm Alexandra but my friends call me Alex."

"Hello, Alex," Vorota said, taking her hand and bringing it up to his have, planting a soft kiss on the top of her palm. "I am Andrei, and it is a pleasure making your acquaintance."

She gently retrieved her hand and reached for her half-drunk mojito, wetting her lips before saying, "I'm from New York. What kind of business takes you there?"

"Imports and exports," he replied, before pointing to his booth, where his bodyguards had already cleared the twin prostitutes, whom Andrei was certain were too happy to get the night off while collecting a full fee. "Shall we?"

She gave the departing man and the blonde a furtive glance before regarding him with the magical eyes.

"Sure," she finally said. "Why not?"

For the next hour they drank, danced, and talked. He was fascinated by her work as a fashion designer in New York and now here in Moscow working with the Chamber of Commerce and Industry of the Russian Federation to coordinate this year's Fashion Week event as part of the country's effort to gain its fair share of recognition by a fashion world that had shifted from Pravda to Prada in order to propel Russian alabaster-skinned beauties into the world's current top models.

And that certainly explained the dress, the shoes, and the overall glamour. Alexandra was a model-turned-businesswoman, which made her all the more interesting to a man bored with the love-for-hire companions who shared his bed in between ruthless business deals.

"Would you accompany me to my penthouse?" Vorota asked after playfully arguing with her about whether one of his bodyguards--whom he had introduced to her as personal assistants--had brought them their sixth or seventh mojito.

She leaned away from him, muscular but thin arms crossed, staring him in the eye while turning serious, considering his proposition.

"I promise to be a gentleman," he added, raising his right hand.

"Why not?" she finally said, standing. "Show me your place and maybe I'll show you mine."

That was all the encouragement the arms dealer required to leap to his feet and walk with her through the crowd, stopping by the coat room, where she collected a beautiful mink, which Vorota draped over her shoulder before donning a long Burberry coat. They reached the entrance, where he tipped the staff while one of his bodyguards fetched their car for them.

The night was cold, clear, energizing. The distant lights from Moscow's historical downtown glowed toward the star-filled heaven. The envious eyes of the crowd lined up half frozen alongside of the building filled him with satisfaction as his black Mercedes sedan slowly pulled up while he stood there holding Alexandra's hand.

Andrei Vorota enjoyed moments like this, at the top of his game, holding all of the cards while a jealous world looked on.

The bodyguard who remained with them opened the door. Vorota held her hand as Alexandra stepped inside first followed by him.

Just as the bodyguard was about to open the front passenger door to get in next to the chauffer-bodyguard, a drunk staggered across the street holding a small flask in a brown paper bag, blocking their exit.

The bodyguard went up to him, while screaming, "*Shto s vami! Pashol von!*" *What's the matter with you? Go Away!*

The drunk resisted, shouting back, "*Astaftye minya pakoye!*" *Leave me alone!*

As Vorota exchanged an annoyed glance with Alexandra, a motorcycle approached the building in the opposite direction, barely missing the drunk, who staggered back and forth. The helmeted driver lost control and struck the Mercedes' left front quarter panel before landing face up on the hood, the back of the helmet slammed the windshield while the cycle skittered across the street, crashing against a lamppost.

Alexandra screamed.

Vorota cursed and snapped his fingers at the chauffer, who opened the door to inspect the figure sprawled on the shiny hood while the other bodyguard started to push the drunk towards the curb while shouting.

In the same instance, the drunk lifted the paper bag and sprayed something on the bodyguard, who immediately collapsed on the street while convulsing. The cycle driver surged from the hood and rammed its helmet into the chauffeur's face while driving a knee into his groin.

As Vorota instinctively sprung for the curbside door, he felt Alexandra's hand on his forearm, holding him back. He tugged to pull free, his survival instinct overpowering any kind of allegiance to this woman.

The arms dealer had to get out of this car, had to--

Her handhold abruptly turned into a vice-like grip that kept him from reaching the door handle.

"Freeze!" she shouted, holding a small gun in her left hand pointed at his groin. "You will talk to us, with or without your penis."

His eyes locked with the burning hazel stare of this woman who had tricked him. Vorota froze, watching helplessly as the drunk and the helmeted figure rushed into the front of the vehicle, the former flooring the sedan, rushing them away from the confused crowd, the latter turning to face his passengers while pointing the spray can at Vorota's face.

"Cooperate and you will be back at your penthouse by midnight."

Vorota's initial shock turned eerily calm as he shifted his gaze from her to him, before slowly asking, "Do you have any idea who I am? The people I know? The power I have in this country? You people are already dead."

"That's the thing, Mr. Vorota," replied Alexandra. "We know who you are. We know the people you know. We know the power you think you have in this country. And, none of it matters to us. You are nothing but a greasy, two-time arms peddler whose day of reckoning has arrived. Before the night is over you will talk to us, Mr. Vorota. You will tell us every last fucking thing we want to know, and then some."

Vorota blinked as the snowy streets of Moscow rushed by. Why were American agents taking the risk of upsetting Russo-American relations by abducting a high-profile and influential business men as Andrei Vorota? Did the Americans think that Russian armament sold itself in the international market? Did the Americans think they owned the market?

"What do you want to know?" he asked, deciding to play their game for the time being to see where it led, and also to buy himself time as he fully expected his people to find him through the Emergency Locator Transmitter surgically implanted in his right thigh.

Alexandra exchanged a brief glance with the drunken impersonator before replying, "Tell us about your recent business with Dragan Kiersted."

❄

Erika Baxter watched the arms dealer closely as he considered the question while Case kept the can of pepper spray trained on his face and a local agent from the Moscow CIA Station drove them to a prearranged location on the outskirts of the city.

Vorota shifted his weight while pursing his lips, before replying, "Isn't he a global climate terrorist? Why would you ask me that question?"

"Don't play with me, Andrei," she replied. "It isn't in your best interest."

Vorota raised her brows while replying, "You are wasting your time. I am an honest and well connected business man who has just been--"

Erika slapped him with the slide of the gun across his left cheek, drawing blood from an inch-long cut.

The arms dealer brought a hand to his face. "You American whore! You will pay for this! You will--"

Erika pistol-whipped him again, cutting his other cheek.

Cupping his face with both palms now, Vorota jerked back, getting out of her immediate range as she leaned forward, weapon ready for a third strike.

"Wait!" he shouted.

As Erika gave him a moment to reflect, the driver turned right into Podsosenskij Street, and after checking the rearview mirror for any potential tail, cut abruptly into the deserted parking lot of a church on the same street. Shutting off the lights, he steered around the towering structure, reaching a smaller lot in the rear bordered by a cemetery veiled in a light haze.

"What are we doing here?" Vorota asked.

Erika ignored him as the headlights of a black SUV cut through the light fog drifting from the snowy graveyard, and drove up behind the Mercedes.

"Let's go, Andrei. Change of vehicles."

Case got out first, opening Vorota's door and guiding the bleeding arms dealer towards the waiting vehicle with Erika checking the rear.

The Mercedes speed off as she closed the SUV's door and settled in next to Vorota in the more spacious club-seating arrangement of the SUV. Case sat across from them holding a FlexScreen while another officer from the Moscow Station held the pepper spray in one hand and an object shaped like the handheld metal detector at airport security in the other.

"What is that?" the arms dealer demanded in sudden panic.

Erika grinned. Vorota was implanted, which explained his confidence.

He thinks someone is coming to get him.

The CIA officer scanned the arms dealer and quickly zeroed in on his upper right thigh, before flipping a switch on the device and running it again over the surgically-implanted transmitter, disabling it with a localized EMP blast. He then switched to scan more once again and confirmed its electronic destruction.

Turning away from a horrified Andrei Vorota, Case said to the driver, "Takes us home."

"Home?" Vorota asked.

"A place where no one will come looking for you, Andrei," Erika explained. "The place where you will tell us more than we need to know in order to stop the pain."

Swallowing while crossing his arms, his face becoming tight with sudden fear, he offered, "I brokered a deal about six months ago between Colonel Lyov Cherkasski, then the head of the

Tessinskij Military Warehouse just outside the city and a Danish trading company."

Erika looked at Case, who immediately began to work the FlexScreen. She handed Vorota a handkerchief before saying, "Continue."

The arms dealer wiped his bleeding cheeks, inhaled deeply, and added, "The name was Solaris Exports out of Copenhagen, which is a company tied to Dragan Kiersted. It was a clean deal, one and a half million dollars worth in three currencies--Rubles, Euro, and Pounds--in exchange for three old Soviet-era machines."

"Are we talking weapons here, Andrei?" Erika asked, concern filling her at the thought of Dragan Kiersted getting his hands on another nuke. Ever since Greenland, the world had gone to extremes to eliminate every last known retired nuclear device.

Vorota shook his head. "They were not conventional weapons I typically deal with. They were also not chemical, biological, or nuclear."

Erika raised her free hand a few inches above her thigh, palm facing the ceiling. "What then? What was it that Dragan purchased?"

"I do not know. I was just the broker for this deal. Cherkasski dealt directly with Solaris after I hooked them up and collected a fee."

Erika just stared at him.

"I swear to you this is true. But Cherkasski should remember. He used to manage the warehouse."

"Used to?" asked Erika.

"Yes, he was dismissed a few months ago."

Case tilted the FlexScreen in the direction of Vorota. Is this Cherkasski?

The high-resolution image features a thin man in his early thirties with fine features and a full head of ash-blond hair.

"That's him."

"Very young to be a colonel," said Case.

Vorota shrugged. "Connections, I presume."

Case turned to the screen back to him while tapping it and reading, "Our records do show that Cherkasski is no longer with the military. But we have no details why. Was it because he got caught with his hand in the cookie jar?"

Vorota gave him a puzzled look. "I do not understand. Cookie jar?"

"Was he caught stealing or doing shady deals like the one with Solaris? Was that the reason why he was dismissed?"

"No."

"Then?"

"He was seen in the company of men at . . . at a gay club."

Erika and Case exchanged a look. He sighed. She raised her brows, before asking, "Where is he now?"

Vorota became silent.

"No more information until we make a deal. I want full immunity and--"

Erika flicked her wrist and cut him across the bridge of his nose with the forward sight of the gun.

Vorota jerked back, stung, his eyes filling as a trickle of blood ran down to his quivering lips.

"You're not going to start crying like a baby, Andrei?" Case teased him while grinning.

Erika remained serious and said, "No deals until we get what we need. First you help us, *unconditionally*, then we may just let you live. Got it?"

Vorota inhaled deeply, wiped his eyes and nose, and slowly nodded.

"Now, where is Cherkasski?" asked Case.

"Where, Andrei? Tell us where we can find him."

"I'm not sure," he replied.

Erika started to move the gun towards his face.

"Wait! But I can find out!" he exclaimed, shielding his face. "I can check with some people!"

Erika slowly pulled the gun back. "Good, Andrei. See how easy it is?"

"Now, where was Dragan taking this equipment?"

The dealer shook his head again. "I do not know these things. You need to ask Cherkasski this after I help you find him."

Case and Erika exchanged another glance before looking at the bruised and bleeding dealer, deciding to cut him some slack until reaching the safe house.

Erika shrugged. "We will see, Andrei. We will see."

12 Another Chance

"The best we can do is size up the chances, calculate the risks involved, estimate our ability to deal with them, and then make our plans with confidence."
--Henry Ford

31,000 FEET OVER THE ATLANTIC OCEAN.

July 11, 2019

Dr. Konrad Malone opened his eyes and stared at a red NON-SMOKING sign in between a pair of overhead vents.

Taking a deep breath, the glaciologist shifted his gaze about him, recognizing what looked like the oval-shaped interior of a business jet.

Where in the hell am I?

How did I get here?

Malone breathed deeply again, his mouth dry and pasty, his ears discerning engine noise, his body sensing slight turbulence, his mind recalling the collapsing glacier.

He frowned, blinking the thought away as he lay on a fully reclined seat, an IV connected to his left arm. He watched the slow drip from a bottle hanging from the overhead baggage compartment before his eyes drifted to the hazy clouds beyond the round window next to him.

Where are we going?

Malone began to fiddle with the side controls of the seat, finding the recliner button, propping himself up, briefly watching the empty seats in front of him.

He checked himself, lifting his legs, moving his feet, flexing his arms. His back sore, a few small bandages on his arms and legs, a slight headache lingering in his temples, Konrad Malone felt damned lucky not only to be alive but to have survived largely unscathed.

"Welcome back to the living Doctor Malone," said a commanding female voice in a heavy Kenyan-British accent.

He turned around in his seat, stared at a tall heavyset African woman wearing white pants and a white T-shirt sporting a red cross above the left breast pocket. A stethoscope hung around her neck. She held a clipboard in her left hand.

"I'm Doctor Elinah Varaiya," she said, standing tall over Malone, who thought he saw admonishment in her dark eyes as she stared down at him and added, "I am with the Kenyan Red Cross. We rescued you from the top of Mount Kilimanjaro by helicopter yesterday and are bringing you to Alaska now by direct orders from the president of Kenya."

"The president . . ."

Varaiya rested her free hand on her wide hip while pointing at him with the clipboard. "You have friends in very high places, Doctor Malone, at least enough for my president to order an emergency rescue operation of such magnitude, pulling many of us away from our work in the villages to search for someone who should not have been at a place closed down by the Kilimanjaro National Park authorities. Hundreds of children die in our villages every day having done nothing wrong, Doctor Malone. You break the bloody rules and get to live. And if that wasn't bad enough, the president ordered me and others to his private jet to escort you back to your home while more children die back at our home."

Malone wasn't sure how to respond to that.

She added, "This is nothing personal, Doctor Malone. It's just that I for one don't understand what makes you so special."

144

Malone closed his eyes and replied, "I'm not special, Doctor Varaiya, but the research I was conducting on the glacier certainly was. It could provide answers that may save many lives . . . millions of lives."

The Kenyan considered his reply for a moment and said, "Well, your friends in high places seem to agree." She glanced at her clipboard and added, "You are dehydrated from exposure, still feverish from a bout with malaria, and endured bumps and bruises from your ice encounter . . . but you will live."

She produced a clear plastic cup filled with a bluish liquid and a small straw. "Here. Drink this."

Malone took it from her and stared at the contents. "What is it?"

"Vitamins and electrolytes."

He took a sip and immediately frowned at the bitterness. "This tastes like shit. How about a pack of Marlboros?"

She grinned, revealing two rows of white teeth, before turning stone serious. "Bottoms up," she said in her booming voice.

"How about a triple espresso?"

She crossed her arms. "Maybe . . . after the medicine."

Resigned, Malone obeyed and handed the empty cup back at her, then pointed at the IV and asked, "What's in there?"

"A cocktail of antimalarial medicine plus more electrolytes and nutrients; everything you need to get another chance. Make it count, yes?"

Malone nodded. "And the espresso?"

"I'll bring you one. We should reach Fairbanks in another six hours.

"Is there a chance I can get a satellite connection with Doctor Natasha Shakhiva? She's the--"

"We know who she is. She observed the collapse of Furtwängler through satellite and got your government to contact ours and get this whole thing started. You could argue that you are alive today because of her. We found you very dehydrated and would not have lasted another day. You're lucky she pushed so hard, moving Heaven and Earth to get you help. That is one bloody guardian angel you have there, Doctor Malone."

His gaze drifted to the sky beyond the window pane, longing to be by her side. "She is indeed," he finally replied.

"I will speak to the pilot about getting you a connection."

"Thank you."

As Varaiya was about to return to the rear of the plane, Malone asked, "Any word on my two guides? They were with me when I went into seizures but were not there when I woke up right before the glacier collapsed."

She dropped a pair of thick brows at him and slowly frowned. "We found you alone. No guides and not much camp or equipment left, just a couple of tents amidst blocks of ice."

Malone shifted his gaze back to the clouds.

13 Truth Be Told

"And you shall know the truth, and the truth shall set you free."
--John 8:32

NORTH SLOPE BOROUGH. ALASKA.

July 11, 2019

The Piper Cub taxied away from shore and pointed its nose into the wind.

Back-dropped by snowy peaks beyond vast fields of bronzed tundra surrounding Shirukak Lake, Natasha Shakhiva watched from the edge of the IARC camp as the yellow and white plane stirred up the smooth surface as it sprung forward when Mario Escobar applied full power. The roaring column of fire from the burnoff vent drowned the Cub's engine.

Dressed in a gray and black down parka, thermal pants, boots, and mirror-tint sunglasses, Natasha filled her lungs with the cold air from a passing Arctic front while crossing her arms.

She had dispatched Escobar to Fairbanks to meet up with Konrad Malone, scheduled to reach UAF in a couple of hours courtesy of Colonel Marcus Stone, who convinced the White House to contact the embassy in Kenya and get the American ambassador to personally call the Kenyan president.

The late afternoon sun cast a yellow-gold hue across the region, battling the orange-crimson glow from the plume of fire spewing at the end of the vent tower. She watched its flickering reflection on the lake's surface as the Cub climbed into a beautiful Alaska sky.

And for an instant Natasha wished she could have left with Escobar, not just to see Malone but to get the hell away from this time bomb.

But she knew she couldn't.

The same Army who had pulled every possible string to rescue Malone and bring him home was now soliciting her help in what Colonel Stone loosely described as a new twist in the battle against climate terrorism.

And besides, the unseasonable cold front had the effect of firming up the permafrost enough to reduce the height of the burnoff vent plume by nearly half in twenty-four hours, lowering the risk of the monster escaping this year.

The Cub gained altitude as Escobar banked to the south, towards Fairbanks.

She watched it for a few minutes, until it vanished beyond the mountains to the south, until the surface of Shirukak Lake gained its mirror-like gleam.

"Hi, Doc."

Natasha turned around. Colonel Marcus Stone stood a few feet away dressed in his camouflage fatigues, matching coat, gloves, cap, shiny black boots, and an equally polished black belt from which a holstered sidearm hung.

"Marcus, hello."

"Feeling better?"

Still hugging herself, Natasha nodded. "Yes, thanks to you and the Army."

"Glad to be of help," replied Stone, before looking into her eyes and adding, "And now we need your help, Natasha."

"Yes, Colonel. You mentioned a new development?" she asked, lifting a brow.

"I'm afraid so."

"Well?"

Stone motioned her towards the large communications tent his team had set up next to the pair of large Superhawks, plus a third Superhawk that had arrived a few hours ago. Unlike the Army Superhawks that Stone had used to transport his team and gear to this camp, the latest arrival sported no markings aside for its tail number. "Come, I'll explain on the way."

A few minutes later they walked past the soldiers guarding the entrance to the large tent. Inside, she saw a small conference table flanked by four large FlexScreens depicting remote conference rooms packed with people.

"What's all this?" she asked, staring at a dozen men dressed in black uniforms sitting about the table.

Stone spoke. "This is a U.S. Intelligence Community emergency briefing on the potential threat of climate terrorism on thawing permafrost. Present here is a team of U.S. Navy SEALs tasked with the protection of this camp as well as this vulnerable region. On the screens we have delegates from the Central Intelligence Agency, the Defense Intelligence Agency, the National Security Agency, and the White House. We also have conferenced-in a dozen officers of the GRU and the Spetsnaz from the Russian Federation, and also present on the phone is the CSIS, the Canadian Security Intelligence Service, as both Canada and the Russian Federation are vulnerable from thawing permafrost. Leading this cross-functional team by presidential order is Daniel Bennett, Director of Central Intelligence."

Natasha knew that the GRU, Russia's largest intelligence agency--often compared to the U.S. Defense Intelligence Agency, the military version of the CIA--also commanded the Spetsnaz, the Russian Special Purpose Regiments.

"Who . . . who is doing the briefing?" she asked.

Stone cocked his head at the climatologist. "You are, Doctor."

Natasha felt a strong jabbing pain in her chest and she realized she had stopped breathing. Slowly, she inhaled, filling her lungs, forcing herself to relax.

"Doctor Shakhiva," said a voice from the closest FlexScreen, before she could reply. A man stood on the remote conference room. He was dressed in a dark suit with silver hair and fair complexion. "Dan Bennett. I called this session at the request of the President to get a real-time briefing on the thawing permafrost to understand the potential ways in which climate terrorists could capitalize on this environmental weakness just as they did in Greenland last year. The people present here in this virtual room represent the largest cross-agency task force ever created under the joint command of the Presidents of the United States and the Russian Federation, and the Canadian Prime Minister."

She turned to Marcus Stone, who said, "Just tell them what you have been telling me for the past couple of days. I have relayed some of the information, but they really need to hear it directly from you. Here is your opportunity to tell your story about the much overlooked threat that the thawing permafrost presents to the human race."

Before Natasha could reply, Bennett asked, "Is it true, Doctor? Is it true that 70,000 million tons of methane trapped beneath the permafrost in the northern hemisphere are dangerously close from being released with global warming? And in your opinion did such a massive release of methane trigger the Permian-Triassic extinction event 250 million years ago?"

Natasha Shakhiva stared at the FlexScreen, before her gaze drifted to the other video feeds. The eyes of the most powerful intelligence agencies were on her, and for a moment she wished that Konrad Malone were here, by her side sharing the burden of educating the intelligence community of the dangers lurking ahead.

It is all up to you today, Natasha thought before slowly, methodically, and factually, she began to speak.

14 Decadence

"With whom the kings of the earth have committed fornication, and the inhabitants of the earth have been made drunk, with the wine of her fornication."
--Revelation 17:2

MOSCOW, RUSSIA.

July 12, 2019

The moon hung high and bright above the Russian capital, its silvery glow staining the Moskva River as it snaked through the city.

Dressed in black leather pants, jacket, gloves, and boots, Erika Baxter glanced at the peaceful sight through the visor of the black helmet while sitting behind the handles of a BWM motorcycle.

Trying not to freeze to death while parked a half block away and across the street from the Samovolka, a raunchy gay club, the operative tapped the tip of the gloved index of her right hand against her thumb, activating the heads-up display on her visor integrated to her SmartLenses. Rubbing the same index finger lightly against the surface of the thumb brought up a pointer on the screen, which she used to navigate through a couple of menus, pulling up the environmental control of her thermal underwear and cranking up the heat by another two degrees.

In the past two hours she had seen many same-sex couples going into the club, a three-story dilapidated building, its exterior

151

red-brick walls adorned with green, pink, and lavender neon palm trees glowing with a varying intensity that matched the heavy base echoing from inside the structure.

Invoking the digital zoom feature on her visor allowed her to digitally probe the faces of everyone coming and going--many dressed in black leather, just like her--as her helmet's CPU performed forty-point facial comparisons with eleven different photos of Cherkasski in the CIA files.

Case Montana, also dressed in leather, was inside, walking about, using his SmartShades for close-up work. Wirelessly interfaced to her helmet unit, Erika could see what he sees, and Case could see what she sees.

Contrary to the weathered exterior, the club's interior was flashy, with multiple platforms at different heights where scantily-dressed men and women danced under a rainbow of light. All of the platforms were clear acrylic, allowing those beneath with unobstructed views of patrons wearing leather skirts.

Three hours ago, Andrei Vorota had provided confirmation that Cherkasski would be here this evening. Case and Erika had left the arms dealer in the company of the local CIA and had reached the club. A CIA chase car with three armed officers parked two blocks away provided back-up for the field operatives.

So far, however, the state-of-the-art facial recognition system had failed to make a match.

Unless Cherkasski had undergone massive facial reconstruction, the forty-point check should provide enough resolution to identify him if they could get at least ten or more points, especially in the shape of the face, the forehead, the distance between the eyes, and the relative location of the mouth, nose, ears, and eyes--which typically required extensive surgery to change, unlike the average nose or chin job.

Erika continued to watch the street while also glancing at the images from inside the club as well as the digital readouts from the computing unit performing the facial matches. The highest reading of the evening had been a three-pointer, hardly a match.

A young man in a shiny red-leather jacket zippered down to expose his muscular chest, smiled at Case as he walked by.

"I think you made a friend there," she said, speaking into the helmet's built-in microphone.

"Not funny," Case mumbled barely moving his lips, the transparent throat mike picking up voice directly from his vibrating vocal cords.

"You should ask him to dance."

"I'm glad you're enjoying this," he replied.

Erika could hear the laughter from the officers in the chase car, whose standard procedure prevented them from speaking.

"Case," she said in a sudden serious tone when the imagery turned the figure of a woman in the club red, denoting a possible match. "I'm getting fifteen points from that woman dancing on the upper left stage."

"Are you talking about that woman up there?"

"That's the best match we have gotten tonight," replied Erika as the camera in Case's SmartShades panned in her direction. "Let's get a closer look."

The video image zoomed in the direction of a voluptuous, middle age blonde in a ridiculously-short miniskirt and tight leather top slow dancing with three younger girls, also barely dressed. One wore nothing but a thong and small round cups over her nipples.

As the video focused in on the blonde from underneath, Erika narrowed her gaze on the digitally-filtered image.

"See what I see?" Case asked.

"Blondie may have breasts," Erika replied. "But the parts below don't match."

The image moved to the face, tracking the head movement as she danced until it snapped a high-resolution still the instance the blonde briefly shifted her face down and to the left, in Case's direction.

153

"Twenty-six pointer," said Case, reading the same information displayed on Erika's visor display. *"Definitely some facial surgery on the nose and chin, but not enough to fool the system."*

"And it looks like he ran out of cash to finish the transformation beyond the face, boobs, lips, and lipo," replied Erika, noticing the trimmed waist and long and smooth legs. For an instant Erika was impressed that the Russian actually looked so good. The facial transformation had been quite good and he looked attractive for a woman.

"Maybe he-she likes it both ways," Case said. *"Or maybe the girls with him like it."*

"Assuming they're girls," Erika noted. "Maybe they're guys who went all the way."

"Good point," Case said, panning to them from underneath, finding another set of male genitalia on one and either surgical or natural females on the other two.

"Told you," she said, grinning.

For the next hour, they monitored Cherkasski's activities as he danced, drank, kissed, and nearly copulated with his companions in a booth.

Case was eventually picked up twice and forced to dance in order to protect his cover--to Erika's delight; once with two men in drag and a second time with two whip-clutching lesbians dressed in see-through plastic skirts and blouses.

She couldn't stop laughing, and neither could the guys in the chase car.

"They're leaving now," Case said, relief filling his voice as the blonde Cherkasski and his three friends headed for the coat closet before reaching the exit.

Erika watched them emerge on the street and flag down a taxi.

"No more socializing, Case! Time to go!" she said, starting the bike and accelerating towards the entrance as the taxi doors closed and the black and yellow vehicle left the curb.

Case rushed outside, jumping behind Erika, who took off after it.

"Dancing with gay men and lesbians, and now riding bitch?" she said, steering them down the street, keeping a respectful half a block through the thin traffic, letting a car get in between them. "You know, I have it all on high-res video? Nice moves."

"Keep it up, funny girl, and you can kiss that drink goodbye," he said, reaching around her with both hands, wedging himself against her back as the streets of Moscow rushed past them.

She smiled, welcoming his nearness, his chest pressed against her back, his arms wrapped around her belly.

"We think it deserves an Academy Award," replied an officer from the CIA chase car, breaking silence.

"Let's keep our eye on the ball, people," Case said.

The taxi continued for another fifteen minutes, reaching a modern apartment complex on Yauzskaya Ulitsa, which, like the Samovolka, also overlooked the Moskva River.

The foursome got out and noisily staggered towards the entrance, apparently drunk, as the taxi drove off.

Erika floored the BMW bike, driving it on the curb, coming to a screeching halt in between the startled group and the building's entrance as Case pulled out two small cans and sprayed their contents on Cherkasski's companions. Erika fired a stun gun at the former Russian colonel, who collapsed in spasms, urinating on himself while continuing to convulse on the asphalt.

"Time!" Case shouted into his throat mike as Erika shutoff the stun gun and Cherkasski stopped trashing.

An instant later the headlights of the chase car cut through the night, landing on them as they dragged the semi-conscious Russian to the street.

Two officers got out and shoved the transvestite into the rear of the sedan before driving back to the embassy.

Erika waited until Case jumped back on before taking off after them.

❋

Thirty minutes later they stood in front of Lyov Cherkasski in a basement holding cell at the American Embassy compound. To Erika's surprise, a contingent from the GRU had been waiting for them in the ambassador's office. Apparently the U.S. Intelligence Community had chosen to join forces with their Russian counterparts in this operation given the likelihood of a terrorist-triggered permafrost event in Siberia.

Moreover, the Moscow Station Chief, by orders from the Director of Central Intelligence, instructed Erika and Case to let the Russians conduct the first round of interrogations--an order that infuriated the CIA operatives who had managed to track down and capture the elusive Cherkasski, who had been on the GRU's most wanted list for a couple of months.

Erika, still dressed in black leather, stood next to an equally leathered Case Montana as two large Russian intelligence agents worked on Cherkasski, who was strapped to a chair with his hands tied behind his back.

The two GRU officers spoke in Russian, which was translated to English and fed into Erika's ear pieces by the embassy's Artificial Intelligence system. Case also wore a similar ear piece to keep up with the conversation.

"Where is Dragan Kiersted now, Lyov?" pressed the older of the two officers--a bulky man named Ivenko with a shaved head in his early fifties--while his younger associate, Alexei, used a pocket knife to slice open Cherkasski's blouse before ripping off the brassiere, exposing a pair of amazingly beautiful breasts that defied gravity.

"My name is not Lyov anymore!" Cherkasski shouted. It is Natalia!"

Ivenko punched Cherkasski in his finely-sculpted nose, shoving his head back as blood exploded through his flaring nostrils.

"Answer, you miserable worm! Or I will disfigure you!"

"No! No! Please stop! Please do not--"

The GRU officer punched him again, nearly knocking him and the chair back. Alexei caught him and planted the bleeding transvestite in front of the massive GRU officer, who slowly removed his jacket, tossed it aside, and rolled up the sleeves of the white shirt he wore underneath, exposing powerful forearms connected to sailor-sized fists.

"I will ask you one more time. Where is Dragan Kiersted?"

"I do not know!" he cried out, tears mixing with the blood over his quivering lips, though Erika found it growingly difficult to think of Cherkasski as a man looking the way he did.

The bald GRU officer pulled out a pack of cigarettes and calmly lit one up, taking a long drag before grabbing one of Cherkasski's breasts and unceremoniously pressing the red-hot cinder against the nipple.

The Russian screamed, jerking and twisting, trying to break free, but Ivenko kept the cigarette in place, rubbing it into the exposed flesh until he put it off.

Taking a step back as he slowly lit up another one, Cherkasski dropped his head, crying, bleeding, chest heaving. "Please," he mumbled. "I swear to you . . . I do not know where he is . . . I just sold him equipment . . . that's all . . ."

Ivenko looked at Alexei and pointed at Cherkasski's miniskirt. The younger GRU officer immediately sliced it off with the knife, leaving him completely naked.

"What is this?" Ivenko shouted in his booming voice, taking a drag, exhaling in Cherkasski's direction while tapping the head of the penis with his shoe.

"Please . . . no," Cherkasski mumbled.

"Did you forget this part?" he asked, kneeling in front of the beaten Russian and grabbing his penis and stroking it multiple times with one hand while Cherkasski continued to cry.

The GRU officer achieved a mild erection before taking the cigarette from his lips and shoving the hot end into the swelling head.

Cherkasski let out an harrowing scream, his model-like face contorting into a mask of agonizing pain as he struggled against the straps, as he tried in vain to break free, shouting, pleading, crying for it to stop as the GRU officer shoved the end into his urethra and stepped back to contemplate his handy work.

In her years with the Agency Erika had seen her share of brutal interrogations, but there was something particular dark about this one--from the subject, who looked like a model except for the groin, to the simple yet massively painful interrogation techniques of the GRU. No fancy drugs or equipment. Just a chair, straps, and a pack of cigarettes.

Russian efficiency.

The GRU officers continued working on Cherkasski for another five minutes, punching, slapping, and burning him in other sensitive areas, and completely humiliating him without even asking any more questions.

Erika understood their technique. Taking the subject through a sudden and massive amount of pain to let him know who was in control, lowering any semblance of defense, of self-control, making him want to tell them everything. But every time Cherkasski started to open his mouth, more pain was inflicted, triggering yet more screaming and sobbing.

The older GRU officer suddenly stopped, grabbed his coat and motioned to his colleague to follow him out the room, walking past Erika and Case while mumbling in heavily-accented English, "He is yours for ten minutes, yes?"

Time for the good cops, she thought, approaching the scourged Russian as the door closed behind the GRU officers.

"Hello, Natalia," Erika said in her friendliest voice while softly lifting the Russian's bleeding face with the fingertips of her right hand. The GRU officers had made a mess of what had been a miracle of modern plastic surgery just ten minutes ago.

The Russian, whose CIA dossier indicated he was fluent in English, coughed, spitting a tooth, which landed on Erika's lap.

She ignored it, staring at Cherkasski's good eye. The other was closed shut from a swelling purple bruise.

"Listen to me, please," Erika said. "You must tell me everything you know right now. I will then try to convince the

158

GRU to leave you alone. You are currently on American soil. We can protect you, but only if you cooperate immediately."

The Russian didn't take long to consider Erika's proposition, lips quivering, nose twisted and bleeding, a dozen cigarette burns on both breasts and abdomen.

"My . . . penis . . . please."

Erika dropped her gaze and gently pulled out the cigarette still embedded in Cherkasski's urethra.

The Russian trembled as a trickle of blood and urine followed, landing on her hand.

She ignored it and asked again, "Natalia, please, I beg you to tell me everything quickly, before they return. What kind of machine did Dragan purchase from you?"

"Not one . . .," he said in between sobbing gasps, his breasts lifting, scorched nipples staring at Erika in the face, a sight which chilled her even if they weren't real. "Four."

"Four? What kind of machines were they, Natalia?"

"Old . . . Soviet era . . . for earthquakes."

"For earthquakes? I don't understand, Natalia. Machines for earthquakes?"

Slowly, the Russian nodded, his one good eye losing focus.

"Get Natalia some water," Erika said to Case.

He reached for the table on the side of the room and filled a cup with water from a jar, handing it to Erika.

She brought it to his lips and got the Russian to take a sip, which he tried to swallow but instead ended up coughing it on Erika's jacket along with bloody saliva.

Erika sighed and tried again, and this time the Russian was able to keep it down. Erika then splashed some water on his face and wiped it with a towel that Case handed to her.

"Now, Natalia," she continued as the Russian regained focus, sitting up, staring at her. "What do you mean by earthquake machines?"

"I do not have all . . . information . . . but they were built to . . . induce mechanical oscillations . . . into the Earth crust . . . along fault lines . . . forcing tremors and . . . maybe even . . . earthquakes."

"Who has more information about them?"

"Yuri . . ." the Russian said, swallowing, breathing deeply and adding, "Yuri Gerchenko."

"Who is Gerchenko?" Erika asked while Case worked the FlexScreen.

"Soviet scientist . . . from the old days. He serviced the . . . systems before purchase."

Case produced a digital photo on the small screen and showed it to him. "Is this Yuri Gerchenko?"

The Russian narrowed his one good eye, spending a moment inspecting it before slowly nodding. "He is older now . . . but it is him."

Erika browsed through the dossier headlines beneath the photograph. Gerchenko had been a young engineer assigned to the legendary Nikolai Telsa, the inventor of the earthquake machine, during the mid 1960s. The dossier indicated that Gerchenko was in his early sixties, and the sole surviving scientist from that project, which was mothballed when the Soviet Union imploded in 1990."

"Where is Gerchenko?"

"Kiersted hire him . . . to help with the machines."

Erika stared at Case before asking, "Where are these machines now, Natalia?"

"I do not know," he said. "I swear."

"You know what the GRU may do to you next?"

Cherkasski's lips began to tremble again before shouting, "I am telling the truth! I do not know!"

"I don't think you are telling us everything, Natalia," Erika said. "When is Dragan planning to use these machines?"

The Russian slowly shook his head while crying, "I do not know! I want asylum!"

"Listen," Case said, leaning down next to Erika, "There is no chance of asylum unless you tell us everything. Only then we will be able to convince our people to take you in. Otherwise, we will be forced to turn you over to the GRU."

"They will disfigure you, Natalia," said Erika.

"And very slowly," added Case.

"Oh, please," the Russian said, the reality of their words shooting a boost of adrenaline into his system. "Don't let them take me! Please!" he cried, mascara running down his face, mixing with the blood on his cheeks, nose, and chin.

"That's entirely up to you, sweetheart," Case said. "What else can you tell us?"

Cherkasski regarded them with his good eye, inhaled deeply, swallowed, and slowly began to speak.

Five minutes later, Erika and Case rushed outside to confer with their GRU colleagues, sharing the critical information they had gathered.

As the Russians headed for the exit while speaking on their mobile phones, Erika and Case headed for the ambassador's office. They not only had to gather every last shred of technical data on Telsa's earthquake machines, but they also needed immediate access to the high-definition video of every satellite within reach of the oil city of Surgat, in the West Siberian Plains.

If Cherkasski was right, they were out of time.

R. J. Pineiro

15 Angel of Death

"And in her was found the blood of the prophets, and of the saints, and of all that were slain upon the earth."
--Revelation 18:24

NORTH SLOPE BOROUGH. ALASKA.

July 12, 2019

The twilight of an Arctic summer midnight stained the sapphire sky with shades of red-gold and mauve as Shin-Li arrested the amphibian Cessna Caravan's steep decent at fifty feet above tundra and meltwater lakes while maintaining 150 knots.

They had flown in from Greenland via northern Canada, over Victoria Island, refueling along the way before venturing into the massive oil complex at Prudhoe Bay, Alaska, where they took more fuel before heading south, inland.

As soon as they had lost line of sight with the oil complex, Shin-Li had activated the large FlexScreen custom-mounted above all horizontal surfaces and the upper fuselage, which replayed the real-time image captured by the half-dozen cameras mounted on the bottom of the wings and the aircraft's belly. Anyone observing the plane from above would have seen it blend with the terrain, including satellites, essentially making them invisible expect for deep infrared imagery, which could spot the engine heat.

As Shin-Li circled the area looking for the right body of water to land while remaining well below radar, Dragan Kiersted watched a herd of caribou grazing in the distant flatlands stretching south to meet the rugged Brooks Mountain Range fifty miles to the south.

The steady wind sweeping down the jagged, snow-capped mountains turned into a steady breeze as it combed through the North Slope's rugged vegetation, rippling the surface of countless lakes, before kissing the leading edges of the Caravan.

Many lakes fed braided streams of meltwater flowing to the Beaufort Sea as temperatures started to creep back up following a brief cold front--one that did little to harden the permafrost he would soon pierce, awakening a monster that had been dormant for 11,000 years.

Just a few miles to the north, the Trans-Alaska Pipeline System connected the Prudhoe Bay oil fields to Valdez on the Pacific Ocean. Its destruction would provide an added bonus to his plan. In terms of recoverable oil, Prudhoe Bay fields was the largest in the United States, more than double the size of the East Texas oil field, the second largest.

And it all gets channeled through the Trans-Alaska Pipeline System right over the thawing permafrost, he thought, watching the unprotected pipeline and the surrounding peaceful scenery while listening to the steady hum of the Cessna's massive turboprop engine muffled by the noise-cancellation headphones.

This is too easy.

But Dragan remembered a similar operation a year ago that had also seemed easy on the way in.

You will not get that lucky again.

He flexed the fingers of his iLimb, wondering if he indeed had been lucky a year ago, or if he would have been better off perishing in Greenland than surviving as half-human, half-machine.

You survived for a reason.

He stared at the distant mountain range and the sea of tundra broken up by seemingly infinite lakes, but his eyes probed beyond the majestic sight, beyond the cosmetics, digging deeper, visualizing the monster breathing below the thawing shield projecting beneath the oversized floats of the descending Caravan.

You survived to fight another day.

But to win this new fight, you can't make the same mistake twice.

This time around Dragan had kept the particulars of this mission completely secret.

This time around no one but those directly associated with the mission--the souls aboard this aircraft--knew that Alaska's North Slope marked the destination of the first strike.

This time around even those who had a need to know were not informed of their destination until *after* departure from Europe with their precious cargo.

But even that had not been enough to satisfy his paranoid mind.

As Dragan watched his mask-like reflection on the Caravan's windshield as Shin-Li selected their landing site, he thought about the machine he had shipped to Siberia along with an expendable terrorist cell to blast through the permafrost near one of Russia's largest oil refineries as a diversion to keep the international law enforcement community looking away from Alaska.

And no one here knows where the last two machines are headed, he thought, regarding the scenery before unplugging the IV connected to his right forearm feeding dinner.

Not even Shin-Li.

His eyes gravitated to the Russian pilot as she used fingertip control to guide the plane over a patch of ash-gold sand bordering a small lagoon.

"That one?" he asked.

Shin-Li nodded while keeping her eyes on the landing ahead, adding flaps, slowing down, trimming, aligning the Cessna's nose into the steady breeze.

Dragan looked over his left shoulder at Hans-Jorgen and Doctor Yuri Gerchenko sitting directly behind them in the club-style seating of the Caravan's Oasis executive interior. Hans-

Jorgen was the young and strapping operative over six feet five inches and 270 pounds who dragged Dragan to safety in Greenland. The elder scientist looked puny and frail by comparison sitting next to him fiddling with a handheld FlexScreen.

"Gentlemen, we're going in. Seatbelts."

Hans-Jorgen gave him a thumbs-up. The scientist barely acknowledged him while working the small computer. For the past two days, Gerchenko had been computing the settings for the machine in the rear to customize its output.

"Call it," Shin-Li said.

Dragan stared at the radar altimeter, which unlike the standard barometric altimeter in an aircraft providing altitude relative to sea level, it indicated altitude above ground level.

"Forty feet," he spoke into his mike, reading the digital display on his side of the panel.

"Thirty feet."

The Caravan rushed over the edge of the water at 75 knots, right on target for the amphibian plane.

"Twenty feet . . . ten feet . . . five feet."

Shin-Li gently arrested the descent and began the landing flare, lifting the plane's nose, forcing the back of the long floats below the rest of the plane while reducing power to idle.

Dragan felt a slight vibration as the end of the floats broke the surface, biting into the water, the added drag rapidly slowing down the heavy plane, dropping the nose back towards the horizon.

Water surging by their sides as the floats cut through the frigid lagoon like a pair of pontoons, Shin-Li increased power to 900 RPM and lifted flaps before using the rudder pedals to steer them towards a beach-like spot on the west end of the lagoon.

As the Caravan conveyed her footwork to a pair of rudders at the rear ends of the floats, Dragan unbuckled his safety belt and headed aft, signaling Hans-Jorgen and Gerchenko to follow him to the cargo compartment.

The machine monopolizing most of the spacious cargo area had two sections, the main oscillator and the rocket booster, each the size of a refrigerator. The Cold-War-era device, based on the mechanical oscillations work of the legendary inventor Nikolai Telsa for the purpose of stressing seismic fault lines, was designed to produce mechanical oscillations of a frequency that Gerchenko had tuned to the resonant frequency of the thawing permafrost to induce acoustic energy deep into the ground.

As the elder scientist had explained during one of Dragan's equipment acquisition meetings with Gerchenko and Cherkasski back in Moscow, mechanical resonance was a well known physical phenomenon. Any structure, whether man-made or natural, such as a stack of soil layers or tectonic plates, had an oscillation frequency--or resonant frequency--which was the frequency at which the structure freely vibrated according to its physical parameters. An external vibration produced driven oscillations, and when the external source frequency equaled the resonant frequency, the oscillation amplitude increased in a positive loop, usually leading to a collapse of the structure. This resonant frequency principle, as Gerchenko had explained, was the reason why hanging bridges would sometimes collapse under heavy winds. It wasn't the sheer strength of the wind that made the bridge collapse but whether the wind direction and intensity triggered a destructive positive loop in the structure.

Today Dragan hoped to use this technology to induce a resonant oscillation into the thawing permafrost, collapsing its structure, piercing the weakened shield by exponentially increasing its methane flux.

Releasing the monster to the atmosphere.

As the Caravan reached the shore and its floats sunk into the soft sand, Dragan Kiersted looked through one of the side windows at the vast sea of tundra expanding as far as he could see.

It was time to scorch the Earth.

16 Biomes

"What is needed is a better way of communicating accurate information to the people in need of such information."
--Jan Egeland, U.N. under-secretary-general humanitarian affairs

UNIVERSITY OF ALASKA, FAIRBANKS.

July 12, 2019

"Here, Mario," Konrad Malone said, pointing to the large FlexScreen. "This is one of the longest samples. I drilled it out a week before the collapse."

Mario Escobar, standing next to Malone in the analysis room adjacent to the freezer basement of the geology department of the University of Alaska, Fairbanks, zipped up his jacket while leaning closer to the large screen. "Definitely a wide layer of dust, Koni. Over 300 hundred years."

"Close to four hundred," Malone said, sipping his third double espresso in two hours not just to stay warm in a room kept at a constant 25°F to preserve ice core samples under analysis, but also to fight off the severe jetlag.

For the past four hours, ever since Malone arrived at the university and Escobar had flown down from Shirukak Lake, the scientists had spent a moment exchanging pleasantries before descending to this sacred basement that stored so much or our planet's history.

Escobar tapped the screen and opened a file containing the last set of core samples he had drilled in Bolivia from the long-vanished Chacaltaya Glacier, once the highest ski run in South America.

"Look here, Koni," the Hispanic glaciologist said, aligning the years to perform an accurate comparison between the sample Malone had extracted from Mount Kilimanjaro a month ago to one of the many cores from Chacaltaya preserved at -30°F in the massive freezer next door. UAF kept thousands of ice cores from over a hundred global expeditions around the world by staff members over the course of forty years. Malone had added dozens of ice cores in the past three months.

"The dust layers do overlap," said Malone.

Escobar nodded. "Not only that, but the element analysis of the particles making up this inch-thick layer, plus the computer analysis of the ice immediately before, indicate a rapid drop in the methane content in the ice, which suggests a decrease of the wetlands thriving in tropics, replaced by an arid landscape."

Malone stared at the digital readouts on the screen right above ice cores from two separate regions of the world but close to the same latitude, near the tropics, noticing the abrupt depletion in oxygen-18 isotopes at roughly the same time, signaling the start of the drought period in Africa as well as a drought period in Bolivia. And that meant that as the rains receded, tropical forests turned into massive wastelands through apocalyptic fires that burned the ecosystem to the ground, crystallizing the soil, turning it into sand. In some regions like South America, the land recovered after a few hundred years as the rains returned the jungles. But in Africa the Sahara remained strong.

"So," Escobar said, fascinated. "This means that we have just made a similar correlation to dust layers, methane depletion in the ice, and a depletion of oxygen-18 isotopes."

"And that means that the famine wasn't limited to Egypt," said Malone, playing with his beard.

"That's right, amigo. It struck both continents."

Malone nodded. "The Egyptians were just better at recording the event in stone."

"Let's upload this into the system," said Escobar, tapping the screen, updating the parameters in the master global climate computer model of UAF.

The massive computing engine absorbed the new correlation and began to crunch the information.

"It may be a few minutes," said Escobar, leaning against a lab table in the analysis room, which was just large enough to fit a pair of FlexScreens, three lab tables with scanners to analyze ice cores, and a collection of tools should the need arose to desecrate a section of a core to thaw out and perform further analysis in liquid or gas form.

Malone yawned.

"That was a very stupid thing you did, Koni," said Escobar, arms crossed. "Tasha was very upset. She really cares about you."

"I know," Malone replied, finding it growingly difficult to keep his personal and professional lives in harmony. "Mario, I really had no choice. I had to get as many cores before the collapse."

"Well, things aren't so good up there," the Bolivian said. "Methane readings are on the rise. The burnoff vent is now going constantly."

"So I heard. At least it does correlate with the theory," Malone said. "The glaciers and the permafrost were created at the end of the last Ice Age. If they froze at the same time, it figures they would also melt at the same time."

Escobar grunted. "I wish we were wrong."

"Unfortunately we're not, pal."

"Unfortunately."

"The question that we need to answer," Malone said, "is how bad do we think it's going to get, and if the projections indeed turn out as bad as I think they will be, how do we prepare the world? How do we learn from what happened to the Egyptians--

and apparently also in South America--four thousand years ago to minimize casualties?"

Almost on cue, the system beeped, indicating the end of the modeling run.

The scientists turned their attention to the screen, and what they saw startled them. Even someone as hardened as Konrad Malone felt a claw gripping his intestines.

The image of the Earth filled the screen as it was that day in July of 2019, with bands of thick jungle in the tropics, ice on the Polar Regions, and heat bands on the desert regions in the correct areas, like the Sahara, Gobi, and Arizona.

But then the computer model began to alter this image based on the data from the ice cores.

"This isn't good, Mario."

"No shit, amigo."

The image of the Earth mutating in front of them forecasted the end of the world as humans knew it today.

Global warming wasn't only going to melt the polar caps and trigger inundations.

Global warming wasn't only going to feed monster storms, consume forests with massive wildfires, and spread droughts around the planet.

If Konrad Malone and Mario Escobar had entered the parameters from the ice cores correctly, and if the computer model was also projecting the data accurately, the results showed the creation of entirely new biomes--major ecosystem types like forests, deserts, grasslands, and tundra around the world. The data pointed to the birth of landscapes which humans have never seen before and in the oddest of locations, starting with the rapid collapse of the Amazon rainforest within two decades, taken over by savannas--the next hottest biome after desert dunes--their lush trees replaced by expanses of tall grass. A thick belt around the Earth projecting five hundred miles north and south from the equator was modeled to exceed the boiling point of water, far hotter than the hottest point in the Sahara today, meaning all life forms in those regions will have to be evacuated within the next ten years, if not sooner.   "These biome displacements are supposed to take hundreds or even thousands of years to play out, Mario," said Malone, not certain if he believed what he was seeing.

"Yep, but our ice cores project this to occur within a couple of decades."

Malone got on the phone.

"Who are you calling?" Escobar asked.

"My grad students. I need more espresso."

The scientists spent many hours holed up in the lab, reanalyzing the cores, triple-checking assumptions, dragging colleagues down to oversee their work, making computer engineers recheck the validity of simulations, which were predicting landscapes the likes of which modern civilization have never seen before.

This was the kind of drastic shift in weather patterns that nearly obliterated the Egyptians and created the Sahara desert where once fertile lands flourished.

And it is happening again.

At the end of a very long day, Malone and Escobar concluded that the data in the tropical ice cores, the computer simulations, the decades of climatology experience under their belts; they were all converging on a very simple message to the world.

Mankind would need to adapt . . . or perish.

R. J. Pineiro

17 The End of Days

"For the form of this world is passing away."
--Corinthians 7:31

NILE RIVER. FIFTY MILES SOUTH OF MEMPHIS, EGYPT. (CAPITAL OF THE OLD KINGDOM, 12 MILES SOUTH OF MODERN-DAY CAIRO).

2210 B.C.

The scream made him blink.

Under a brutal late afternoon sun, Pepi II Neferkare shifted his stoic gaze beyond the cedar wood planks and oars of his massive barge towards the left bank.

That any scream would rattle him seemed impossible. The pharaoh and veteran of many wars had seen men wailed while skinned alive, or dismembered, or simmered in boiling water.

But for reasons he could not explain, Neferkare had cared enough about the guards suffering in the adjacent raft enough to grace them with a brief stare as the fire consumed them while they continue to bail water in clay buckets and propel it in the direction of his barge, preventing the dry wood from igniting.

The godking watched the thatched roof made of papyrus and halfa grass dripping from the incessant barrage of water splashed by endless teams of guards in the dozens of escort ships that accompanied Neferkare in his short expedition to survey his dying country, cooling off the royal barge at the price of disregarding their own vessels.

Sometimes the men aboard the escort vessels would be able to divert the water to quench the fire on their ships before it got out of control. But most often, the super dried papyrus plants would ignite like oil under the merciless sun, spreading too fast across the small boats, narrowing their choices of death to two.

Death by fire or death by crocodile.

The pharaoh watched as three guards made the latter choice, diving into the reptile-infested water and attempting to swim ashore.

But they didn't make it.

They seldom did.

The same famine that had killed over half of the country's once thriving population had turned the normally aggressive Nile crocodile into monsters.

The men screamed as several reptiles converged on them, losing themselves in a feeding gorge of howls, open jaws, whipping tails and foamy blood. The rest chose an even worse death, desperately rowing to shore when the flames engulfed them, finally jumping ablaze into anxious jaws.

Neferkare saw it all; heard it all.

Yet, one by one the escort vessels took their turn, throwing bucketfuls at the barge's roof, at its wooden flanks, on its deck, until they were given the order to push back and cool themselves and their vessels while another pair of escorts took their place.

But sometimes the vessels would catch fire before their rotational shift was finished.

And death choices would be made.

Neferkare watched one vessel successfully approaching the shore, half the men aboard quenching the fire while the other half rowed as crocodiles followed.

Teamwork.

They jumped off from the burning ship as its bow went up on the bank, using wooden oars to keep hungry reptiles at bay as they rushed inland.

Unfortunately, the surviving crew would be dead before sundown.

The relentless sun had turned the once fertile and prosperous banks filled with farms, markets, and villages, into a wasteland of disease, famine, and cannibalism. And if that didn't kill them, the intense heat, enough to ignite papyrus wood, would boil them alive before they could reach shelter.

Neferkare turned to Harkfuf, his chief military officer who accompanied him in this short expedition.

"My Lord," the elderly general said, his bronzed and muscular chest filmed with sweat as he stood beneath an awning shielding the entrance to the pharaoh's quarters as his men measured the speed of the boat relative to land and calculated their remaining travel time. "At this rate we will reach Memphis before sunrise. I would not recommend such a trip again until winter."

Neferkare stared into the aging eyes of his most trusted adviser, military chief, and friend, and said, "Let it be done."

The youngest military captain under Pharaoh Merenre, Neferkare's father, Harkfuf had protected the young pharaoh and his mother, Ankhesenpepi II, during his early ruling years until he became of age. In return, Neferkare provided him with a lifetime of power and riches.

Neferkare placed a hand on Harkhuf's shoulder as his loyal subject bowed his head. "I know you will deliver your Lord and your queen home safely, my friend," he said, before turning around and going inside his much cooler refuge while two chamber maids drew the entrance curtains.

Dressed in a veil-thin white-linen tunic, her head pulled back with lapis beads, keeping her long and thin neck clear, Queen Nitocris turned away from the chamber maids fanning her with palmiforms in the shape of the blue lotus, and walked toward her husband and king.

She took a soft and damp cloth and pressed it softly against his face, cooling him.

Neferkare closed his eyes in pleasure.

Three years has passed since the day she nearly died on that altar, and yet Neferkare still shuddered at her touch. So much had the former Nubian princess captivated him that the pharaoh had ordered his other wives entombed to wait for him in the afterlife.

Neferkare embraced his wife as all maids in the royal chamber looked away while freezing, like living statues, not uttering a sound as the pharaoh sought release for the horrors he had witnessed today, and the days before.

Entire cities had been decimated--most completely obliterated--by unimaginable temperatures, by a relentless heat wave that had turned lush valleys into inhabitable deserts, by an obstinate Nile that refused to expand, and that would no longer overflow its banks. The Nile was narrowing, sun-baked and cracked soil replacing the once majestic shores as the angry gods would not allow the rain to provide his superheated kingdom with much needed relief.

Nitocris held him, washing away the anger, the frustration, the fear worming in his gut at the rising number of dissenting Nomarchs, at the growing number of royals questioning his heavenly powers, at the numerous death plots his spies and guards had uncovered, making the traitors die the worst kind of deaths.

Neferkare clutched on to his wife just as he used to clutched his mother, tensing at his inability to deal with his growing opposition.

It didn't matter how many he tortured, how many he had killed publicly. Traitors would continue to surface, more plots would flare, more rumors would spread about his failing powers, and more priests stopped believing in his divine right, challenging his godking lineage.

Perhaps he wasn't the son of the esteemed Merenre.

Perhaps Ankhesenpepi II had not been impregnated by the great pharaoh.

Perhaps Neferkare was a bastard, a mortal, incapable of reversing the tide of death sweeping through this once prosperous and powerful nation.

As the maids fanned them without looking, Neferkare ripped her tunic and took his wife hard, in anger, on their large bed made of a thick and soft woven mat on a wood frame supported by legs shaped like the same crocodiles consuming his escorts as they continued to cool down his barge, keeping temperatures inside the royal chambers comfortable.

Nitocris accepted him in silence, allowing him to release, to purge his frustration, his rage, his fears.

When he finished, they stepped into a massive alabaster vase filled with fresh Nile water, where they cooled off while the maids washed them, while the screams continued as another vessel caught on fire, the flames roaring just outside one of their windows.

Neferkare stared at his wife, who briefly closed her eyes, bowed her head, and said, "My lord, my love."

The last pharaoh of Egypt's Old Kingdom gazed into the magical eyes of the only woman he had ever loved besides his mother, and whispered, "When we reach Memphis I will face more danger, more traitors, many more attempts on my life."

The Nubian woman whom he trusted as much as Harkfuf narrowed her magical eyes, pouting those incredibly soft and moist lips, her perfectly-shaped breasts barely breaking the water surface.

"My Lord, my love, I am always here for you."

"Our world is ending," he continued. "Our nation is dying."

"Egypt will rise again, my Lord," she replied. "This too shall pass."

"Not in my lifetime, Nitocris . . . not in my lifetime."

She didn't reply. Instead she shifted over to him in the large tub and held him from behind, her long and thin arms around his stomach, her hands below, providing pleasure.

Neferkare closed his eyes and surrendered to her touch, but not before turning his head and whispering in her ear, "If they wrong me . . . you must avenge me."

18 Holy Warriors

"Believers, make war on the infidels who dwell around you. Deal firmly with them."
--Surah 9:121

SURGAT, RUSSIA.

July 13, 2019

They moved swiftly, quietly, with purpose under a moonless night in the West Siberian Plains.

Ivenko led the strike followed by Alexei and a contingent of ten Spetsnaz operatives dressed in NanoSuits and clutching automatic weapons. Erika Baxter and Case Montana followed them also wearing the advanced bullet resistant assault gear to shield them from the climate terrorists believed to be holed up in a large waterfront cabin around the bend in a trail in the middle of the vast expanse of forest dominating the scenery in this remote oil outpost.

Three days ago, high-definition satellite coverage of the region caught a medium-sized plane landing at a remote airstrip west of the place locals called Refinery City. Five men transported two crates from the plane into a waiting truck.

Which is still parked in front of the cabin, Erika thought, inspecting the trail ahead before shifting her gaze to the towering pines around her, most tilted at varying angles as their roots lost their grip in the thawing permafrost.

Drunken trees.

She wiped the perspiration on her forehead as unseasonal high temperatures plagued an area which had seldom left the high forties even in the height of summer. Yet, today temperatures had climbed into the low seventies, and this early evening they still hovered in the sixties.

Which explains why the ground is so damned mushy.

Erika frowned as her water-proof boots sunk in the mud, creating light suction sounds every time she took a step, making it difficult to keep up with the well trained Russian forces, which continued advancing single file with a ten-foot spread.

Her thighs burning from the effort, Erika forced control into her breathing, inhaling through her nostrils and exhaling through her mouth, filling her lungs with the pine-resin fragrance of her surroundings.

Insects hovered about her but didn't settle, their incessant buzzing mixing with the splashing sounds drifting from the direction of the cabin, confirming satellite imagery of a stream running in front of a vacation property registered to an imports & exports company based in Copenhagen, confirming the information extracted from Lyov Cherkasski.

The bulky Ivenko stopped and signaled the group to spread.

Shifting in the darkness, the Spetsnaz team vanished like shadows, taking pre-assigned positions around the target.

Ivenko dropped to a crouch behind a clump of boulders before extending the middle and index fingers of his free hand at Erika and Case, signaling to approach him.

They joined him a moment later, and Erika was glad to take a breather, dipping her right knee into the soft and wet ground.

The large, two-storey cabin—what locals called a *dacha*—was nestled between the scenic rapids of a wide river and a dirt road connecting the property to the main highway into the Surgat refinery complex.

Ivenko, his face and bald head smeared with dark green and black camouflage paint, pointed at the 4-inch FlexScreen on his wrist, depicting real time satellite infrared imagery of the *dacha*, where four figures moved about.

"You take the east side," the Russian said, "but do not go inside. The orbs will . . . secure first, yes?"

Erika slowly nodded as her surgically-implanted SmartLenses linked to overhead U.S. Intelligence satellites positioned to observe the cabin from four different angles. Their computer-enhanced deep-infrared imagery was fed directly in near-holographic form to her ocular implants, providing her with the equivalent of X-ray vision.

In an instant, she could see through the thick walls of the vacation cabin, and so could Case, who slipped on a pair of SmartShades.

Four figures moved about inside, confirming the information displayed on Ivenko's wrist. But unlike the Russian's five-year-old system, the CIA-issued 3D imagery Erika and Case used didn't require users to constantly take their eyes off the target while trying to read the information on the FlexScreen. The American interface superimposed the imagery over the real world in front of them, also conveying that all four targets were in the large living area in the middle of the first floor.

But like anything new, the Russians were hesitant to trust it, especially when provided by the Americans.

"Where are the SmartShades we provided to you and you men?"

Reluctantly, the Russian reached into a Velcro-secured pocket on the armored vest he wore over the NanoSuit and produced them. He frowned while staring at them. "Is this necessary?"

"Amuse me, Ivenko," said Erika, already regretting the arrangement her country had made with these technologically-lagging troops, who were still relying on 2D IR imagery to guide them through an assault.

"Put them on and look at the *dacha*," Case said. "Tell me what you see."

He pointed at Erika. "But you do not wear them, yes?"

"Mine are surgically implanted lenses over my corneas," she explained.

Ivenko frowned. "We don't have time for this, yes?"

"We're not moving in until you put them on," said Erika. "Or would you like me to contact the embassy?"

Ivenko mumbled something in Russian and slipped them on. The nanotech compounds recognized the shape of his face and adjusted the frame real time to conform, creating an instant perfect fit.

Slowly, the Russian turned his head toward the dacha and mumbled something else Erika could not make out but which tone indicated surprise.

"This is . . . impossible . . . how do you—"

"The technology will be made available to the *Spetsnaz* as a token of our appreciation for the collaborative effort between our governments."

"Amazing," he said, inspecting the cabin with enhanced vision, before ordering his troops to do the same.

Erika smiled a moment later as she heard similar reactions from the rest of the troops.

"We agreed to keep them alive, Ivenko, remember?" said Case, his hard-etched features softened by the camouflage cream. "We need to be able to question them to find the other machines . . . to find Dragan."

The Russian nodded solemnly. "We agreed this is our intention, yes?"

"Yes, Ivenko," said Erika, reaching inside Case's backpack and producing one of a half dozen black spheres stored inside, each the size of a softball. "First the Orbs release the gas, then we wait three minutes for it to become inert, then we go in."

Ivenko stared suspiciously at the black ball in her hand. "These things will really go in undetected and neutralize them, yes?"

"Correct. This is proven technology, Ivenko. You must trust it. But if any of the terrorists manages to figure out what is going on and uses a gas mask, then we use stun rounds. Real bullets are a last resort. Agreed?"

Ivenko nodded reluctantly, then spoke into his throat mike in Russian, hopefully relaying the objective, before looking at the American operatives whom he had been ordered to obey.

He turned to them and said, "My team is ready. Take your positions and release them in one minute. I will then give them exactly three minutes before my team goes inside from the south, west, and north ends. You two will cover the east, yes?"

Case and Erika nodded in unison.

"See you inside," he whispered, before vanishing in the forest, joining his team.

Case looked at Erika, watching her reflection in the mirror tint of his SmartShades. "They'd better not screw this up."

"Come," she said, walking in a crouch past the edge of the waist-high shrubbery, her eyes on the weathered cabin, confirming that all four terrorists remained inside and away from the windows.

Her objective, a tall pile of firewood adjacent to a large chopping block and two rusty axes, would place them a dozen feet away from a side entrance, which her SmartLenses showed led to a narrow hallway connecting the entrance to the main open area where the terrorists moved.

She reached it first, breathing rapidly as she slid into place with Case in tow, huddling by her side, so close she could smell coffee on his breath from the cup he had on the way from the airport.

He took off his rucksack and together they removed the six Orbs, the brainchild of a team of nanotechnology scientists from Los Alamos two years ago. The units, coated with bullet-resistant layers of Kevlar and armed with a potent sleeping gas, used GPS navigation to reach targets as far away as a mile.

They pressed their thumbs against the Orbs' activation windows, booting them up. A dozen portholes opened around each sphere, and they immediately started to hover around them under the power of their micro fans.

Case tapped a set of commands on his wrist FlexScreen, enabling the stealth mechanism. Micro cameras deployed around each unit recorded their independent fields of view and played them in real-time reverse synchronization on their LCD skins, mirroring their environment, making them invisible to the naked eye.

As they blended away, Erika's ocular implants presented them to her as spherical blue grids floating about them.

"Looks like we're in business," she said, still amazed at the units.

"Here we go," said Case, tapping additional commands, which caused the blue-gridded globes to rush towards the cabin. One pair went up to the roof and vanished inside the fireplace chute. Two others snuck in through open windows on the second floor. The last pair surrounded the house while spewing gas in case the terrorists decided to make a run for it.

Twenty seconds.

Case and Erika waited, their advanced ocular gear also confirming that the Russian troops remained put, per their agreement.

Forty seconds.

The terrorists continued to move inside the cabin undisturbed, when suddenly one reached for his throat and collapsed. As the others began to run in different directions, realizing something was wrong, a small heat signature materialized in the middle of the cabin.

Erika frowned, uncertain what that was as the three figures reached the front entrance, running away from the cabin.

A terrorist collapsed by the steps connecting the front porch to the driveway as the gas did its magical work. The remaining two, clutching weapons, opened fire blindly into the forest while dashing for their truck.

Somebody from the Spetsnaz team panicked and returned the fire, but contrary to the agreement, did not use stun rounds.

Bullets ripped through the chests and faces of the terrorists who collapsed on the dirt road.

Silence, broken by Case Montana as he shouted, "Damn it, Ivenko! Stun rounds! Stun rounds!"

Three Spetsnaz operatives appeared on the clearing west of the cabin, rushing to the target.

"Ivenko, tell your men to hold back!" barked Erika, "The gas is active by the cabin for one more minute."

Instead of acknowledging, two more Russians appeared on the clearing from the north end. Both of them dropped to the ground within a dozen feet from the cabin just as the three from the west also fell to their knees before collapsing.

"Dammit, Ivenko!" shouted Case. "Hold your men back!"

Now fast-spoken Russian flooded the frequency.

More silence followed as Erika stared at the bodies littering the clearing, though thankfully, most were just sleeping.

"Time!" announced Case, rising from behind the pile of wood with Erika as the rest of the Spetsnaz unit surged from the tree line and zigzagged towards the house.

Erika raced after her CIA colleague, her enhanced eyes probing the cabin, the surroundings, making sure the—

The heat signature from the living room had nearly tripled in size.

"Case," she said, reaching the side entrance.

"I know," he replied, yanking the door open, going in.

She followed, the smell of musk, wood, and garbage tingling her nostrils reminding her of a saw mill as they raced through a narrow corridor, their boots clicking hollowly on bare pine floors.

Pictures of people fly fishing adorned walls leading to a large living area with a panoramic view of the river.

That's when she first saw the machine described by Lyov Cherkasski.

Larger than two refrigerators on their side, its charcoal hunk rested inside a hole where the terrorists had sawed off the pine floor, placing it in direct contact with the ground.

With the permafrost.

Lights blinked on the humming unit, but the small solid rocket booster atop one side of the machine had not yet fired.

Ivenko and his troops rushed through the front door, catching up to them as they surrounded the earthquake machine.

Erika continued staring at a contraption that looked so simple, so fragile, yet supposedly powerful enough to unleash apocalypse on the world.

Controlling her breathing, feeling in some strange way like a holy warrior fighting to save the Earth from the worst form of evil, Erika said, "Cherkasski told us that as the booster fires, its energy drives the oscillator system to inject a resonant frequency deep into the ground, inducing a positive loop. We need to stop it."

"How?" asked Ivenko.

Case and Erika exchanged a glance. Dragan Kiersted had the only surviving scientist who knew how to work this contraption.

The humming intensified, signaling that it would soon go active.

"Well? The Russian commander asked. "How do we stop this?"

Erika stared at Case, then at Ivenko, before her gaze landed on this mysterious machine, whose increased pitch told her they were out of time. Once the solid rocket booster fired there would be no turning back.

"Shoot it," she said.

"What?" Ivenko asked, obviously surprised.

"Shoot the fucking thing!"

"But the solid fuel?"

"Shoot the opposite side!" She said, realizing they were out of choices. "If the machine goes off, it will release Gigatons of methane gas! This is our only chance! Shoot now!"

Ivenko barked an order in Russian, and his troops readied their weapons, training them on the section of the machine away from the booster and its solid fuel.

"Stand back!" he ordered Case and Erika, who rushed behind the line of Spetsnaz commandos lined up like a firing squad.

She grabbed his hand as Ivenko barked a final set of instructions to his team before giving them the signal.

The rattling of large caliber machine guns deafened them inside the enclosed structure as they opened fire, depleted uranium rounds tearing into the mechanism, breaking it apart.

Erika stopped breathing, certain that any moment now a stray round would pierce the fuel cells.

The panoramic windows shattered as chunks of equipment and uranium slugs peppered the glass in an ear-piercing crescendo that shook the structure of the cabin as the massive panes collapsed in shards reflecting the sun's wan light.

The Spetsnaz team persisted, concentrating their precise fire on the core of the unit, carving a white-hot track through the middle of the machine, disintegrating its many components while avoiding the rocket section, muzzle flashes casting a stroboscopic, nearly surreal effect on the room.

Ivenko suddenly raised a fist.

The Russians stopped firing, the smoke coiling from their weapons mixing with the thickening haze hovering above them as the commandos lowered their weapons.

Erika took a deep breath, the smell of cordite hovering around her, her eyes staring at the sizzling hunk of metal, relief sweeping through her that somehow the Russians had managed not to detonate the solid fuel.

Ivenko raised his brows at Erika and Case while exhaling through his mouth.

"Let us not do that too often, yes?" he said.

"No shit," replied Case.

Satisfied that they were safe for the moment, Erika went straight for the sleeping terrorist on the far side of the living room while asking Ivenko to get his men to drag the one by the front steps back inside.

"Scan him," she said to Case, kneeling by the unconscious terrorist, a man in his mid thirties with ash-blond hair dressed in jeans, hiking boots, and a plain black T-shirt. The red, blue, and yellow emblem of the *Fromandskorpset*, the Danish Navy Seals, was tattooed on his left forearm.

Case produced his portable FlexScreen and set it to scan the retinas of the unconscious terrorist. The information was uploaded to the CIA database, where his ocular signature would be matched in chronological order to the terabytes of retinal data collected by the millions of high resolution cameras located at most street corners, airports, train stations, hotels, restaurants, and stores across Europe.

"Most terrorist cells operate independently," Erika told Ivenko as the Spetsnaz team brought in the second operative and Case scanned him. "That means that irrespective of the amount of pain you inflict on these two, the information they have will be incomplete, or worse, incorrect, pointing us in the wrong direction. But the retinal scan system will tell us where they have been for the past couple of months, and that, combined with whatever we can extract, might just be enough for us to piece together the likely location of the other three machines."

"And of Dragan," added Case as he produced a pair of small hypodermics from the rucksack and injected the contents into the sleeping terrorists, awakening them.

"Show time, Ivenko," said Erika as his men took each terrorist to a separate room to prepare them for questioning while the rest swept the house for clues.

Slowly, over the course of the next hour, they learned that one of the terrorists, Udo Deppe, had last seen Dragan at a small airfield outside of Copenhagen, where the mastermind of the Greenland disaster had dispatched them to this corner of the world with orders to activate the earthquake machine. But Deppe claimed he didn't know where Dragan had sent the other units. In fact, both terrorists claimed they were not aware of other such machines in existence, confirming Erika's fears that Dragan had learned from his mistake in Greenland and had managed to keep each cell operating independently from the others.

"What now?" asked Ivenko, his uniform splattered with the blood of multiple questioning rounds.

Erika did a retinal signature check against the data collected by the cameras at the Danish airfield and got an instant match. Deppe had indeed been there on that date.

As Ivenko watched with interest, Erika accessed the digitized video of the cameras installed at the airfield on the same day and played it back on Case's FlexScreen, using the computer's retinal and face recognition programs to scrub the video in high-resolution mode in an attempt to get a visual on Dragan Kiersted. Such detailed search could only be done once the target area had been narrowed down.

Erika stopped breathing when the computer froze an image of Deppe meeting with a man she recognized as Dragan Kiersted, getting a visual on the elusive terrorist for the first time since Greenland.

"Damn, Erika," Case said. "Is it really him?"

"It is and it isn't," she replied, noticing the slight facial deformation.

"That looks like a facial plate," Case observed, his face a few inches from the screen."

"Jimmy told us he was seriously wounded back then but surgery and implants brought him back."

Case nodded. "Looks that way."

"So they did meet there five weeks and four days ago," she said.

"Now what?" asked Ivenko.

"This," Case said, pointing at a large single engine plane on floats parked on the ramp behind Dragan and Deppe. The master terrorist shook hands with Deppe before heading for the plane, where an Asian woman met up with him.

"European Arctic Research Agency," Case said, reading the large emblem on the side of the plane.

"Never heard of it," said Erika as she commanded the FlexScreen to match the tail number with its registered owner, which indeed turned out to be the agency whose logo was painted in black on the side of the white plane.

"That's because it's probably a front company," said Case as he began to work that lead on another FlexScreen.

Meanwhile, Erika commanded her machine to match the plane's tail number with the records from Air Traffic Control, which allowed her to access all flight plans for the Cessna Caravan starting on that day until today.

"Case," she said a moment later, as her eyes read through the ATC list. "I think I know where they went."

"Where?"

"Get Langley on the line," she replied, her finger pointing at a section of text on the FlexScreen. "We need to access our satellites over northern Alaska."

"Alaska? Are you sure?"

Breathing deeply once more, realizing the extreme danger facing that entire state, the modern-day holy warrior in Erika shouted, "Now, Case! Do it now! We are out of time!"

19 Gathering Storm

"The sun will be darkened, the moon will not give its light, and the stars will fall from the sky."
--Matthew 24:29

NORTH SLOPE BOROUGH. ALASKA.

July 13, 2019

The main rotor of the Superhawk helicopter rattled Natasha Shakhiva as it lifted the heavy craft high above the soft permafrost north of the IARC camp in tight formation with a second advance transport helicopter carrying the SEAL team. Their call sign for this mission was Hawk Two, while the SEAL team's chopper was Hawk One.

Colonel Marcus Stone sat next to her in the spacious cabin customized as a VIP carrier for ten, though only three other seats were occupied by the colonel's aides. The rest of his team remained behind in the operations tent to act as mission command. His other second Superhawk sporting a utility configuration for their cargo remained at the IARC camp on stand-by.

The carbon-fiber machines reached five hundred feet before the twin turbofans mounted on the tail ignited, accelerating them to 230 knots in thirty seconds, pressing her against the soft seat.

She gave the column of flames burning above the camp a furtive glance before dropping her gaze to the GPS map on the FlexScreen on her lap, which was slaved to the displays in the Superhawk glass cockpit.

Colonel Stone had received word from the White House that CIA officers in Russia had discovered a climate terrorist plot that included an attack on the Alaska permafrost by some sort of earthquake machine designed to increase the methane flux in the thawing soil.

Unleashing the monster.

The CIA in conjunction with a team of Russian Spetsnaz had destroyed a similar machine before it could wreck havoc in the West Siberian Plains, including the likely destruction of the oil city complex of Surgat.

Satellite data began streaming into Stone's operations tent thirty minutes ago, pinpointing the shores of a lagoon just fifty miles west of their position, where an amphibian Cessna Caravan had landed the day before.

According to the official FAA flight plan, the Cessna was registered to the European Arctic Research Institute, which the CIA report indicated was sponsored in part by Solaris Industries, a front company of Dragan Kiersted, the Greenland mastermind. The Caravan held motion picture permits to shoot caribou movies, but the plane had vanished from radar soon after departing Prudhoe Bay.

Stone had asked Natasha to come along as technical consultant. Their plan called for the SEALs aboard the lead Superhawk to neutralize the terrorists before the scientific team tried to disarm the machine.

She filled her lungs and crossed her arms. Natasha had wanted to alert Malone at UAF but Stone had insisted that the mission was classified by the White House as need-to-know. Aside for Stone's team, she was the only one who knew about the terrorist threat, and that meant the rest of the IARC camp would continue with business as usual.

"The whole region is very vulnerable, Marcus," she said into the mike of her noise-cancellation headset while tilting the FlexScreen in his direction.

Stone frowned. "And our Trans-Alaska Pipeline System goes right above it all."

"The same reason this region is rich with oil explains why there is so much methane, just like in Surgat."

"A package deal, huh?" Works nicely for the terrorists."

"I'm afraid so, which makes it that much more vulnerable," she said.

"A threat multiplier," Stone said more to himself than to her.

She nodded while tundra, lakes, and rivers rushed past them beneath clear skies as the pilots kept the stealth machines at one hundred feet above the flat terrain to avoid tipping their presence to the terrorists they expected to still be at the site, though the last satellite imagery no longer showed the Caravan anchored by the lagoon's shoreline. Stone's cross-functional team back at the National Photographic Interpretation Center was still trying to figure out where it had gone.

"Five minutes," the pilot warned. "Going stealth."

The craft slowed down as rotor noise decreased to a mere whisper. Natasha narrowed her eyes as she watched Hawk One becoming nearly invisible.

"FlexScreen tech," Stone explained. It plays back the image on the opposite site of the ship."

"Incredible," she said, watching the space where the Superhawk carrying the SEAL team had been just a moment ago, now replaced by a slightly distorted horizon, reminding her of seeing through thin haze.

Natasha watched the sea of tundra expanding south, towards the Brooks Mountain Range.

She closed her eyes and inhaled deeply, longing for the smell of pine trees, of fresh, clean air. Her legs ached for the exercise she denied them while working at the IARC camp.

Natasha sighed while opening her eyes, while staring at the jagged peaks, her mind probing further, across the Alaska peninsula, reaching Fairbanks, where Konrad Malone was now safe and sound—where she wish she were at this—

"Two minutes. Target lagoon in sight," reported the pilot. "Hawk One is going in while we circle at five hundred."

"Any sign of the Caravan?" Stone asked.

"Negative, sir. But there is some sort of equipment by the lagoon's north shore. Hawk One is dropping the SEALs in two minutes to investigate."

Natasha watched with interest as Hawk One broke formation and descended steeply towards the target and Hawk Two started a shallow turn.

"Prudhoe ATC just reported a contact 10 miles south at five thousand feet and climbing," reported the pilot of Hawk Two.

Stone frowned. "Is it the Caravan?"

"Can't tell, sir, though its speed and climb profile matches that of a turboprop."

Natasha felt a chill gripping her gut as she watched Hawk One approach the target zone, the rotor's downwash flattening the shore vegetation and rippling the water's surface.

At that instance, before the helicopter reached the ground to deliver the SEAL team, the top of one of the boxes ignited in a plume of fire that engulfed the helicopter.

"Hawk One! Get out of there! Get out of there!"

Instead of a reply, agonizing screams filled the frequency as the intensely-hot plume tore through the hovering craft while pushing it skyward.

Natasha watched in paralyzed shock as the pilots made a brave attempt to move the helicopter away from the white-hot billowing column that reached one hundred feet in seconds.

As screams continued to rattle the operations frequency, the helicopter pulled out of the rising flames just to enter an autorotation, plummeting back to earth and crashing a few hundred feet away, exploding on contact.

"Sweet Mother of God!" exclaimed Stone, his fists tight, his eyes fixated on the helicopter.

"The rocket booster, Marcus!" said Natasha. "The machine is active! Do we have any means of shooting it?"

Stone turned to her, anger in his eyes as he said, "Destroy the target! Repeat, destroy the target!"

"Roger that," replied the pilot.

The helicopter entered a sharp left turn as the pilot maneuvered for a shot.

The ground grew hazy for an instance before fire erupted around the rocket booster, spreading rapidly across the tundra in every direction.

"The methane!" Natasha shouted. "The machine is collapsing the soil structure, releasing the methane!"

"Damn! Destroy the target! Now, dammit! Now!"

"Fox Three!" shouted the pilot as two missiles dashed from the helicopter's underside towards the burning target, reaching it an instant later.

The ensuing blast echoed across the meadow as the high-explosive warheads tore into the machine, igniting the remaining rocket fuel in a massive bowl of flames that threatened to swallow them.

Natasha shielded her eyes at the ensuing brightness lighting up their surroundings an instant before the explosion echoed across the land.

But instead of shrinking, the flames rapidly grew in intensity, fueled by the free-flow of methane.

"Oh, Dear God!" Natasha shouted. "The monster, Marcus! It is the monster!"

Bright orange and red-gold, the eruption licked the helicopter's underside as the pilot fought for altitude.

She grabbed the arm rests, terror seizing her intestines.

Gasping, her throat going dry, Natasha almost screamed as the helicopter trembled, as the rotor noise peaked to a deafening roar, as she sensed severe upward motion.

The last thing she saw out of the side windows before the flames and the smoke surrounded them was a massive sheet of fire stretching in every direction as far as she could see.

R. J. Pineiro

20 Armageddon

"And there will be strange events in the skies – signs in the sun, moon, and stars. And down here on earth the nations will be in turmoil, perplexed by the roaring seas and strange tides. The courage of many people will falter because of the fearful fate they see coming upon the earth, because the stability of the very heavens will be broken up."
--Luke 21:25

NORTH SLOPE BOROUGH. ALASKA.

July 13, 2019

The shockwaves injected into the ground to a depth of fifteen hundred feet altered the composition of the soil as far as one mile in every direction from Ground Zero, destroying the semi-frozen balance of its crystal lattice across several square kilometers, exponentially increasing the methane flux of the permafrost, creating a massive burnoff vent for the pressurized methane trapped for the past 11,000 years.

The gas hissed through this circular tunnel of weakened soil almost as if it were not there, reaching the surface just as the missiles blasted a crater at Ground Zero the size of a basketball court.

The resulting fireball, resembling a monstrous torch, spread out at fifty miles per hour as the mechanical oscillations receded.

But by then a deadly positive loop was formed.

The fire stopped momentarily at the edges of the altered soil structure, but the white-hot inferno scorched the walls of this vertical tunnel, tearing into the permafrost, thawing it from the surface down to the methane deposits, enlarging the radius at the rate of one mile every thirty seconds, exponentially expanding the opening.

The sheet of fire reached the IARC camp in less than ten minutes, as scientists, technicians, and even Stone's personnel struggled to evacuate.

The intense heat incinerated every soul on the camp as the wall of flames propagated through the area like a sizzling sandstorm of inky smoke and pulsating flames, swallowing all that stood in its way. Heavy objects, like the helicopter, vehicles, and heavy equipment sank in the smoldering quicksand-like soil, as if swallowed by hell itself.

A few souls jumped into the freezing Shirukak Lake, their backs on fire, only to be boiled alive as the flames reached far beyond the shores, heating the surface water in seconds. Their final agonizing screams were shunted by the roaring blaze and blinding smoke.

Within one minute all life ceased at the IARC camp as the scorching monster continue to eat away the soil, expanding its opening to the deposits, consuming some while igniting new ones in a chain reaction that threatened to devour the entire North Slope.

21 Scorching the World

"After there is great trouble among mankind, a greater one is prepared . . . rain, thirst, famine, and disease. In the heavens, a fire seen."
--Michel de Nostredame (Nostradamus)

NORTH SLOPE BOROUGH. ALASKA.

July 13, 2019

"Mayday, Mayday, Mayday, Hawk Two has turbine failure! Repeat Hawk Two has turbine failure and is going down sixty miles southwest of the IARC Camp!"

Natasha clutched Stone's hand as their world spun around them while immersed in their own smoke spewing from the malfunctioning turbines and main rotor.

They had managed to rise above the initial blast but the chopper had endured excessive engine damage as they made a dash south towards the Brooks Mountain Range, where she knew the terrain was firm, solid, where the permafrost ended.

But they were still over ten miles away.

"We're not going to make it!" Stone shouted as the smoke cleared, as she got another glimpse of the fire burning in the distance but heading their way in what she knew was a deadly positive loop. The monster had been unleashed and only the massive Brooks Mountain Range would be able to hold it back, sparing the rest of the state.

But to spare themselves they needed to reach it first, needed to—

The helicopter began to auto-rotate as the main turbine failed while flying at five hundred feet above the tundra.

Her world vibrating and gyrating around her, quickly losing perspective, Natasha watched in a blur as Colonel Stone opened the Superhawk's side door.

A rush of cold air and smoke invaded the cabin, the clear surface of a lagoon projecting beyond the rectangular opening.

Stone reached across her and unbuckled her seatbelt.

"Wait!" she screamed. "What are you doing?"

"Out! Everybody jump out!" Stone shouted over the intercom, before yanking his headset and also Natasha's, and lifting her frame with one of his massive arms.

"Wa—wait! What do you think you are—"

The colonel stared into her eyes for an instant and screamed, "Run to the mountains! Survive! Fix this!"

And he tossed her outside.

The blue-gray water, rocky shores, clear skies, and the smoke trailing from the dying helicopter exchange places in her field of view as she fell, for an instant feeling the heat from the burning turbines before diving feet first in the lagoon, the water chilling her.

She gasped, controlled the urge to vomit from the piercing cold, from its stabbing pain, feeling as if she was rolling on a bed of nails puncturing the sanity out of her shocked mind.

Kicking her legs, she began to swim to the surface, reaching it a moment later, filling her lungs with cold air just as the helicopter crashed a hundred feet away into the jagged rocks by the shoreline.

A cloud of smoke and debris engulfed the crash site but she heard no explosion.

Get out of the water!

Natasha immediately began to swim as hard as she could, realizing she only had minutes before hypothermia set in, her eyes on the helicopter, praying it would not explode as it sat crushed on the shore, thin coils of smoke rising from its main rotor and aft turbines.

Her clothes began to slow her down; began to make it difficult to move, to swim.

Realizing what she had to do to survive the climatologist removed her jacket, jeans, sweatshirt, undershirt, and boots, but did not dispose of them, knowing she would need them later.

Down to her panties and no bra, Natasha clutched her clothes against her bare chest while floating on her back and kicking her legs as hard as she could, propelling herself towards the shore just to the right of the crash site.

Her skin goosebumping, quickly losing sensation in her feet and hands, she pressed on, realizing she would die if she stopped, forcing savage control to fight off the panic, the nearing fiery storm, closing the last dozen feet, until her toes touched the rocky bottom.

Straightening up, shivering, she looked for anyone else through the haze enveloping the wreckage as she walked rapidly out of the water.

Nearly paralyzed by the appalling cold, Natasha glanced to the north, to the scorching tempest they had managed to escape only to crash short of the protective rocky hills and caves of the Brooks Mountain Range.

Lips quivering, her body trembling, feeling light headed, dizzy, about to collapse, Natasha Shakhiva mustered strength, ignoring the stinging pain, approaching the wreck.

She stopped.

Wedged in a clump of jagged boulders protruding through the surface between her and the helicopter was the body of Marcus Stone. He had also tried to jump but had fallen on rocks.

She approached him, controlling the urge to vomit from the cold as well as from the sight of his maimed body, impaled by the sharp boulders, limbs twisted at unnatural angles.

His blue eyes on a face packed with freckles stared at the darkening sky.

Run to the mountains! Survive! Fix this!

Forcing control, his words echoing in her mind, she closed his eyes, said a brief prayer, and continued to the wreckage, reaching the side of the helicopter, peeking through the same side door that Stone had thrown her out of moments before, saving her life at the price of his own.

Inside the murky, hazy interior she spotted all three of Stone's aides plus the pilot and copilot—all still strapped to their seats.

Dropping her wet clothes and reaching for one of two Arctic survival kits, Natasha unbuckled the front straps of the hard case, opened it, and grabbed a one-piece thermal body suit. She ripped the clear protective cover, unfolded the bright-yellow garment and unzipped the front. The jump-suit-like survival device had a single zipper from the crotch to the neck.

She unzipped it with numb fingers, before stepping into it with her right leg first, then the left, welcoming the advanced material, waterproof and thermally insulated, against her prickly skin. She slid both feet into built-in foot covers that stretched to conform to her shoe size.

Lifting the top over her shoulder, she ran each arm into it the long sleeves before reaching down and zipping it up to her neck.

Arms crossed, feeling the material developed by NASA some years back starting to hold on to her heat, she looked towards the still passengers, trying to see if anyone was—

Natasha gasped, bile reaching her throat when noticing their smoking entrails by their feet.

Oh God, she thought, realizing that a section of the main rotor had sliced through the cabin, almost cutting them in half.

She looked away, rushing towards the cockpit, hoping to find a survivor, but the pilots lay inert in pools of their own blood as the jagged rocks had pierced through the canopy of the Superhawk, impaling them.

Sweet Mother of God, she thought, controlling her breathing, bile once more reaching her gorge.

This time she couldn't hold it back, and kneeling in the space between the aviators, she vomited, tears blinding her, every muscle in her body tense, on edge.

Breathing in short sobbing gasps, she stopped, stood, tried to get a hold of herself.

It was then that she got a glimpse of the scenery beyond the rectangular opening of the chopper's side door, and she realized that she could not stay here much longer if she intended to survive.

Run to the mountains! Survive! Fix this!

She had been damned lucky that Colonel Marcus Stone had thrown her out when he had, but she was still in extreme danger.

Get away from here now.

Hastily, Natasha turned away from cockpit and looked about the cabin once more. She stared at the dead aides next to her, whispered, "I'm so sorry," and unbuckled the restraining belt of the smallest of the three. Nearly decapitated by the blade, his head swung back at a grotesque angle. She removed his thick Army jacket, which albeit bloody, would provide protection from the elements.

Stepping away, she put it over the thermal suit before removing the officer's trousers, which fit her good enough, as well as his Army field boots, which she laced quickly.

Her mind on automatic, her survival instincts overtaking all other emotions, Natasha knelt by the Arctic survival case and extracted the large survival backpack, putting it on, feeling its weight, not nearly as balanced as her hiking gear but certainly lighter.

She also removed the aide's belt, including a holstered .45 caliber Colt semiautomatic, standard U.S. Army issue.

Finally, she pulled out both portable ELTs--Emergency Locator Transmitters--from the side wall, and turned them on to verify their operation and also to start broadcasting her presence to potential rescue crews. In addition, she grabbed a handheld transceiver—two-way radio—from a cubby hole next to the ELTs and powered it on, verifying functionality, before switching it to the Guard frequency, 121.5Mhz, typically monitored by most aircraft and Air Traffic Control.

If she managed to outrun the incoming storm, she would need them in order for a search-and-rescue party to find her in the mountains.

Satisfied, she shoved the small ELTs into Velcro-secured pockets in her Army trousers while hanging on to the transceiver, which she planned to use to broadcast her situation every thirty minutes.

She jumped off the chopper and headed for the mountains, her eyes focusing on a familiar peak, where she knew would be many caves for shelter from the elements.

Looking back once, Natasha Shakhiva narrowed her gaze at the distant firestorm heading her way, at the boiling clouds of smoldering ash rushing in her direction.

And began to run.

22 Alarm Bells

"The scientific consensus presented in this comprehensive report about human-induced climate change should sound alarm bells in every national capital and in every local community."
--Klaus Topfer, United Nations Environment Program, commenting on the IPCC's Third Assessment Report, January 2001.

UNIVERSITY OF ALASKA, FAIRBANKS.

July 13, 2019

"What in the hell is *that?"* asked Malone, sitting next to Mario Escobar in the analysis room adjacent to the freezers dominating the basement of the department of geology.

Escobar stared at the real-time satellite feeding a window on the large FlexScreen, where they had been reviewing core samples non-stop for the past 12 hours, since Malone arrived here.

The Bolivian dragged the cursor to the window and enlarged it while narrowing his eyes. "It . . . please tell me this isn't what I think it is."

Malone stared at a satellite image of the state of Alaska and its neighbors, the Yukon Territory to the east and Washington state to the south. A deep crimson stain covered ten percent of the state, or roughly 50,000 square miles.

"This must be a mistake," Malone whispered, his mind doing the math. The methane flux was not high enough to justify such outburst. "Check the satellite link and data integrity."

Escobar typed a few commands and shrugged. "It all checks out, *amigo*. The fire is real."

Malone sat there contemplating the surreal image painted on the FlexScreen, his mind going in different directions.

"Call the IARC camp," he said, heading upstairs to the radio room.

Escobar put a hand on his forearm and said, "Hold on, amigo. Let's take a closer look."

The Hispanic glaciologist superimposed the location of the camp on the real-time image and zoomed in.

"Oh, God, no," Malone said, staring at the inferno surrounding Shirukak Lake, his vision tunneling at the thought of Natasha Shakhiva--

"Maybe they got out," Escobar said. "She was always escorting Colonel Stone from the U.S. Army who arrived in these fancy transport helicopters. Maybe they all got the hell out of there in time."

A glimmer of hope.

Maybe they got out.

Maybe she got out.

"The video, Mario!" he said, taking a deep breath, praying that she managed to get out in time. "Rewind the video to the hour preceding the fire."

Escobar did. Watching in slow motion as the fire broke out from the shores of a lagoon some fifty miles west of the IARC camp. Infrared imaging worked best, clearly depicting Ground Zero as well as the Army helicopters converging on the site.

"Get the Pentagon on the horn, Mario. These guys were on a mission up there. That's the only explanation why they would be headed for Ground Zero moments before it went up in flames."

"And I think this is who they were after," Escobar said, pointing to the IR signature of a mid-size general aviation aircraft leaving the shores twenty minutes before the military arrived.

"Let's track them separately and feed their flight path to the Pentagon. Bastards on that plane scorched the world, Mario. They're not going to get away with it. Hurry up. After we speak to them we're going up there."

"We are? Are you looking at the same picture I am?"

"Natasha was on that second chopper, Mario. I want high-res video tracking the flight path of the chopper. Then you and I are going on a little search and rescue mission."

R. J. Pineiro

23 The Last Hour

"It is the last hour; and as you have heard that antichrist is coming."
--John 2:18

NORTH SLOPE BOROUGH. ALASKA.

July 13, 2019

The initial flash reminded him of Greenland, only this time he was in full control.

Sitting in the co-pilot seat of the amphibian Cessna Caravan, Dragan Kiersted watched the massive fire propagating beneath them as they reached ten thousand feet heading back to the ocean at full speed to get away from the rising charcoal clouds building up like an apocalyptic storm.

He took a deep breath, the magnitude of the destruction surprising him, never having expected for the Russian earthquake machines to work so well so fast. But then again, there were Gigatons of methane trapped beneath the permafrost.

Dragan watched the North Slope vanishing beneath a pulsating blanket of dark clouds alive with flames, redeeming the failure in Surgat even though the Russian oil city had always been the distraction.

"The American helicopters were caught in the fire," Shin-Li reported. "No one will follow us."

Dragan sighed, almost refusing to believe his good fortune. There was indeed something poetic about using a terrorist strike to also protect the getaway route by blocking pursuers.

"How long before reaching Canada?" he asked as they left the spreading fire behind while leveling off at fifteen thousand feet and accelerating to 200 knots.

"Thirty more minutes," she said.

Dragan leaned back in the co-pilot seat and watched the navigation system as well as the on-board radar system, which searched the sky for any nearby traffic.

"There's someone on the Guard Frequency," reported Shin-Li, tapping a couple of switches to pipe in the audio to Dragan.

"Mayday, Mayday, Mayday, this is Doctor Natasha Shakhiva, sole survivor of the IARC camp in Shirukak Lake. I'm headed for Brooks to seek shelter. Any aircraft listening please relay the following coordinates to Alaska Search and Rescue."

Dragan listened to her GPS coordinates, which placed her just a short distance from the foot of the mountain range.

"There is no help headed your way, Doctor," Dragan mumbled while watching the clear skies ahead before focusing on the radar display.

The screen was devoid of any traffic in this remote region of North America, though he knew that was all about to change in the next hour, as the world woke up to the massive ecological disaster he had triggered.

They remained on course until ten miles before crossing the border with Canada, when Shin-Li put them in a steep descent to five hundred feet, where they remained for another twenty minutes until overflying the mining town of Old Crow in northern Yukon in a southerly direction.

Shin-Li then climbed to seven thousand feet and contacted the Yukon Territory arm of NAV Canada, the country's centralized Air Traffic Control, where she had filed a flight plan for a Cessna Caravan registered under Canada Air Care, a nonprofit organization dedicated to providing free air transportation for medical and humanitarian purposes. According to the flight plan, they were carrying a cancer victim from Old Crow to a treatment center in White Horse, a city in the southern end of the Canadian territory. Their new call sign was Air Care 65R.

"Air Care Six Five Romeo, Yukon Center," came the reply from NAV Canada. *"Radar contact ten miles south of Old Crow. Climb and maintain ten thousand, expect fifteen thousand in ten minutes."*

"Yukon Center, Air Care Six Five Romeo. We are noticing strange dark clouds forming in the distant eastern horizon. Looks like a large fire in Alaska. Please advice."

"Air Care Six Five Romeo, infrared satellite confirms a very large fire on the North Slope propagating rapidly in all directions. Unknown origin. Alaska's Forestry Division in Fairbanks has already been contacted."

"Roger that, Yukon," replied Shin-Li while grinning at Dragan, who winked back.

The climate terrorist gave one more glance to his handy work monopolizing the eastern horizon before removing his head set and heading aft, where Hans-Jorgen and Doctor Yuri Gerchenko sat while watching the fire through side windows.

"Enjoying the show, gentleman? You have the best seat in town."

They looked at Dragan momentarily before returning their attention to the incredible sight.

Dragan Kiersted sat in the rear of the plane and peered at the massive clouds, at the extent of the devastation, an omnipotent feeling descending on him.

He was punishing the human race, slowly eradicating them. A million here. Ten million there. Many, many more in the future as the long-term effects of his global hammer settled in, destroying their lives of excess, of immense waste, of irresponsible consumption.

The Earth will recover, he thought, *just as it has countless times before following extinction events.*

But the insatiable parasite that is the human race will not.

I have drowned them.

I have frozen them.

Now I will burn them.

And tomorrow I will burn them again and then drown them.

Water. Ice. Fire. The Earth's basic elements, its basic forces.

Dragan swore to continue using them to destroy those trying to destroy the Earth.

Burn them and drown them.

He stared at his reflection on the window and frowned at his deformed face, at the plate he had been forced to wear for the rest of his life. He hated it as much as he despised hi liquid diet, his mechanical limbs, and the knowledge that he would forever be considered a half-human abomination.

But the fires beyond his reflection gave him solace, comfort, filling with the satisfaction of having punished those who had taken so much from him, from his father, from the Earth.

Burn them and drown them.

He lowered the window shade and turned his attention to the FlexScreen unrolled before him displaying real-time updates of the effort underway to repeat Alaska in the highly-populated Toronto.

Burn them and drown them.

He intended to make personally sure that the last two machines would surpass Alaska and Greenland.

24 Ashes to Ashes

"The first angel sounded, and there followed hail and fire mingled with blood, and they were cast upon the earth: and the third part of trees was burnt up, and all green grass was burnt up."
--Revelation 6:15

NORTH SLOPE BOROUGH. ALASKA.

July 13, 2019

Broiling clouds of smoldering ash spread across the darkening skies of Alaska, swallowing meadows and forests whole, devouring the thousands of rivers and lakes that defined the western tip of North America.

Trees and vegetation ignited in the superheated air, sizzling embers reaching a mile high, exterminating all species in its scorching wake in a biblical conflagration the Earth had not seen for millions of years.

The hungry monster leaped across rivers, stretching its blistering wrath like a relentless plague, scourging the woods and all its creatures, heating the streams, boiling alive all creatures who had sought refuge from the inferno, as well as all the fish, which floated dead on its simmering surface.

Steam hissed from the evaporating rivers, their bubbling cry ignored by the roaring flames pulsating from the surrounding tundra, orange and red-gold fists flickering through the rising haze as millions upon miles of cubic miles of organic fuel fed this insatiable beast, this unyielding curse consuming the North Slope Borough of Alaska.

Against this apocalyptic hell a lonely figure caked in gray dust scrambled across the dying valley at the foot of the mountain range; a lonely creature under the shadow of her planet's darkest hour struggling to escape the inescapable, the end of days.

The echoing cries of the dying at her back, she ran as fast as her tired legs allowed, rushing towards the mountains that marked the southern end of Alaska's North Slope, her only hope in a place losing all hope.

Staring into the barren scarlet tundra at her world's setting sun, Natasha Shakhiva forged ahead, no longer looking back, her nostrils alerting her to the sizzling curtain of death threatening to devour her just as it greedily consumed any creature that had failed to flee in time, from fulmars, bears, squirrels, and caribou, to ravens, geese, and swans--many burned alive as they cried out for a relief that never came. The rest had long fled or dashed past her, reaching the safety of the mountains, escaping the growing inferno.

But something else reached the sensors lining her nasal passages.

A gathering storm, but not behind her.

Her eyes probed the thawing terrain before her, searching for the distant sight that would corroborate her sense of smell.

A storm was forming ahead, high above the mountain range.

But not any storm.

A hail storm.

Her brain evoked images of dense clouds packed with flesh-ripping hail, powerful enough to kill her in seconds.

Hail storms.

Lightning gleamed in the distance, above tundra on fire behind her and blasted with a fast-moving curtain of falling ice pounding the peaks before her in a whirlwind of certain death blocking the sinking sun as night fell over Alaska.

Monster hail storms.

They had begun five years ago in this region, their origin still unknown, but certainly the byproduct of shifting weather patterns.

Natasha screamed over the roar of the incinerating cyclone at her back, the incoming hail storm shrouding the mountain range, and the thunder clapping above it all.

She screamed in anger, screamed in frustration, and cursed the dark skies as the world closed in on her.

Lightning flashed as the sun vanished, as a trembling reddish glow spread across the mountains, a reflection of the surging fire against the wall of shredding ice. Scorching clouds of death shooting ahead, accelerated by southern winds, reached beyond the edge of the inferno, stretching mercilessly across the dying landscape like a relentless chastisement, hungry still, threatening to engulf her.

Sheets of lightning arced across the northern sky, bridging the forces of nature accelerating towards each other in a direct collision course, briefly illuminating the path ahead, the patch of tundra by the foot of the mountains untouched by an angered world, the eye of this Apocalyptic storm.

And that's when Natasha's keen eyesight, amidst the flashes casting a stroboscopic glare on the burgundy land, spotted the ragged edges of rock formations protruding through the desert floor off to her right, the caves used by her and Malone to escape the elements during previous hiking trips.

Natasha risked a brief backward glance, her eyes assessing the gap separating her from the expanding crimson shroud, before glaring at the incoming hail storm, alive with forks of lightning.

She grunted, but not out of desperation. The guttural shrieks echoing straight from her lungs with all her might, clashing with the roar and the thunder, echoed inside her mind as she pushed herself a final time, sprinting towards the serrated formations projecting before the Brooks Mountain Range, back-dropped by the towering wall of falling ice accelerating towards her with flesh-ripping force.

The growing heat roasting her back, her lungs protesting the toxic air she had to inhale deeply in order to keep up her speed, Natasha focused on the looming rock formations, on her only way out of this predicament.

Screaming in pain, in fear, in near-blind panic, her vision tunneling, her mind pushing everything aside, Natasha Shakhiva took leap after agonizing leap, her survival instincts refusing to give up, refusing to acknowledge the futility of her situation: a lonely figure racing towards her only hope for safety in the middle of the most destructive forces of nature.

Against the fall of night.

At the end of time.

She pushed, kicked, and hurdled, soaring over the tundra while covered in ash, like a white ghost, taxing her endurance to the brink of complete exhaustion.

But through the swirling haze of a world gone mad, through the insane heat threatening to set her on fire, Natasha found solace in the granite terrain she had just reached, hard and solid ground, methane free.

Just a little longer, she thought, her lungs protesting the abuse, her tired legs propelling her toward the nearing jagged shapes against the incoming hail storm, remembering its narrow entrance leading deep below the mountain.

A cloud of falling ice descended over Natasha, blinding her as she neared the entrance, pounding her as the smoldering ash behind blistered the back of her neck, scourging her.

Closing her eyes, she persisted, ducking her head, pushing her way through the colliding squall, holding her course, until it all vanished abruptly, the heat, the punishing ice, the toxic fumes-- replaced by the cool humidity of the interior of a cave, its musk bringing back memories of yesteryear, of times she spent with Konrad Malone sharing a sleeping bag, enjoying each other's company during their--

The roaring collision outside brought her back around. She had momentarily collapsed from the final sprint, had briefly passed out from the heat, the scarring ice, the sheer exhaustion from three hours of constant running.

But the misty interior injected her with renewed hope, with new strength as the titanic fronts collided outside in an earth-shaking rumble of fire and ice.

Slowly, Natasha stumbled to her feet, soothing her lungs with the fresh and humid air oozing from deep within the cave.

She blinked repeatedly, clearing her eyesight from ashes and dust, snorting heavily to unclog her nasal passages before testing the air, confirming the presence of what she needed most besides shelter.

Water.

Inhaling deeply while standing tall, she ignored the world above her exploding in an ear-piercing crescendo that propagated down the tunnel, rumbling the walls, shaking the marble floors.

A few stalactites fell from the rocky ceiling, dislodged by the mighty heavens clashing.

The brittle formations thundered as they shattered on impact, kicking up a cloud of dust that mixed with the sandy haze and heat exhaled by the monsters into the cave's entrance.

It's not safe here. I need to go deeper.

Reaching into her backpack, she produced a flashlight, which she used to guide her in the murky interior as she followed the steep gradient of a narrow chute with caution, her rugged boots gripping the damp granite surface leading to a large chamber, tall enough to fit a three-storey house.

Here the air was cleaner, purer, still untainted by the firestorm, its thick marble walls insulating her.

But Natasha went deeper, the clashing madness on the surface receding, the crimson glow fading, the deafening sounds giving way to her steady breathing mixed with the gurgling sound of an underground stream as the grading shallow and she reached a foot bridge that led to a spacious chamber divided by a narrow stream that flowed slowly over a light gravel fill, disappeared beneath a ledge.

She walked slowly towards the stream, going around a few stalagmites, rock formations protruding from the floor up to the ceiling, before kneeling by the edge, closing her eyes for an instant before dunking her entire head in the cool water, washing away the layer of white dust caking her head, her hair.

She tasted the stream, deciding it was safe to drink, before swallowing it.

Resting the flashlight on the granite surface, she removed her backpack, unzipped it and inspected its contents for the first time.

She found several packs of beef jerky, dehydrated fruits, peanuts, chocolate, and two MREs—Meals Ready to Eat—one with chicken and the other with beef.

She tore the plastic wrapper of a string of beef jerky and took a bite, chewing it slowly while rubbing her aching legs.

As she ate, she rummaged through the backpack, finding a sleeping bag made of the same insulated material as her body suit. It had a built-in inflatable pad and pillow, which she gladly inflated.

As she rested on it, she assessed the rest of her survival gear, including a compass, a handheld GPS, the two ELT transmitters, a waterproof plastic poncho, two knives, a stainless-steel dish and canteen, waterproof matches, fishing line and hooks, a transceiver radio capable of reaching aircraft, two flare guns, a signaling mirror, and some first-aid gear.

Enough to last a few days if she rationed the food and also was able to leave the cave and make it to the mountains, where she could fish and hunt until help arrived.

After consuming two strings of beef jerky, a pack of peanuts, and a small chocolate bar, she dipped the canteen in the stream, filled it, and then took several sips, before closing it.

Yawning, she stowed all of the food into the backpack, crawled into the sleeping bag, switched off the flashlight and, clutching the pistol in case a bear ventured into the cave seeking refuge, fell asleep.

25 Consequences

"The era of procrastination, of half-measures, of soothing and baffling expedients, of delays, is coming to a close. In its place, we are entering a period of consequences."
--Winston Churchill

PRUDHOE BAY, ALASKA.

July 14, 2019

The wall of methane-fueled fire marching south stopped at the foot of the Brooks Mountain Range. To the north, the progressively colder permafrost slowed down the monster, but not before it reached Deadhorse, the oil city on the shores of Prudhoe Bay.

Evacuations started within the hour after the methane gas explosions, but being the height of the drilling season, there simply weren't enough transports to get everyone to safety.

Smoldering clouds reached the oil complex thirty minutes before the flames, raining massive amounts of embers on the panicked population as they sought shelter that didn't exist. The fire from the sky ignited all wooden structures, from the famous Caribou Inn in the center of town to all residential and commercial properties. Over a thousand souls perished in the most inhumane of deaths--their skin blistering from the heat, their brains boiling inside their craniums, their organs melting inside their shriveling bodies from the broiling ashes. Even their clothes ignited as they ran towards shore, away from the inferno.

Explosions followed the clouds as the extreme heat ignited storage tanks. The Trans-Alaska Pipeline fed by the tanks blew next, propagating south like a massive fuse towards the methane fires nearing the dying city.

The fires continued propagating to the northwest, approaching Barrow, the borough seat of the North Slope Borough of Alaska, North America's northernmost settlement and home to 5000 souls.

Evacuations at the Barrow airport and seaport began almost immediately. The city had long been warned about the possibility of methane explosions by UAF's IARC team and had set up emergency evacuation procedures for the dangerous summer months, when the permafrost was most vulnerable.

But, like in Deadhorse, there wasn't enough time to get everyone out to safety. Women and children boarded the ferries first, chugging out of port and into the calm Arctic Ocean as the wall of fire reached the outskirts of the city, rocketing temperatures, burning hundreds of wooden homes built on pylons due to the thawing permafrost. The blaze and the clouds finally descended over the sea front, engulfing the crowded docks, exterminating nearly three thousand men, women, and children in minutes and in plain sight of camera crews aboard helicopters hovering above departing ferries. Seagulls and fulmars winged to sea, many failing to escape the accelerating clouds, igniting in mid air.

The president declared Alaska a federal disaster area and ordered the immediate evacuation of towns south of the Brooks Mountain Range, including Fairbanks, as a precaution, and had ordered all available forest fire fighting units in the American West to the region.

A massive southerly migration began in the hours following the devastating news from Barrow and Deadhorse as hundreds of thousands of panicked residents took to the highways with every possession they could pack in their vehicles, clogging up the road system.

Above this unprecedented evacuation, a lone Piper Cub flew at ten thousand feet heading north.

Konrad Malone watched the madness below with mixed sadness and anger. The scientific community had issued warnings for years that this could happen, that the thawing permafrost might not be able to contain the methane deposits, and it looked as if it had finally happened, exploding with Biblical powers, wiping out in hours a hundred thousand square miles of tundra and everything that lived within it that failed to make it to the mountain range looming in the distance.

Spread on his lap was a FlexScreen playing back the satellite video feed that had prompted him to disregard the government warnings, convincing Mario Escobar to fly north, towards the monster. The high-definition satellite images of the crashing helicopter by the lagoon just north of the Brooks Mountain Range, followed by the incredible transmissions on the Guard frequency, confirmed that somehow she had survived and was headed for their old hiking grounds.

The world below them in havoc, their radios switched off to stop listening to ATC instructing them to turn around, Konrad Malone focused on the mountains looming in the distance, growing larger with every passing moment. At this altitude, he could also see the clouds behind the range, charcoal and billowing, but apparently held back by the leeward winds blowing steadily from the south, sparing the rest of the state.

At least for now, he thought. But the unpredictable winds could easily shift in the opposite direction tomorrow, spreading the terror that consumed the North Slope Borough.

The government was already deploying most of its teams of forest fire fighters to the Brooks Mountain Range. These teams of Hot Shots, as they were called, specialized in controlling massive forest fires that consumed millions of acres of forest each year in the American West.

Malone returned his attention to the FlexScreen, to the last known transmission from her Emergency Locator Transmitter by the foot of the mountain range almost four hours ago.

"You realize how crazy this is, Koni?" asked Escobar from the front. "You never get closer to a fire than the Hot Shots. They're the experts, amigo."

Malone shrugged. He was asking Escobar to fly to a spot north of where the Hot Shots were headed to hold back the fire. Common sense told him to remain behind the fire-break line the Hot Shots were going to carve along the range to prevent the flames from spreading further south. But then again, common sense had also told him not to camp so close to the dying glacier in Mount Kilimanjaro.

"Just set me down close enough, Mario. I will go the rest of the way on my own. She's a survivor, like you and me. I will find her and bring her back."

"But the odds are—"

"Fuck the odds, man. She's alive. I can feel it."

"Koni, I also hope she is alive, and I will not just drop you off. I'm in this thing with you one hundred percent," he replied over the intercom as they flew in and out of clouds while climbing to get past the southern peaks. "I'm just concerned that there has not been any two-way-radio transmission in the past four hours. Her ELT also went dark at the same time."

"That just means she found shelter, Mario. She got to one of our caves and is in deep hiding, riding out the storm, just as I would have done. Like I said, she's a survivor."

"I hope you are right, *amigo*," he replied. "I hope to God you are right."

I am right, he thought.

I must find her.

I will find her and rescue her.

Just as she rescued me.

Konrad Malone had vowed to find Natasha Shakhiva.

Or die trying.

He continued watching the madness below as well as the apocalyptic scene ahead.

The world was on fire.

Just as it had been on fire 4000 years ago.

26 An Eye for an eye

"If any harm follows, then you shall give life for life, eye for eye, tooth for tooth, hand for hand, foot for foot, burn for burn, wound for wound, stripe for stripe."
--Exodus 21:25

MEMPHIS, EGYPT
(CAPITAL OF THE OLD KINGDOM, 12 MILES SOUTH OF MODERN-DAY CAIRO).

2210 B.C.

Nitocris stood to the side of the room as she watched the enemies of her husband gorge themselves in the most succulent of meals.

It had been months since anyone in Egypt had seen such delicatessen served, and the widow of the late Pepi II Neferkare had saved them for this occasion.

Standing next to her was the loyal Harkfuf, whose role was now that of protecting the queen as their country imploded, as the relentless heat wave propelled the world's most advanced society into utter chaos, into complete anarchy. Hundreds of thousands had perished, and the priests had finally placed the blame squarely on the shoulders of Neferkare, who died days later at the hand of an assassin, proving to the entire kingdom that he was not a godking.

And that revelation had also placed Nitocris in severe danger, especially as a council of Nomarchs and priests took over whatever semblance of an army still existed across the land, a mere shadow of what it had been just two years before.

And this council, which she knew was responsible for her husband's death, now feasted in a special chamber in the bowels of her husband's burial temple, a massive pyramid constructed over the past decade by the shores of the Nile.

Nitocris smiled politely at them, an eclectic group of priests, Nomarchs, merchants, and military chiefs. They ate, drank, and fornicated with Nubian slaves, before eating and drinking some more.

"How much longer?" asked Nitocris.

"As soon as my messenger arrives we leave the chamber," he replied.

"You must protect Pepi III," she said. "They will come after me for what I'm about to do, but not after my son."

"I vow to protect him," the military chief said.

Nitocris watched in silence as slaves brought in course after course, as the drinks flowed, as naked slaves copulated with council members right on their chairs, sometimes while they ate and talked.

Nitocris despised them all for what they stood for, for what they had done to her beloved husband, for the plots she knew were underway to kill her as well.

But I will kill you first, she thought. You will die here, tonight, in a chamber lower than where my beloved rests.

Harkfuf's messenger arrived just before dawn, along with a fresh group of whores and more food, bringing a round of applause from her guests, who were thoroughly impressed at her ability to produce so much fresh food in a time of extreme famine, of death across the land.

Nitocris and Harkfuf bowed while slowly retreating, presumably to give room to the arriving entertainment, but they continued walking back, finally turning around when losing line of sight with the party.

The narrow corridor led to the anteroom, where Nitocris reached for a stone at waist level protruding just a little more than the rest. To the average observer, it would appear as a minor defect in an otherwise perfect work of architecture. But this stone had been placed here as the trigger of a mechanism conceived by her husband's finest builders.

As designed, the stone glided softly into the wall, releasing the blocks holding back the massive boulder that formed the roof of the connecting corridor.

In an instant, the boulder dropped into place, completely blocking the main chamber from the anteroom, sealing the party behind a wall of rock the width of three horses.

Forever.

She wished she could have heard their screams as she entombed them, but perfectly smooth limestone did not allow any sound to propagate.

Nodding to Harkfuf, they walked up the incline passageway to the surface.

The predawn skies were indigo with faint streaks of orange in the horizon.

My last sunrise, she thought, perspiration already forming on her forehead and in between her breasts from the blistering temperature, even at this early hour.

As agreed, the chief of the military activated the second hidden architectural feature of the pyramid by pushing three rocks down a long slide towards the side of the structure butting into the crocodile-infested Nile.

A window opened below the surface, sucking water and beasts into the much deeper chamber.

"It is done, my queen," he said as the escorts of the entombed royalty approached the structure to retrieve their principals back to their residences before the sun rose and temperatures became intolerable for humans.

"Then complete your task," she ordered. "Do what you must!"

Clenching his jaw, inhaling deeply while slowly nodding, the large warrior proclaimed the crime committed by Nitocris to the dozens of incoming guards.

The queen stepped back as the armed crowd approached her.

And, just as planned, she retrieved a dagger beneath her garments and drove it into her abdomen.

27 Persistence

"Energy and persistence conquer all things."
--Benjamin Franklin.

30,000 FEET OVER THE NORTH ATLANTIC.

July 13, 2019

Erika Baxter settled next to Case Montana in the rear of a Cessna Citation as they read the information browsing on one of the LCD panels. CIA analysts worked the other terminals.

"Dear God, Case. We were too late," she mumbled while staring at what now appeared to be roughly 150,000 square miles of destruction. In plain terms, the north section of the state of Alaska was on fire, and the conflagration was sending clouds of smoldering embers ten miles high, where the jet stream carried them around the world.

"This one's going to hurt . . . at the global level," he said, before running a finger along the middle of the Brooks Mountain Range and along the western end of the Yukon Territory. "This is where the Hot Shots are going to try to hold the line. They're going to try to keep it from spreading into northern Canada as well as south of Brooks."

"They won't be able to," she whispered. "There aren't enough fire fighters to control something of this magnitude."

Case just stared at her.

During her college years, Erika had done an internship with one of the nearly one hundred Hot Shot teams in the American West, each around ninety fire fighters strong. She spent three

229

unforgettable and grueling months controlling forest fires in Idaho as part of the Idaho City Hot Shots. The experience had drilled into her the dire consequences of global warming. Where twenty years earlier the largest forest fires measured tens of thousands of square acres, now fires averaged over one hundred thousand square acres, with the largest reaching seven hundred thousand acres.

And all that caused by just an increase of one miserable degree in temperature, she thought, also recalling that it took an average of two hundred Hot Shot fighters to control a forest fire of around 100,000 thousand acres. The monster in Alaska was 150,000 square *miles,* or close 96 *million* acres.

"There aren't enough fire fighters . . . in the entire world," she mumbled again. "And besides, the way the Hot Shot teams work is by surrounding the fire and cutting off its fuel supply with burn lines ahead of the inferno to keep it from spreading and letting it burn itself out after exhausting the available wood and other fuels in the affected area. I'm not sure how they're going to kill the fuel supply to this one though. It's not being fueled above the ground like a classic forest fire. The fuel is coming from deep in the ground. Sort of like an oil well fire but multiplied times a million."

"Well, there are oil fires mixed in with the methane blaze. The Prudhoe Bay oil fields are on fire as well as a huge section of the Trans-Alaska Pipeline System," Case pointed out.

The comment only made her feel worse. This was her home state they were talking about, the place where she grew up. She spent many weekends on hiking trips to the Brooks Mountain Range and on the North Slope.

Now it's all gone.

"What will happen?" Case asked.

Fighting hard to control her emotions, Erika slowly shook her head and said, "I'm not sure, Case, but there isn't much we can do about Alaska. The damage is already done. We need to focus on the next strike. There are two more of these earthquake machines out there. What's our ETA to Toronto?"

"Two more hours," Case replied.

The CIA, assisted by the Pentagon, had broadcast a field report about a plane departing Ground Zero in Alaska shortly before the fire broke out, and heading into Canada. The airplane, which Erika suspected to be Dragan's Cessna Caravan, mysteriously disappeared as it neared the border with Yukon, but twenty minutes later Yukon ATC had picked up a Cessna Caravan operating as an Air Care unit heading into Whitehorse. Unfortunately, before any interceptors could be launched, the Caravan once more vanished from radar, only to be found an hour later by members of the Canadian Special Operations Regiment (CSOR) at a remote lake three hundred miles north of Whitehorse.

In the middle of nowhere in Yukon.

"But you're still sure Dragan is going for a strike in Canada next?" Case asked.

"I'm trying to think like him," she replied. "There are three major permafrost areas in the northern hemisphere. The first is the West Siberian Plains. The second is Alaska and parts of the Yukon Territory. The third is on the entire eastern section of Canada, including the area just north of Toronto, and within close range of New York City. In fact, archeological records show that people had been living in the Toronto area since the last ice age eleven thousand years ago. The entire area is sitting atop a massive pocket of methane. If I were a climate terrorist, that's where I would focus my energy. Imagine a disaster like Alaska but in a highly populated metropolis like Toronto, and then imagine the clouds of fire burying New York City under a dozen feet of red-hot embers. I would first go for places like Surgat and Alaska to create a diversion before striking hard in densely-populated areas."

Case raised his brows and sighed before saying, "Okay, I follow the logic. What about the fourth machine?"

She lifted her shoulders. "Maybe it's for back-up. Maybe he plans to use them both in that area. He sure as hell doesn't need it for Alaska or Yukon, and we destroyed the one in Surgat, and the last report from Ivenko is that they combed the entire area and it's clear."

"Or maybe there is a fourth target," he said.

"Then is not related to permafrost in the northern hemisphere."

Case leaned over and put a hand on her shoulder. "Now, I know this may sound a bit stupid, but how else would you use an earthquake machine?"

She raised a brow and pushed out her lower lip, pouting, before saying, "Well, my guess would be to trigger an earthquake somewhere. That's why the Russians built them in the first place, though not as a terrorist weapon. The original concept from Nikolai Telsa was to induce oscillations along fault lines to cause minor tremors and thus reduce the tension between tectonic plates to minimize the chance of a major earthquake. But it's unclear if they actually worked in that application."

"Well, it sure did work in Alaska, so the design does something to the soil structure."

"No doubt there," she replied, dropping her gaze.

Case stood up and stretched. "Trigger an earthquake, huh?"

She tilted her head while looking up at him. "That would be my guess."

"That narrows down the potential target to a hundreds of spots on the planet," he said yawning. Neither had slept much in almost two days.

"Maybe we will get lucky and collect some intel in Canada."

"Well, unless I get some shuteye I will be worthless in Canada," he said, heading to the front, where he collapsed in one of the seats.

Although her emotions were in havoc, the trained operative in her ordered Erika to also try to get some rest before landing in Toronto.

Rest is a weapon.

Erika nodded to herself. Despite how she felt, her training told her she also needed to rest, to prepare for the next round. Of course, that was easier said than done, but she still had to try. A member of the CIA analyst team would wake them if something came up in the meantime. The analysts poured through the data emerging from the NPIC satellite imagery as well as the National Security Agency's phone conversations, plus Air Traffic Control's logs would wake them up if something came up in the mean time.

Settling next to him, Erika rested her head on his shoulder while putting his arm around her and saying, "Don't say anything, Case. I just need to be held at this moment."

He did just as she asked, holding her gently as they both fell asleep.

R. J. Pineiro

28 Mass Extinction

"The end of all things is at hand."
--Peter 4:7

BROOKS MOUNTAIN RANGE, ALASKA.

July 14, 2019

The trail from the mouth of the cave to the first hill was layered with ash and dust, remnants of a colossal battle that resulted in temporary retrieve from the massive fires burning in the north.

Just past midnight, Natasha Shakhiva trekked up a steep incline as lightning gleamed in the distance, casting a brief flash across the face of the mountain.

She waited to hear the ensuing clap of thunder, but this early evening the remote lightning strike was followed by a massive quake that shook her high ground.

The smell of fire soon tickled her nostrils.

It's returning, she thought, watching the shifting winds starting to blow the charcoal clouds back towards the valley below--and everything and everyone within its vast expanse.

Shaking her head, Natasha peered again at the incredible sight, at the massive plumes of billowing smoke rising above the scorching land as far as the eye could see. She heard distant agonizing howls and screeches in the distance--bears, wolves, birds of all kinds, some wounded, others scared.

Entire species were being exterminated in front of her tired eyes as she also noticed the changing color of the distant fire, becoming bluer as surface vegetation was consumed and only pure methane fed the monster.

Keep hiking.

And she did, for six hours straight, finding it harder to breathe not just because of the altitude but from the reduced oxygen content as the nearing inferno consumed massive amounts of it, which also explained the breeze sweeping towards the flames, drawn by the suction force created by the flames.

She kept one ELT on while conserving the batteries of the second for later, after she cleared the tallest peaks and got a visual of the valleys leading to Fairbanks. She also knew that reaching the other side of the range would increase her chances of being heard on the Guard frequency. So far her emergency calls had proven fruitless.

She spaced her meals, maintaining a steady pace on trails she knew would lead to a passage in between the mountains, leaving the North Slope valley behind as eruptions burst through the layer of flames now reaching the very foot of the range, pulsating above a sea of flickering fire, licking the darkening sky, obscuring it with charcoal clouds.

Birds rushed overhead in massive flocks which at times blocked the skies, their deafening screeches echoing against the mountains while winging south, away from the inferno. Plumes of fire punched through the blistering valley as the land released more gas, feeding the monster, the boiling swirls of grey spiraling to the sky.

Ina dying world, the climate scientist at the devastation below, at the massive extinction event she was witnessing.

Soon the sky would darken with ashes and the deadly black rain would reach the northern edge of the range, suffocating anything that survived the inferno.

Soon night would fall.

Vast herds of mammals, mostly caribou, raced south, toward the vegetation-rich valleys on the other side of Brooks. She had spotted a grizzly once, which made her reach for the holstered semiautomatic, but the beast seemed far more concerned in getting away from the fire than in the possibility of a meal.

Erika was tired, but she still couldn't stop, even though she had difficulty breathing, while her lungs fought for the same oxygen greedily consumed by the conflagration.

Natasha Shakhiva needed to increase the gap, to distance herself from the flames before hypoxia set in, before she passed out from lack of oxygen.

Keep going.

And she did, step after tiring step, her legs protesting the abuse, her feet blistering, her eyes burning from the haze, her lungs screaming for the oxygen she could not deliver despite her deep breaths.

Keep going.

Following her GPS, Natasha headed for a small lake nestled deep in the mountains, where an old hiker's cabin by its shores provided any hiker with shelter from sudden blizzards, hail storms, or any other unexpected climate change—the place where Mario Escobar would drop her off for her hikes.

The roaring fires receded in the distance as she immersed herself in the heart of the mountains, watching the twilight of an Alaska summer evening, which provided enough light to see the trails ahead, to see her GPS without using the unit's backlight to conserve batteries, without having to use her flashlight, to continue her escape south.

She no longer heard any animals, any birds or mammals around her, which meant that the creatures had either perished or had already reached safety on the other side.

You are all alone.

And that sinking feeling sent a chill down her tired body.

But you are not alone.

You are never alone.

Natasha Shakhiva thought of Konrad Malone, thought of their times hiking these mountains, these trails, wishing he were by her side.

Keep going.

She persisted for five more hours, breathing through her mouth now, fighting off a stinging headache, her mind growing cloudy. She clutched the GPS in her trembling hands and struggled to read it, her eyesight worsening as she struggled to follow the course she had plotted earlier in the day.

Only two miles away.

Natasha tried to go on, but her body would no longer obey her, would no longer respond to her commands.

She fell to her knees on a clearing high up in the mountains, her right hand reaching for the second ELT, activating it as back-up to the first one before she collapsed on her back.

The predawn skies, indigo and stained with burnt orange and yellow-gold, were dotted with stars.

Natasha watched it through her tears before everything faded away.

29 Risky Business

"Only those who dare to fail greatly can ever achieve greatly."
--Robert F. Kennedy

BROOKS MOUNTAIN RANGE, ALASKA.

July 14, 2019

"We got a signal, amigo," reported Mario Escobar over the intercom of the Piper Cub as they circled the southern end of the mountain range at ten thousand feet in moderate turbulence at four in the morning. "Fifteen miles northwest. That's on . . . son of a gun."

"Good girl," said Malone, reading the information on his FlexScreen just as it streamed into Escobar's cockpit display. "She went to the lake; Mario . . . looks like a couple of miles from the cabin. How come we can't reach her on the radio?"

"Don't know. My guess is that her transceiver must be out," said Escobar after trying to contact her on the Guard frequency repeatedly in the past hour, after refueling at Coldfoot, a former mining camp reincarnated as a construction town while the pipeline was being built, and shifting shape again in the early 1980s as a trucker stop and tourist attraction for being "The Farthest North Truck Stop in the World."

They had landed in the nearly deserted airstrip, where a lone attendant topped off their tanks before heading this way.

"Can you land on the lake before dawn?"

"That's the beauty of Alaska, Koni," the bush pilot replied. "It never gets dark enough. We'll be there in fifteen minutes."

Malone looked towards the north, to the crimson glow behind the mountains, pulsating with hues of orange and gold. The view would have been majestic if the reason for the enchanting backdrop wasn't a giant climate leap towards a radical shift in weather patterns similar to what our planet experienced 4000 years ago.

But he noticed something else. The mountain peaks, clearly visible minutes ago, grew hazy.

"Is that what I think it is above the mountain range?" asked Malone.

"Looks that way," said, Escobar, confirming his observation.

The winds had indeed shifted, pushing the charcoal clouds south, just above the tip of the range.

While Malone doubted that the prevailing winds would let them continue too far south of the mountains, the fact that they were over the mountains meant not only bad news for Natasha Shakhiva, but also for them if they couldn't get in and out fast enough.

"We can't afford to linger around, Koni. The ash stored in those clouds will shred the skin of the plane in a matter of minutes."

"How much time do we have to go get her before the clouds cover the range?" he asked, concern filling him.

"I'd say no more than an hour."

"Then you'd better get me on the ground in five minutes. We didn't come this far to quit this close to her."

As he said this, Malone's gaze remained locked with the angered charcoal clouds pulsating with flames looming above the range.

30 Permian Dream

"And they went up over the breadth of the earth, and compassed the camp of the saints about, and the beloved city: and fire came down out of heaven, and devoured them."
--Revelation 20:9

BROOKS MOUNTAIN RANGE, ALASKA.

July 14, 2019

The engine noise reverberated in the periphery of her subconscious, as her world spun out of control, as she stared at Marcus Stone's face swirling around her, tight with tension while moving his lips, shouting something she couldn't hear.

Natasha tried to listen but the roar from the helicopter drowned his words. And that's when Stone pointed at the other passengers in the rear of the helicopter, and she saw Sergei Shakhiva strapped to a seat across from her.

Sergei? My love, what are you doing here?

But the Russian climatologist did reply, staring at her with his hypnotizing blue eyes, which shifted to the other passengers in the cabin, Stone's aides, their bodies maimed, their ghostly faces turning towards her, their lips moving just as Stone's had, their voices drowned by the reverberating rotor noise.

She turned to Stone, his face now as ghostly as that of his aides, highlighting his orange freckles, his closely-cropped orange hair. He leaned over and shouted straight into her ear.

You don't belong here, Doctor! You survived this!

Natasha blinked and found herself falling from the helicopter as it exploded in scarlet flames pulsating across the barren landscape.

She fell, landing in sand instead of water.

Sand?

That's when she saw the nearing inferno and began to race away from it, from the incoming wall of fire, sheet lightning gleaming, thunder whipping the valley.

Her legs burned, her lungs protesting the heat, her mouth and throat raw from the ashes.

She watched animals rush by; bears, caribou, geese, and foxes trying to escape the inferno.

That's when she saw the strange creatures, a mother and two large cubs. They looked like tigers but much larger, with massive saber teeth flanking their muzzles. Their streamlined bodies, light-brown in color with darker streaks down their torsos, shot ahead of her through the swirling haze, their strong and elastic muscles pumping against the desert floor in long cat-like strides. They studied her briefly through large oval yellow eyes before darting ahead.

Gorgos! They are Gorgos!

The mother growled, her guttural shrieks clashing with the roaring thunder.

The Permian beasts dashed ahead of her, leaping over a sand dune as volcanoes erupted in the distance.

Sand dunes? Volcanoes?

Confused, Natasha tried to run faster, but her boots sank in the sand as lighting arced across the angered sky, as she stared across the arid terrain at an incoming cloud packed with super-fast sand.

A sandstorm? Here, in Alaska?

Lightning flashed in the distance, above a desert hurtled into the dusky horizon by invisible claws stirring up the surface, blasting tons of sand into the air with the power of a million tornadoes, creating a whirlwind of certain death blocking the sinking sun as night fell over her world.

Natasha followed the Gorgos as they shifted direction toward the ragged edges of rock formations protruding through the desert floor off to their right, the caves used by their kind to escape the day's heat during their winter hunting season.

She followed them while risking a brief backward glance, her eyes assessing the gap separating them from the expanding crimson shroud, before glaring at the incoming sandstorm, alive with forks of lightning. She understood the Gorgos' strategy, their last-ditch attempt to avoid getting caught right in the middle of the colliding fronts.

But she wasn't fast enough.

The Gorgos reached the mouth of the cave and turned around to watch her, three pairs of golden eyes staring out from the darkness, three lonely creatures from a long-forgotten past roaring at her to hurry, to sped up, to save herself from the apocalypse closing in on her.

The Gorgos vanished as the cloud of sand engulfed her, suffocating, blinding, tearing into her, skinning her alive as the sizzling breath of hell scorched her mind, her senses, her very soul.

Natasha screamed in pain, in agony, in anger at the heavenly chastisement, at the claws raking her body down to the bone.

But through the flames, the shredding sand, the madness, she heard his voice calling out to her in the distance.

He was here.

He had come to rescue her, to save her from this inferno.

Natasha stretched her arms at the spinning darkness and felt his warm embrace, his strong arms lifting her, holding her tight, so very tight, and soothingly whispering in her ear.

You are not alone.

You are not alone.

❉

Konrad Malone pressed Natasha's light frame tight against his chest, carrying her as he would an infant, close, very close.

Racing back towards the lakeshore, his throat sore from the haze rapidly descending over the mountains, his shoulders burning from the stress, he forged ahead, finding his surroundings eerily devoid of any animals, any creatures.

He heard nothing except for the distant drone of the fires on the north end of the range mixing with his heavy breathing. Gone were the birds, the caribou, the bears and foxes. And as he struggled to keep up his pace with a gradual depletion of oxygen content—as measured by the wrist-mounted FlexScreen he wore, the scientist understood why, and also understood the reason for Natasha's current state.

Unlike Malone, who had spent the past three months atop Mount Kilimanjaro, becoming quite conditioned to low-oxygen environments, she had lived by the shores of Shirukak Lake, one thousand feet above sea level.

But that doesn't mean you will last forever, he thought, following the same familiar trail he had used twenty minutes ago, after Escobar had pulled up to shore and Malone had jumped off armed with a handheld GPS map marking the precise location of her ELT transmission.

She stirred in his arms, and he realized just how much he missed holding her as he pressed her tight against his chest, right arm holding her upper body, her head tucked against his chest, his left arm under her legs.

The trail veered to the right before gradually dropping to the rocky bed leading to the water, to the waiting Piper Cub.

A brief upward glance confirmed what his lungs protested: the cloud cover descending over them slowly turned into a dust-rich fog.

His eyes burning and itching, his mouth completely dry, Malone maintained his pace, his rugged boots providing enough traction to keep his momentum forward, pointed straight at the single-engine amphibious plane looming around the bend in the trail.

"Crank her up, Mario!" Konrad Malone shouted at the top of his lungs, finding it hard very to breathe now as he raced across the rocky clearing surrounding the spring-fed lake. "Let's get the hell out of here!"

Escobar ran up to meet him and together they carried her down to the shores as the inky clouds completely blocked the sun and temperatures started to drop below freezing.

Since the Piper Cub was designed as a two-seater airplane, Malone sat in the rear seat first holding Natasha on his lap. Escobar jumped in the front seat and they were airborne in five minutes.

They remained at five hundred feet above the rugged terrain to stay clear of the toxic and abrasive clouds, which, like volcanic ash, would strip the metal skin of the Piper in minutes while flying at 100 knots.

As they reached the southern tip of the range, the skies opened up and they were able to climb while heading straight for Fairbanks, where only military personnel, fire fighters, and scientists were exempted from the evacuation.

"How's she doing?" asked Escobar over the intercom as they reached cruising altitude.

"Steady," he replied, monitoring her pulse as he took a deep breath and filled his lungs with clean air.

Malone looked over his right shoulder at the nearly vanished mountains as charcoal clouds swallowed the entire range.

Natasha's breathing became heavier as her body detected the increased oxygen content and started drawing it deeper each time she inhaled, replenishing her system, feeding the cells in her bloodstream.

A moment later her eyelids fluttered and she opened her eyes, blinking, gaining focus, staring straight into Konrad Malone.

"Hey there, stranger," he said, grinning.

"Hey there," she replied, smiling and holding him tight before drifting back to sleep.

31 11,000-Year Journey

"Climate change is the most severe problem that we are facing today, more serious even than the threat of terrorism."
--David King, UK government chief scientific adviser, January 2004.

THIRTY MILES NORTH OF TORONTO, CANADA.

July 15, 2019

Dragan Kiersted stood in a heavily wooded valley next to Shin-Li as the members of his North American cell pulled the earthquake machine from a shipping crate labeled as weather monitoring equipment from the British Weather Bureau that had arrived at one of Toronto's piers via a merchant ship the week before.

One of his smallest cells working North America had loaded up the crate onto a flat bed and taken it to this location, remote, secluded, layered with the thawing permafrost that gave the towering pines around them the same slant as the forests in Surgat, where his team had failed him.

But we are not failing today, he thought, filling his lungs with cool air, with the invigorating pine resin fragrance of a forest that had been around since the last ice age, a place where people had lived when mastodons and saber tooth tigers roamed the land, moving into the cold sub-arctic landscape from the south to pursue the big game animals that preceded them.

But it all ends today.

And there would be no one getting in his way. He had taken the utmost precautions, even ditching Shin-Li's coveted Cessna north of Whitehorse, hiking into town, and renting a charter plane at the regional airport to take them to another regional airport just east of Toronto, where they rented a helicopter and met his North America cell an hour ago at this location, right on schedule.

The local cell was one of his youngest, made up of four men and one woman, all in their late twenties to early thirties and hand-picked by Dragan himself from large pools of revolutionaries and ideologists from South America, Indonesia, Serbia, and the Middle East. Each had a profound reason to hate America and her allies, including Canada and England, and Dragan had merely provided them with an opportunity to channel their anger. This team was hungry, willing to do anything to make a difference, to strike terror into the heart of the American people.

It truly amazed him just how easy it was to recruit teams to strike against the West.

He watched as Doctor Yuri Gerchenko instructed two members of the young team how to remove the machine and start the assembly process at the bottom of a shallow ravine, below sight from anyone roaming the forest.

And also providing added protection against an unexpected raid, Dragan thought, having selected this location because of its proximity to the gravel road his cell had used to transport the Russian hardware from the major highway out of Toronto to this secluded location—the same access road leading to the nearby clearing where Shin-Li had landed their rented helicopter from the short flight from Toronto.

His plan was identical to Alaska. Set up the machine, get everyone on the chopper, and activate it via remote.

Hans-Jorgen and the other three operatives had formed an elaborate perimeter defense system around the soon-to-be Ground Zero and were now standing guard at each point of the compass several meters inside their high-tech defense shield. In addition, Dragan, an old-school commando, had set up his own inner perimeter surrounding the ravine with a dozen Claymore mines linked to a simple handheld detonator. He had also installed mines a few dozen feet up and down the ravine connected to trip wires and to his detonator in case anyone tried to sneak up on him through the creek.

The top climate terrorist in the world smiled.

He felt good today.

Greenland had drowned the world and had frozen Europe. Alaska was burning, and with it America's largest oil producing state. Despite the failure in Surgat and the severe physical punishment he had endured in Greenland, Dragan Kiersted was making a difference.

Dragan stared at the iLimb holding his assault rifle and grinned, standing firm on his advanced artificial legs. He was punishing the world for what they did to him, to his father, to the earth's natural resources. He was punishing them for their arrogance, their stubbornness, for their refusal to listen to the truth.

Burn them and drown them.

He continued to watch his team with growing satisfaction.

Toronto and New York would die today.

By fire.

32 Tightening the Noose

"This is not a battle between the United States and Terrorism, but between the free and democratic world and terrorism."
--Tony Blair.

FIFTY MILES NORTH OF TORONTO, CANADA.

July 15, 2019

Her face smeared with camouflage cream, Erika Baxter followed Case Montana as they approached the terrorist cell from the north. Canadian forces covered the southern perimeter, while commandos of the Navy SEAL Team Two from Naval Amphibious Base Little Creek, Virginia closed in from the east and west.

Stealth Unmanned Aerial Vehicles controlled by a circling AWACs ten miles away hovered the area, their deep infrared cameras providing an accurate count of the terrorists and overlaying that information on the GPS maps displayed in the wrist-mounted FlexScreens of every member of this cross-functional team.

The plan called for the SEALs to go in first guided by SUAV imagery, neutralize the enemy with real bullets--by presidential order after Alaska--and destroy the target with precise surgical fire.

Fearing the events of Alaska, where the final video feed from the Superhawks depicted a missile attack that may have contributed to the initial explosion at Ground Zero, the SEALS would take a similar approach as the Spetsnaz commandos did in

251

Surgat, disabling the machine without igniting the rocket fuel--and, of course, the methane.

Erika sighed, her boots sinking in the soft terrain as she followed Case Montana, as she came to terms with the reality that they once more were walking over an apocalyptic time bomb. If the monster reached the surface, her brain would not be able to even register it before the intense heat would vaporize everyone and everything else in a ten mile radius.

Focus.

Her operative side ordering her to stay the course, to continue the approach, gloved hands clutched a Heckler & Koch graphite MP7 assault rifle packed with armor piercing rounds.

Together they followed the uneven terrain, past tilted trunks rising to a clear sky, across a dry ravine flanked by clumps of jagged boulders, the leaf-littered ground giving gently to every step, her heart beat steady, her breathing slowing as they reached the outer perimeter of the SEAL killing zone.

Case took a knee behind a row of waist-high bushes bordering the area where only the SEALs could enter for the next three minutes.

"Team Three, Eagle, how do you read?" Erika called out to the CIA team aboard the AWACs in this joint mission.

"Loud and clear, Team Three. All systems go."

"Team Three in position," she reported through her throat mike.

"Team One in position," answered the Canadian team lead.

"SEAL Team Two moving in," reported Commander John Towers, leader of the SEAL team. Unlike Ivenko and the Spetsnaz team, Towers and his SEALs were a delight to work with, including allowing the CIA to quarterback this mission since Erika and Case had the most exposure to the threat they were approaching. Towers had readily understood the nature of the beast they were fighting and quickly agreed to tone down his team's firepower in order to avoid inadvertently setting off the Russian machine. This meant no grenade launchers or heavy

caliber machine guns, limiting his commandos to their silenced Heckler & Koch MP7 new generation assault weapons.

Erika settled down next to Case, shoulder to shoulder, exchanging a brief glance.

He winked while grinning, exposing two rows of white teeth beneath a face darkened by hues of dark green and face paint.

She had fallen asleep in his arms and had woken up to his smile during final approach into Toronto. He had kissed her forehead, whispered, "Morning sleepy head," and offered a cup of orange juice.

That close moment, staring into each other's eyes, was broken by the sudden jerk of the landing gear touching down and the onslaught of planning and coordination that followed to orchestrate the attack underway.

Erika returned the smile before checking her FlexScreen, verifying the location of the threat, depicted as crimson returns by the SUAVs, as well as the incoming SEALs, the twelve dark-blue circles now completely surrounding the target.

"Releasing the Orbs," said Commander Towers.

She watched as blue specks—fifteen of them—propagated beyond the SEAL team.

"Incoming," said Shin-Li, watching her FlexScreen, depicting Hans-Jorgen and his three operatives deployed per plan inside the orange circle marking their defense system around the shallow trench where Gerchenko was hard at work. Small blue dots--gas spheres--were approaching from the east and west.

"Masks," ordered Dragan Kiersted, donning a small gas mask that resembled a pair of skiing goggles with a mouth piece connected to a tiny oxygen canister built above the top of the nanotechnology apparatus designed to provide him with air for twenty minutes.

She looked at Dragan, her dark eyes waiting for his order.

He nodded and said, "Blast the bastards. Blast them to bloody hell."

The master climate terrorist watched as his most trusted operative activated the countermeasures unit, which deployed a circular ray of smart blue-green light that expanded from their perimeter system as it became brighter.

The radial proton flare propagated through the forest like blue lightning, altering the molecular structure of any object carrying an electrical charge and lacking the protection password signature embedded by the high-tech flare.

The Orbs trembled as their nanotronic brains melted from the inside, turning carefully designed circuitry into a brew of boiling alloys firing random commands at their propulsion systems, shooting off in multiple direction.

"Reported movement from the east and west," advised Hans-Jorgen through his password-protected two-way radio as his team spotted incoming figures in the forest.

Dragan and Shin-Li took up defensive positions on the east edge of the ravine, and he ordered the two operatives assisting Gerchenko to do the same on the west end, leaving the elder scientist in the middle of the trench giving the final touches to the equipment.

"How did they find us so fast?" asked Shin-Li.

"It doesn't matter," he replied. "Activate the shield."

She tapped the touch-sensitive FlexScreen and said, "We're hot. Repeat. We're hot."

"Let's dig in," he said.

Most of his body protected by the ravine, Dragan rested his elbows on the top of the five-foot inclined wall of their trench, right hand on the handle of a massive M60 machine gun, right hand under the wide barrel, pressing his body against the wall for balance.

He gathered leaves within reach and used them to visually shield his exposed shoulder, head, and arms keeping his weapon just above the edge of the ravine pointed at the seemingly endless drunken trees. Shin-Li did the same, though she held a 9mm Uzi, compact but deadly.

He watched in satisfaction as she mimicked his moves from a few feet away.

"We have visual," said Hans-Jorgen. "Two targets east, one west, and two south. Five contacts . . . they stopped short of the shield . . . they look like SEALs."

Shin-Li whipped her head at Dragan. "Navy SEALs?"

Dragan inhaled deeply. During his years with the *Fromandskorpset*, he had conducted joint exercises with the American elite fighting unit, and they were virtually unbeatable. They were also invisible. SEALs relied heavily on stealth. The fact that his perimeter team could actually see them told him something was seriously wrong.

"They can see it," Shin-Li hissed, watching on her FlexScreen as the incoming team stopped just short of the outer high-tech defense circle. "They can see our shield."

Dragan didn't reply, his mind going in different directions, considering his rapidly narrowing choices.

"And if they can see it they can also neutralize it," she added. "What are we going to do, Dragan? They can see our defenses."

Dragan sighed. Shin-Li was a super pilot, and she had saved his life in Greenland, but at the moment she was beginning to annoy him. "Hans-Jorgen, do you have visual on targets?" Dragan asked.

"Affirmative," he replied.

"Open fire when able. Buy us time."

❄

"Stay where you are, Team Two," said Erika, reading the downlink from the SUAVs. "They killed the orbs and are using an active shield of infrared trip wires. Don't get any closer until I can disable it."

"Roger that," replied Towers. "We have spotted some of their men. My snipers are in position. Four contacts on outside perimeter. Permission to engage."

"Engage," she said while exchanging a brief glance with Case as they waited.

"Team Two engaging," Towers replied, adding a few seconds later, "targets neutralized."

Just like that, she thought before saying, "Recommend flares, Commander. "Use them to trip the shield, detonate hidden charges, and open access channels to Ground Zero."

"Roger that," Towers reported.

❊

Dragan Kiersted frowned. Hans-Jorgen should have opened fire by now. Yet the outer perimeter was deadly quiet.

"Come in, Hans-Jorgen," he said.

Silence.

"Why isn't he answering?" asked Shin-Li.

A deep sinking feeling gripped Dragan as he turned to Gerchenko, still fiddling with the hardware. The SEALs must have had snipers in position in addition to the commandos that had chosen to show themselves to draw attention. Hans-Jorgen and his young team had fallen for the ruse.

"They've been compromised," he finally said, before asking, "How much longer, Yuri?"

"Just a few minutes," the scientist said, his hands holding odd tools as he worked the Russian machinery. "All we need is a few—"

The explosions rocked the forest from every direction. The perimeter shield had been pierced, triggering the outer Claymore directional charges covered by leaves.

"Let's hope that took care of enough of them," Shin-Li said.

Peering into the murky forest through the sights of his weapon, Dragan Kiersted doubted any of his perimeter defenses would make a difference when SEALs were involved.

Still, not all was lost. He still had his inner defense system, the dozen Claymore antipersonnel mines he had placed just a few feet from the edge of the ravine and also inside the ravine's north and south channels.

Our final stand.

"You have less than one minute, Yuri," Dragan announced in a calm voice that even surprised him considering they were about to be overrun by the Americans.

But he was ready to die, ready to sacrifice himself for this noblest of causes; he was ready to take one more step towards exterminating the race who had ravaged the Earth with a society built on excess, on the irresponsible exploitation of precious natural resources.

They don't deserve any of this.

They will drown.

They will freeze.

They will burn.

The figures appeared in the distance, amidst once towering pines now tilted in every direction as a direct effect of human gluttony.

He aligned the closest figure and opened fire in unison with Shin-Li, though he knew their muzzle flashes would mark their location for the enemy.

The figure dropped but others rushed behind him, and silent rounds stirred the ground around them, though nowhere near the trademark barrage of overwhelming firepower that he would have expected the SEALs to unleash.

Still, the incoming fire forced them to duck, to use the terrain as shield.

With his back against the inclined wall as suppressed rounds zoomed overhead, Dragan watched his younger operatives beyond the equipment, on the east wall, failing to react in time, the rounds from the SEALs approaching, tearing off chunks of their heads.

His young operatives landed on their backs at the bottom of the creek already corpses, dead eyes staring at the green canopy overhead.

Damn.

He clenched his jaw in anger, the sight evoking memories of Greenland, of his maimed team.

Focus.

"Cover that side!" Dragan ordered Shin-Li.

The former Chinese military pilot rushed around Gerchenko still fiddling with the system, reaching her new post.

He took a deep breath and resumed his post, searching the forest, keeping his head as low as possible while sweeping the terrain with--

Two SEALs materialized from behind trees and opened fire on his position.

A burning pain on his left shoulder told him a round had found its mark.

Cringing, he didn't utter a sound as he took aim and fired, taking out the right figure as the left one dove for cover.

Bastards.

He had been shot. But his iLimb remained firing at the shadows materializing behind the SEAL who had dropped from sight behind a line of short bushes, taking down one of them as they emerged from behind wide trunks just to disappear again.

Ignoring the arresting wound, he stepped to the right along the wall, taking up a new position, and firing at a SEAL rushing from one trunk to another, a shadow in the darkness, scoring a direct hit.

Three down on this side, he thought, trying to focus despite the loss of everyone but Shin-Li and Gerchenko.

He risked a backward glance at the middle of the trench, only to see the scientist dead in a pool of his own blood.

And the machine was still not active.

But it was close.

He now saw motion around him in the forest in every direction. The SEALs were rushing in. One of the Claymores rigged to a trip wire up the ravine detonated, followed by screams.

"The system!" he screamed at Shin-Li. "Get it ready!"

She dropped to a deep crouch and abandoned her post to finalize the power-up sequence, giving Dragan a thumbs-up. "Good to go any moment!" she screamed over the noise of gunfire, holding up the remote control device. "Hey, you are bleeding!

"It doesn't matter for now! We're about to be overrun!"

Dragan Kiersted reached in his pocket for the detonator and stared into her captivating Asian eyes.

"The moment the Claymores go off, we run north along the bottom of the trench to the gravel road. We need to reach that chopper and get the hell out of here!"

She nodded.

Dragan toggled the switch and the blast rocked the forest, lighting up the murkiness in a blinding flash of orange flames followed by more agonizing screams.

"Now! Run!"

❊

"Towers? Come in Team Two!" Erika shouted into her throat mike right after the massive blast coming from the middle of the SEAL kill zone.

"Not a good sign," he said, pointing not just at the two infrared emissions rushing away from the center of the terrorist nest but also at the stationary but growing heat signature in the middle. "Remember Surgat? The machine is on."

"Team One, you copy?" she asked, knowing exactly what that was.

"Team One here," replied the head of the Canadian detachment to her relief.

"Head into the middle of the kill zone, Team One," she spoke into her throat mike. "Team Two is not responding. Destroy the machine *then* search for wounded. Repeat. Destroy the machine *before* searching for wounded. We're going after the bastards."

"Roger that, Team Three."

Case led the way as they raced across the forest, up trails and around bends in the uneven terrain in full pursuit of two terrorists painted red in her FlexScreen by the circling SUAVs. Their most direct route took them down into a shallow ravine, which they followed, skipping over rotting logs, branches, and massive amounts of fallen leaves and pine needles.

"They're about a half mile ahead of us!" she said, staring at Case's dark silhouette as they pressed on. "Team One, are you in position?"

"Almost there, Team Three. My men are almost in position! There's wounded men everywhere. Calling medical evac now."

"Roger that, Team One. But first priority is the machine. Repeat, first priority is the machine. Please acknowledge, Team One."

"Team One acknowledging, Team Three."

"Advise when . . . machine is disabled," Erika Baxter said into her throat mike, taking in large gulps of air as she kept kicking her legs, thigh muscles burning while running as fast as she could.

They had to catch up.

They had to intercept the terrorists not only to prevent a remote-control activation before Canadian forces could destroy the equipment but also to interrogate, to find the location of the last machine.

"They've stopped . . . shit, Case, they have a chopper!" Erika hissed while transitioning her surveillance from the FlexScreen to the SmartLenses as they got closer to the terrorists, providing her with telescopic x-ray vision. "They have a chopper!"

"A helicopter? How come we missed with . . . the overhead surveillance?" Case asked as they kept the pace, closing the gap.

"Camouflaged," she said, looking at the images superimposed on her field of view as fed to her from the SUAVs. Two figures were removing a tarp cover and getting inside.

They were still a quarter of a mile away over rough terrain when they heard the high-pitch whine of a turbine revving up.

"We're not going to make it!" Case said.

"Eagle, Eagle, Team Three. Emergency request," said Erika.

"Team Three, Eagle, go ahead."

As Erika put in her request with the CIA controller, Case looked back for an instance in pleasant surprise.

❈

Dragan Kiersted watched in satisfaction as the main rotor accelerated, lifting them off the soft terrain. Maybe they would make it after all. Maybe they would—

"Radar contact," she replied, reading the information streaming on her Primary Flight Display system from the onboard radar unit. "Incoming. Three o'clock, two miles, five hundred feet and closing in fast."

As she pulled on the collective and the helicopter lifted about ten feet off the ground, Dragan slid the door open, unstrapped his safety restraints, and peered in that direction while clutching the M60.

Nothing. He saw nothing but skies that had begun to become hazier from the fires in Alaska.

"Are you sure?"

"Three o'clock, one mile, two hundred feet," she said.

Damn.

Dragan pointed his weapon in that direction and started firing blindly, before he spotted the black shadow.

What in the hell is that? He thought as the shadow loomed bigger.

He pressed on, adjusting his fire for a few more seconds, but failing to detonate whatever type of missile the Americans had fired on them.

"Ten seconds to impact! Jump!" she shouted.

Instinctively, as Shin-Li began to unbuckle her safety harness while setting the chopper in a shallow dive, Dragan tossed the weapon out and jumped.

He fell a dozen feet, landing on his titanium and graphite iLimbs, listening to the hydrogen pistons bleed pressure from the pistons, cushioning the initial impact, and immediately forcing his body into a roll.

As he surged from the roll, the shadow of the incoming threat rushed above him an instant before it collided against his side of the helicopter, setting it ablaze before Shin-Li could jump.

"No! No! No!" he shouted. "NO!"

As he looked on in horror, he could hear her screams from inside the burning wreck plummeting to the ground fifty feet away.

A loud explosion marked the crash site, the flames boiling up to the sky.

Bastards! Fucking bastards! He thought, producing the remote controlled device with his artificial left hand while reaching for his sidearm, clutching it with his right.

I will make them pay, he thought. *They will all burn today! They will all—*

The silent shot exploded through his artificial forearm, taking off his iLimb at the wrist.

He watched in shock as the artificial hand fell by his feet holding the detonator.

"Drop it! Drop the weapon," screamed a female voice from behind him.

Slowly, the climate terrorist turned around to face his foe, a man and a woman in camouflage gear clutching MP7s fitted with slim sound suppressors. He looked down by his feet, his eyes on the remote control device.

"Now! The gun!"

He complied, tossing the weapon at them, before reaching down for the detonator.

"Stop!" she shouted. "Don't do it!"

Dragan managed to place his right hand on it just as two silent rounds punched him in the chest, pushing him on his back, his finger never able to hang on to the unit.

❄

Erika Baxter walked right up to the terrorist, quickly frisking him to make sure he didn't have a back-up weapon or had strapped himself to dynamite.

That's when she recognized him.

He looked like his most recent shot on the CIA file but different. The right side of his face was covered by a flesh-colored molded plate including a new generation ocular implant, which moved in perfect coordination with the left eye. Like the artificial hand next to him, this was all part of the damage he sustained in Greenland according to what James Payden had told her.

She frowned.

Like Case, who had fired the round that amputated Dragan Kiersted's fake hand, her two bullets had been placed carefully, on the shoulders, meant to disable not to kill. And that didn't explain the blood and foam forming on his mouth. Dragan had been shot before, probably during the exchange with the SEALs.

As the terrorist stared at her, she checked the wound and sighed. The round had punctured a lung. Dragan needed immediate assistance or he would drown in his own blood.

"Case, get a medic here ASAP and also get me a chopper. We need to get him to a hospital!"

"On the way," Case shouted back, adding, "Area is clear."

In the distance a fusillade of gunshots confirmed the Canadian forces were opening fire on the third machine.

Erika leaned down and applied pressure on the worst wound, which bled profusely.

"Where is the last one, Dragan?" she asked. "Tell us the location of the last earthquake machine and we may be able to help you."

The terrorist opened his mouth and whispered something she couldn't make out.

"What did you say? I couldn't hear you," she replied, leaning closer, her right ear just an inch over his lips.

"Burn . . . drown . . ."

Erika pulled back, staring at the dying terrorist, a grin on his face as he locked eyes with her and mouthed the same words.

"Burn . . . drown."

"Where is the last unit? Tell me!" she shouted, pushing her fingers into the wound.

The terrorist tensed, quivering lips smeared with blood. He stared at her defiantly, his natural eye turning red while the artificial one remained steady.

"It's over, Dragan," she insisted, growing angry at the dying half-human half-machine terrorist. "Cooperate and you may get leniency. But you must do it now. Where is the last system?"

Instead of replying, his natural eye rolled to the back of his head while the other just stopped moving.

"Case! Where's that medic!"

The climate terrorist went into more convulsions, blood and foam oozing from his mouth and nose as his breaths became raspy, irregular.

He is drowning in his own blood.

The thought made her wonder if what he had meant was that he was drowning.

"Dragan! Stay with me, Dragan!" she shouted, shaking him as one of the Canadian medics reached them and began to apply pressure to the wounds.

"Is he going to make it?" asked Case as he knelt by her side while the medic, a dark-haired man in his thirties sporting a goatee, dressed the wounds before jabbing an IV into his arm.

"Hard to tell," the Canadian replied. "He's hurt pretty badly and is going into shock."

"Can you bring him back for thirty seconds?" she asked.

The medic nodded, adding, "It could kill him."

"Fine," she replied. "I must speak with him!"

The medic injected something into the same forearm as the IV and a moment later the terrorist's eyes realigned and began to move in unison, regaining focus.

"Listen to me, Dragan. It's over. We disabled the machine in the woods, and you are in our custody. Tell me where the last machine is, and I will make sure you get leniency."

Dragan Kiersted stared back at Erika Baxter, then at Case Montana, before grinning and saying, "You will burn. You will drown."

Case leaned down and said, "Wrong, pal. You are the one who is going to burn . . . in hell."

Erika stood there as the terrorist continued to glare at them, eyes burning with a hatred she had seen before in fanatics, in ideologists, and that told her that Dragan Kiersted would rather die than disclose the location of the last machine.

They watched as the medic tried to keep him alive, but the climate terrorist crashed before the helicopter arrived, taking the secret of the final earthquake machine with him.

And just like that, the chase was over, the monster responsible for Greenland and Alaska was dead, terminated along with several members of his team while trying to repeat the same holocaust in Toronto and New York.

Yet, Erika Baxter felt utterly unsatisfied, disappointed, and not just because they had not yet located the final machine. Somehow she had expected to feel much better knowing that they had managed to prevent another disaster while also neutralizing the world's most wanted terrorist.

"This is a bit anticlimactic, huh?" commented Case as Canadian units and the surviving SEALs hauled their wounded comrades to the arriving helicopters for their short trip to Toronto-area hospitals.

"Reminds me of that old quote from President Kennedy about nuclear warfare . . . you know, where victory would be like ashes in our mouths?" she said, her throat feeling dry and raspy from the growingly hazy skies as the winds aloft carried the ashes from

Alaska around the world, staining the heavens with an eerie orange shade.

"Unfortunately . . . this isn't victory," Case said looking to the west. "Unfortunately, this is far from over."

33 Cracks

"At first it seemed a terrible disaster, a terrible tragedy. But I think as the days have gone on, people have recognized it as a global catastrophe."
--Tony Blair

EAST RIFT ZONE. FORTY MILES SOUTHEAST OF HILO. HAWAII.

July 15, 2019

Doctor Aeko Nahinu trekked along the bottom of the 50-foot-deep crack collecting samples of Keanakakoi ash to bring back for analysis at the geology department of the University of Hawaii in nearby Hilo.

Dr. Nahinu paused to wipe the sweat filming his bronze forehead with the sleeve of his cotton T-shirt, and took a moment to admire the amazing rift walls towering above him, filled with parallel laminated fine ash deposits.

The East Rift Zone, together with the Southwest Rift Zone-- known as the Great Crack--and the Koae Fault System formed the north and west boundaries of the South Flank Block of Kilauea.

Identified as a high-risk landslide that could generate a massive tsunami, the earthquake-prone South Flank Block had been under the careful study of geologists such as Dr. Nahinu for many years.

Nahinu continued his inspection of the fissure, reaching the first of many steel markers he had drilled into the volcanic rock two decades ago. Using the red marker as a reference, Nahinu snapped photos of opposing walls, before downloading them to his mobile FlexScreen, comparing them for form and fit. Like a giant jigsaw puzzle, the opposing walls continued to fit together well. But a comparison to the same shots from five years ago, revealed an alarming trend.

The crack was widening.

Nahinu frowned. The rifts had been largely unchanged for most of the 20th century and even the first decade of the 21th century, but then something changed. The rifts began to enlarge. Slowly at first, a mere few inches per year, suggesting possible soil settlement. But in 2014, when Nahinu published his observations that the widening rate exceeded three feet per year, the old theory about the South Flank Block breaking away from the island was instantly revived.

Now, five years later, the crack had expanded by thirty feet, strongly suggesting that the island was tearing apart along this seam.

And that means fifty square miles of land could one day slide into the ocean.

The question was when. In 10 years? In 100 years? In 1000 years? Longer?

The scientist shook the apocalyptic thought away as he continued to gather the evidence that may provide him with a defendable answer. This was the primary reason behind his monthly tours, collecting more ash, taking more pictures, slowly piecing together the widening rate, which he viewed as the best way to provide answers, in a way similar to the sliding rates in glaciers used to predict their collapse.

The broadening rate so far suggested a linear progression, which further suggested a longer time span before the collapse, probably in a few centuries.

But he needed to be sure.

In the past thirty days this section of the fissure had widened by two inches, which could be the start of an exponential trend, drastically reducing the time table.

Or the past thirty days could be just an anomaly in the data, what statisticians called an outlier in the trend chart.

Which is why you must keep collecting monthly data, he thought, for a moment wondering if it would be prudent to go weekly for the next month just to be safe.

Dr. Nahinu had a number of graduate students returning to school early for the fall term that he could put to good use until the semester began in a few weeks. And he could even keep them taking samples during school by justifying to the board that this phenomenon was quite worthy of multiple masters' thesis.

But as far as the world was concerned, he didn't have enough information to recommend any course of action beyond the warning signs posted every kilometer along the perimeter of the South Flank Block about the danger presented by the shifting landmass.

Unfortunately, like the active lava flow site of Hawaii's Volcanoes National Park, such warning signs only served to attract more tourists, who regularly started visiting the South Flank Block soon after news of the widening crack reached travel agencies.

Fortunately, only scientists such as him were allowed into the deepest and most active crevices after a series of rock slides killed a dozen tourists last year.

And unfortunately for him, this high-risk area was where the best data could be collected.

Nahinu sighed while staring up the towering walls, deciding not to think about the deadly consequences of falling rocks, before resuming his work.

Over the next hour he made his way to the deepest and most active section of the fissure, far away from the tourist areas, photographing the walls, checking markers, using a small laser to measure distances, before entering the data into the FlexScreen, which information was uploaded real time to a server in the geology department for analysis.

That's when he heard strange beeping sounds coming from around a sharp bend in the gorge.

Intrigued, he hiked over to the jagged edge, by a large metal marker anchored deeply into the west wall, and looked beyond a cluster of volcanic rocks from a recent avalanche, spotting a strange machine resting on volcanic ash at the lowest point in the fissure.

He narrowed his gaze and used the spotter in the laser as a telescope to get a closer look. As large as a pair of refrigerators on their side, the machine sported what looked like a rocket booster with the nozzle pointing up on one side and a number of blinking lights on the other.

What is that?

And how in the hell did it get down here?

He looked up the wall and spotted the long neck of a crane protruding above the east lip of the fissure.

As he approached the unit, Nahinu heard the whop-whop sounds of a helicopter overhead and watched the dark silhouette of the craft hover high over the gorge back-dropped by clear blue skies.

What is going—

The blast was sudden, deafening even from a distance of a few hundred feet.

The rocket booster atop the machine ignited, its plume blinding, deafening as it shot straight up the gorge.

Sweet Mother of—

The rocks began to shake under him, forcing him to reach out for the three-foot-long metal marker, gripping it as the canon trembled, as a massive earthquake shook the crack and began to stretch it eastward in front of his eyes.

The scientist held on to the marker with his left hand while controlling the camera with his right, filming the event as clouds of ash descended on him.

He watched in a mix of fascination and horror as the rocket booster continued to burn while the east wall slid away from him, shifting towards the distant ocean, the fissure deepening, widening.

A massive roar and an avalanche of rocks rained down the gorge as the floor gave out from under him, swallowing the machine, its gleaming plume vanishing in a black abyss.

Nahinu reacted like the trained scientist he was, hugging the marker still anchored to the east wall, clutching it without dropping the camera.

His legs swung beneath him as he kept filming the event, as the handheld unit automatically uploaded the high-resolution video stream to the university servers.

He continued to video the event through the haze, even as he felt the rising heat beneath him.

Risking a downward glance, he watched in horror as the ripping crust exposed a sea of pressurized molten lava surging a hundred feet below him, its sizzling vapors rising towards him, suffocating, burning his nostrils, his trachea.

Nahinu dropped the camera as he started to vomit, instinctively clutching the rebar with both hands now as a blast of superheated air enveloped him.

He screamed, howled as his skin blistered, as his clothes ignited in the scorching cloud erupting through the gorge.

Relief came swiftly and mercifully when an avalanche of volcanic rocks careened down the west wall, crushing him, killing him instantly before plunging into the rising lava.

The South Flank Block ripped cleanly from Hawaii's Big Island, as the released pressure shot a wall of lava the length of the fissure a mile into the sky, its roar heard across all of the islands as the land plummeted into the Pacific, displacing 80 cubic miles of ocean in thirty seconds in an explosive show of earth, foam, and lava.

The resulting swell rose up above sea level almost five hundred feet with a forward velocity of four hundred miles per hour in a radial pattern propagating east, towards the American continent.

The Biblical tsunami, packing ten times more energy of the Greenland tidal wave, obliterated hundreds of vessels in its first hour, from sailing rigs to megaships, as it rushed towards the mainland, where it would hit southern California first.

Across the entire West Coast, Emergency Broadcasting Systems prompted the largest evacuation in history, but there were just too many people, not enough roads, and too little time.

In the coastal plain of Los Angeles, millions took to the highways trying to reach the San Gabriel Mountains, only to clog all access roads in a matter of minutes. Riots broke out, turning the entire metropolis into a death zone. In northern California, residents hoped the high cliffs of the Coastal Range would be enough to protect the state's 400-mile long Central Valley, which encompassed the Sacramento and San Joaquin Valleys. But that still didn't prevent residents from San Francisco to Silicon Valley to attempt fleeing east towards the Sierra Nevada mountain range.

The tidal wave slowed down to two hundred feet as it approached the continental shelf while rising to a monstrous eight hundred feet.

The mountain of water drowned the entire Los Angeles metropolitan area, toppling every skyscraper with apocalyptic force, ripping buildings and roads from their foundations, drowning four million souls in less than five minutes, before continuing inland for another forty miles until colliding against the mountains bordering the east and north end of the valley.

To the north, the wall of ocean clashed against the Coastal Range in an earth-trembling explosion that shot foam and dirt two miles high while shifting the tall mountains inland by a dozen feet, stressing the region's tectonic plates to the breaking point, triggering a massive earthquake across the entire state.

As the tsunami collided against the coastal peaks, it gushed inland through the Sacramento and San Joaquin River deltas, at the heart of the San Francisco Bay, penetrating deep into the

Central Valley, forcing millions of cubic feet of high-pressure sea water in the form of a hundred-foot-high tidal wave into the long and narrow bowl-like valley, as high as Redding at the north end and Bakersfield to the south.

In San Francisco the soaring torrent leveled every structure, from shacks to skyscrapers, uprooting piers, streets, trees, and bridges, including the Oakland and Golden Gate bridges, tearing deep into the soil, triggering massive landslides in its wake as it flashed down Palo Alto, Mountain View, Sunnyvale, San Jose, and Santa Clara, burying everyone and everything under a hundred feet of boiling sea water, mud, and debris.

The tidal wave struck along the entire Pacific Cordillera, rushing inland through every river delta on the western seaboard, charging through marshlands, century-old forests, large cities and hundreds of villages and towns, inundating the valleys beyond, from Alaska and Washington State to Mexico and Central America, where the massive coastal plains leading to the central mountains became a death zone of sea water, uprooted vegetation, mud, and debris.

The wave surged across the Gulf of Panama, bursting a barrage of seawater three hundred feet high up the channel leading to the Miraflores Locks of the Panama Canal, flooding Balboa and Cocoli, tearing the Bridge of the Americas from its foundations and sending hundreds of tons of mud, concrete, steel, and logs against the lock system, before flooding the Miraflores Lake, the single-stage Pedro Miguel Lock beyond it, and reaching as far as the Centennial Bridge by the continental divide, before starting to recede.

From the top of Ecuador to the southern tip of Chile and the northern coast of Antarctica, the tidal wave struck, tearing into hillsides, cities, and icy headwalls, crushing icebergs, spreading the kind of destruction the Earth had not witnessed for thousands of years.

Before the waters receded, leaving the land barren, smooth, devoid of any sign of human existence.

34 Farewells

"We must accept finite disappointment, but we must never lose infinite hope . . ."
--Martin Luther King

SAN GABRIEL MOUNTAINS. CALIFORNIA.

October 15, 2019

Erika Baxter held Case Montana's hand as they walked on the trail leading to the Remembrance Gardens, the large memorial park hi on the mountains overlooking the San Fernando Valley and the Los Angeles Basin beyond it.

She held his hand as tears welled into his eyes while walking past the recently completed archway leading into the simple, yet powerful clearing visited by so many Americans since it opened two months ago, a few weeks after the waters wiped the state clean of its major cities, towns, and highways with the power of a thousand Katrinas.

But unlike the New Orleans disaster, this time the ocean took it all, dragging entire societies to the bottom of what now looked like a tranquil sea, the deep grave of thirty million people. There were no bodies to bury, no streets to clean, no buildings to reconstruct.

The sea took it all down to soil and limestone.

Erika felt Case tightening his grip on her hand as they approached the now famous picture wall, where surviving family and friends of those tens of millions of casualties pinned pictures

275

of those stolen by the sea, by the largest single-most destructive event in all mankind.

Thirty million.

Erika sighed as Case reached for his back pocket and produced his wallet, where he extracted two pictures Erika had first seen on their trip to Russia what seemed like a lifetime ago even though it had only been three months.

Thirty million people.

But to Case Montana there were two in particular that had had a devastating effect. Cameron and Ashley. So young to have perished under the wave.

So young.

His hands trembling, Case Montana placed the pictures on the south end of the angled wall, amidst so many other pictures, messages, kids' drawings, flowers, and cards, in many ways reminiscent of September 11 and Katrina, when so many were lost to terrorism and global disasters.

Thirty million people.

Erika hugged him as he wept, just as he had wept so frequently for the past three months, since they had seen the impossible on that LCD screen on that hotel in Toronto the day after killing Dragan Kiersted.

Burn . . . drown . . .

Drown.

Case had had a nervous breakdown right there, shortly after they had spent their first night alone.

The CIA had placed him on temporary leave, and Erika had taken a sabbatical to be with him in his time of need. Case had no one now, and the devastation of losing two kids had been more than the formerly confident operative had been able to take.

So she had walked out of the GCCU for a few months to become the shoulder that would allow him to cry, to mourn, just as so many Americans mourned not just California but also Alaska, where the fires finally receded as winter set and an Arctic front hardened the permafrost enough to shut off the methane feeding the flames.

But not before consuming more oxygen than the world's ecosystem could replenish, resulting in a percent reduction significant enough to dilute sea level concentrations to those found at 7,000 feet, which made certain cities up in the mountains, especially in Colorado and Arizona in the United States, habitable only to those who could adapt to living in altitudes over 13,000 feet.

The low-oxygen world also had devastating effects on ocean life, where many species perished as the world's seas content also dropped.

The mortality rate was on the rise around the world, especially in the population above fifty, whose bodies were less capable to adapt to the Earth's rapidly evolving biomes. Temperatures on the equator belt were already five degrees hotter than normal, triggering droughts, killing tens of thousands, thinning the rain forests, and causing people to start migrations north and south to more habitable climates.

And speaking of climates, the fires in Alaska had only worsen the situation in Europe, where the near-permanent haze from the ashes carried by the jet stream had dropped temperatures another two degrees, propelling that continent into an even deeper freeze.

The events, however, had apparently awakened the world to the fact that not only did global terrorism have to be eradicated, but also a dramatic reduction in the generation of greenhouse gases had to occur.

At the moment there was a large convention in Rio de Janeiro, Brazil, where the world's nations were meeting to discuss steps towards fighting climate terrorism on a global basis as well as global warming.

Case slowly pulled away from her and stared into Erika's eyes, also filmed with tears. It pained her to see him like this, which also told her than for better or worse, she had fallen for Case Montana.

"I have mourned them and I have said my farewell," he said, staring at the pictures, then at the vast valley projecting to the distant ocean.

"Time to move on?" she asked.

"Yes," he replied, starting for the exit. "Time to move on. Together."

35 Denial

"The warnings about global warming have been extremely clear for a long time. We are facing a global climate crisis. It is deepening. We are entering a period of consequences."
--Vice President Al Gore

RIO DE JANEIRO. BRAZIL.

October 17, 2019

Natasha Shakhiva-Malone stepped out to the balcony of their hotel overlooking the beach wearing her husband's white tuxedo shirt.

A full moon hung high on the South American sky this late evening, casting its gray light on a peaceful ocean.

For the past two hours the recently married couple had celebrated the honeymoon they never really had following their narrow escape from Alaska.

So much has taken place, she thought, remembering the endless press conferences, media events, and meetings with government officials from ten different countries.

For a while it seemed that that everyone wanted to hear what Natasha and Malone had to say regarding global warming, the permafrost, the new biomes, and the future of the world.

And tonight had been a particularly promising evening. The couple had shared the stage at the World's Climate Change forum, where high-ranking officials from fifty countries, including the presidents of the United States and Russia, as well as the premier of the People's Republic of China, had listened to their theories and the data supporting them. Natasha and Malone had spoken about accelerated rise in sea levels, trapped methane beneath permafrost, and apocalyptic deserts near the equator. They had presented their findings in the accepted scientific formats of the day. They had issued warnings to the nations where computer modeling showed drastically changing climates, as captured in hundreds of ice cores from long-melted glaciers. In the end, they had left the stage amidst a shower of applause and praise for their work.

But as to be expected, what started as pure scientific work began to turn political a month ago, when a team of scientists from Beijing challenged their theories.

Tonight, on the limo ride to the hotel, they heard a story on the BBC about scientists from the Ëcole Normale Superieure, in Paris, one of France's most eminent universities and research centers, claiming to have data contradicting UAF's methane threat research, proposing that the Permian-Triassic event was nothing more than another asteroid, similar to the one which killed the dinosaurs over a hundred million years later.

Already the on-line news services were questioning their findings.

"Hey there," Malone said, stepping out barefoot to join her wearing only his tuxedo pants and holding two glasses of red wind. He no longer wore a pony tail, though his hair was still long, but above his shoulder, and he was clean shaven. "Courtesy of the hotel manager."

"Thanks," she said, taking a glass and staring out to sea while taking a sip.

"The Beijing team speaks in the morning," he said. "Their claim is very reminiscent of the post-Kyoto Protocol talks about curving greenhouse gases on a per-capita basis, which gives them a huge advantage because they have so many people."

Natasha didn't reply. Her eyes on the moonlit ocean.

"The ENS team goes after them, and their PR person sent me a note informing me that their theory and supporting data continues to contradict ours," he said. "I guess the French want their five minutes."

"Darling, I don't want any fame," Natasha said, looking at him for a moment before once more staring out to sea. "I'm a scientist, as you are. We look at facts, and we let them speak for themselves."

"But sometimes even facts are not enough."

"Then they have to face more consequences, like Greenland, Alaska, the Hawaiian Tsunami, and much worse, like what is coming our way next summer. The world was told today that of the thirty Gigatons of methane trapped beneath the permafrost, less than five percent was consumed in the Alaska fires before the winter closed the valve. If that isn't enough to scare them, then nothing short of the full Permian-Triassic event will."

Malone rested his forearms on the balcony, standing shoulder to shoulder with his wife. "The world, it appears, has the attention span of a gnat. They forget very quickly."

"But the Earth doesn't forget. While the world continues mourning California, global warming continues its unforgiving trend, Greenland continues to melt, sea levels continue to rise, and Europe continues to freeze. Meanwhile the permafrost is barely hanging in there, holding back a monster that can do to the entire world what that tsunami did to the Pacific coast of the American continent. Alaska was just a warning, Koni. It just gave us a taste of things to come."

"Not according to our Chinese and French colleagues," Malone said. "They will show evidence that the Permian-Triassic event was caused by a meteor."

She shrugged. "Summer will most certainly come again, Koni. It is only six months away. It will arrive, just as it does every year. No PowerPoint presentation and well-delivered speeches by the French and the Chinese will stop the Earth from circling the sun. You and I know what's beneath the Earth's permafrost. And when summer does arrive . . ."

As Malone put an arm around his wife and kissed her gently on the cheek, Natasha Shakhiva peered into the dark horizon and

281

took a sip of wine, her mind inexorably thinking of an event the world still may not be ready to accept.

An event that took place a long, long time ago . . .

Epilogue

"And all living things upon the earth perished--birds, wild animals, and reptiles . . . all existence on earth was blotted out."
Genesis 7:21

KAROO BASIN (MODERN DAY SOUTH AFRICA).
PANGAEA SUPERCONTINENT.
LATE-PERMIAN/EARLY-TRIASSIC PERIOD.

250 Million Years Ago

Parting a wall of conifers with a snout full of wicked teeth, the adult female Gorgonopsian, the Permian equivalent of the saber-tooth tiger, surveyed the river bank projecting beyond her hunting hideout.

Her quarter-size nostrils probed further, past seed ferns lining the uneven tundra sloping down to the herbivores' feeding grounds by the shoreline.

Her body completely caked in mud, both to hide her scent from potential prey as well as for protection against flying insects that fed at night, the Gorgo, a creature more mammal than reptile, surveyed the herd.

A pack of Deltavjatias, Triceratops-like creatures lacking protective horns and just over ten feet long, grazed on the herbaceous plants near the water. Their smooth armored plates, dark green with bluish shades, reflected the bright moonlight this breezy and unusually warm evening, when the Gorgo female reached the end of the wide river following a long migration from the winter hunting grounds to the north.

The Gorgo sniffed the familiar dung-aroma of the herbivores, confirming identification.

Among the Deltas roamed several pups, their dark torsos telegraphing the tender skin that will not be protected for another season, though seasons themselves had become less prominent, with warmer weather lasting longer and the white zone retreating farther south each summer.

The mouth of the river and the ocean beyond it no longer remained hardened during the summer, preventing the Gorgo female from completing her migration to the summer feeding grounds of her youth, to continue south across the ice sheet that led to a land blessed with cool temperatures, fresh meadows, and many herds of herbivores that also used to migrate there to escape the extreme summer heat.

Instead, the Gorgos had to evolve hunting tactics during this time of the year and cope with the increased heat, the mosquitoes, and fewer herds. Heading back north meant living through little shade as the clouds that used to shield the land during her youth in the summer had all but disappeared. Lacking their shade, the sun scorched the land, triggering droughts that even a desert-adapted hunter like the Gorgo would have difficulty surviving. Lack of heat meant lack of water, which also meant a lack of prey.

But adapting to hunt here in the summer had also not been easy. As the herbivores' ranks thinned from increasing temperatures and low rainfall even this far south, they grew more aggressive.

The Gorgo's scars on her torso reminded her of this each day. She had endured deep lacerations last year from the sharp claws of an angered Delta female while the Gorgo stole a youngster. Her mate and other Gorgos had perished here then, while trying to adjust, making mistakes, testing new techniques--as well as developing new survival strategies when hunters became hunted.

The vanishing cloud cover and increased heat this far south had also brought a new threat to the Gorgos: the disease injected by mosquitoes at night. It had claimed many lives in the rolling meadow flanking the river, which had shrunk in size from last year. Protection for the female Gorgo had come by accident one rainy night when her clan ended up covered in mud, whose aroma fended off the mosquitoes.

The Gorgo sniffed the air to the south with melancholy, longing for the hunting grounds barely visible in the distant horizon and beyond the reach of the dreaded flying insects that thrived in the hotter regions.

Her hungry stare returned to the movement of the herd as it slowly made its way down the receding shoreline, where the water was fresh, safe to drink.

She took her time, waiting for a pup to stray from the protection of the adults, giving her enough time to approach silently using the shallow trenches formed over previous seasons in this changing tundra to get close enough to lunge and steal it before the slow-moving Deltas could reach her.

That's when she saw a Delta youngster laying on its side on a bed of river stones where water had once flowed.

The Gorgo's muscles tightened; her salivary glands filled her snout.

But something was wrong. The pup was convulsing.

Her mind provided an explanation: the young Delta was sick.

Exhaling in a barely audible grunt, the Gorgo realized it had probably been infected by the disease from the flying insects because the pup lacked the protecting armor shielding the skin of the adult Deltas.

It is not safe to eat, she thought, watching the herd move downstream, away from her while protecting the healthy youngsters.

Albeit hungry from the month-long migration, she would not touch the diseased pup just as she didn't attempt to attack the herd without a clear opening, having learned a hard lesson a year ago, when such an attack had cost her the loss of her mate, who was cornered by a mob of aggressive Deltas and clawed to death.

The Gorgo female let go a soft whimper, recalling how her mate had drawn the Deltas to create a distraction while she snatched a youngster. But the attack had backfired. The well-organized Deltas had mounted an effective counterattack, nearly killing her as well, which would had also resulted in the death of the unborn cubs she had carried in her womb at the time.

But she had healed, in part by rubbing the wound against the dark-green ferns that grew amidst conifers flanking the shores of dry river beds, just as her mother had shown her long ago, allowing her to birth two healthy cubs, a male and a female.

Keep looking, her orange-size brain commanded, shifting her muzzle to the right of the Deltas, her sharp eyesight recognizing the long and furry silhouette of a Therocephalia feeding on a lizard, a sight that the female Gorgo had not seen for some time.

In her youth, the Gorgo's mother had taught her how to approach the three-foot-long slippery hunter from the rear, the creature's blind spot, snatching it by the long and weak neck and clamping hard to rip off the head before the creature had the chance to whip its sharp snout around and bite off an eye.

The Gorgo inhaled deeply, her brain triggering distant memories of the Thero's tender, moist, and salty flesh, filling its muzzle with milky saliva, which began to pepper the sand in between her clawed paws.

Withdrawing her head from the veiling conifers, the Gorgo inspected her cubs, nearly half her size and also covered in mud, sitting by her hind legs facing the opposite direction, guarding her flanks and rear as she had taught them, constantly sniffing the air, looking for danger.

The dark and quiet forest behind her had changed significantly following the vanishing clouds in recent seasons. Trees no longer stood erect, as had been the case in her youth, but tipped to one side, as if pushed by some invisible force--perhaps the same force that had robbed the land of its smoothness, shaping the shallow hills and valleys that the Gorgo had learned to use to sneak up on prey. The uneven terrain did make it harder to charge in a straight line, but the Gorgo had since developed a technique for half running and half leaping that allowed her to cover much ground very fast without tripping.

The male cub looked back, making eye contact, before purring loudly, *I'm hungry.*

The female Gorgo swatted him with a hind paw for breaking silence. Absolute stealth was paramount for the successful execution of a hunt, and also to prevent telegraphing their presence to larger predators in the area.

The offending cub shook his head and quietly returned his attention to his observation quadrant while exchanging a glance with his sister, who exhaled through her nostrils in silent reprimand for his brother's blunder while leering, exposing two rows of glistening teeth. This was a family effort and all had to perform their jobs flawlessly, or no one would eat tonight.

The Gorgo gave the listing tree line a suspicious scan until she was satisfied that her cub's telegraphing noise had not attracted any unwanted attention before resuming her search.

The Thero continued to work on the dead lizard, apparently undisturbed by the noise. The direction of the wind, sweeping in from the river delta, told the Gorgo that the purr had been carried away from the prey and into the forest behind them.

It had been a few seasons since she had seen a live Thero, not since the slow-flowing river and the ocean beyond it began to bubble with the gas that turned into fire, causing thick waves of dead fish to wash ashore.

Many species, including Theros, had feasted that day long ago, only to die soon after.

Most of the Gorgos in her old pack had shown restraint. Her survival instincts, triggered by the faint but different smell, which had also caused flying insects to fall from the skies, kept her from consuming something already dead.

Larger species, like the dreaded Titanophoneus--nearly five times the Gorgo's size, sporting a snout large enough to tear her in half--had fed on the many dead Theros, and some of them started to die within days.

The Gorgo female, her mate, and other Gorgo's from her old pack had escaped north, away from the poisoned air and the fields of death until the following season, when all that remained were rolling tundra layered with the massive bony carcasses of dead Titans.

But that Thero has survived--and has also adapted, her logic told her as her early recollections of the long and furry creature showed it feeding on fish. And just like the Gorgo, the skin of the Thero continuing to feast on the lizard was also caked in mud for protection against the large mosquitoes.

And that realization triggered two additional threads in her brain. First, the Thero would be safe to eat. Second, the Thero had adapted to its environment like the Gorgo.

Those two thoughts led her mind to a conclusion: the Thero would require new tactics to outwit.

Unfortunately, successful hunts had been growingly difficult without her mate, as two predators were far more efficient than one, and her cubs would need another season before they would be ready to assist beyond guarding the rear. In addition, the rest of the Gorgos from her old clan had long perished while trying to adapt to the changing landscape.

I am alone on this one, she decided, once more slowly parting the thin layer of conifers, surveying the landscape, the dark-brown ginkgos beyond her veil swirling in the same breeze that tickled the Gorgo's nostrils, carrying with it the chemical promise of a meal if she could do this right for her and her hungry cubs.

Slowly, she drifted through the vegetation effortlessly, snout first, parting soft branches before her aerodynamic body flowed through while dropping to a deep crouch, her belly brushing the sphenophytes layering the tundra's flood in between ferns, her senses heightened, her eyes on the prey.

Off to her far left, the Deltas continued to graze on the thin shrubbery amidst river rocks, their thick plates mirroring the grey light from the rising moon as well as shielding the youngsters splashing on the shallows while producing soft screeches to the delight of their elders, who groaned in return. One adult female looked back at the dying youngster by the shore, still convulsing, and she shrieked several times, before turning away.

The Gorgo welcomed the noise as it helped mask her own.

The Thero continued to feed, front paws clutching its prize, long muzzle buried in the lizard's entrails.

The breeze rustled the surrounding vegetation, the long branches overhead of a large marattialean tree fern and surrounding conifers, breaking up the moon shadow.

She now moved swiftly, quietly, with cat-like grace, four clawed paws moving with synchronized precision, barely sinking in the sandy terrain, her adaptive brain transitioning from survey mode to attack mode. Ten million years of evolution combined with multiple seasons of drastic adaptation guided her as she closed on her prey, as she began to--

The Gorgo paused the instant the Thero stopped feeding.

Instinctively dropping to the sandy floor, hiding behind a pair of seed ferns, the Gorgo slowly raised her eyes--conveniently located near the top of her skull--like two periscopes barely protruding above her hiding trench.

The Thero had dropped its meal and lifted its bloody snout to test the air, nostrils flaring.

It doesn't make sense, she thought. The breeze was coming from the water, carrying any smell not covered by the mud away from her prey.

On the periphery of her vision, the Gorgo noticed the Deltas had also stopped feeding, their heads stretched above their stocky bodies while surveying the forest lining the rolling tundra.

The forest?

The Gorgo sniffed the air again, this time deeper, more carefully, identifying a new chemical signature that made her hind legs twitch. She had not smelled it for a long time--not since the day when the bubbling gas killed so many animals.

A shriek echoed in the tundra. It came from her male cub. *I smell something strange!*

As the Gorgo's meal scurried away and the herd of Deltas stampeded along the shore with an earth-rumbling racket that shook the branches of the ferns around her, a single Titan crashed through the tree line, its semi-hunched body four times longer than her and three times as tall.

Breaking the silence of the feeding grounds with a deafening growl, the Titan stomped onto the sandy meadow kicking up puffs of dust and dirt with its massive paws as it charged toward her cubs.

Charcoal grey with an immense, top-heavy long head at the end of a very thick neck and an equally disproportionate muzzle crowded with oversized white teeth, the Titan moved clumsily, but what it lacked in speed and grace it made up in sheer size and terror. Powered by muscular hind legs and strong but smaller front legs sporting long and ragged claws--which she had seen it use to disembowel prey, including Gorgos--the Titan roared again.

Her maternal instincts burning in her mind, drowning all other senses, the Gorgo raced up the meadow as her cubs broke through the wall of conifers rushing toward her in long elastic leaps. They were fast, but the Titan took longer strides, and it would eventually catch up to them.

But not before the female Gorgo would plant herself in between. A lifetime of hunts had trained her mind to quickly calculate relative velocities, which told her she could reach the cubs before the Titan did.

Once the Gorgo and her mate had killed a Titan, but it had required a very coordinated effort.

Tonight she was alone.

Her frightened cubs reached her, their long and slanted brown eyes displaying raw fear, nostrils flaring, their whimpering grunts almost drowned by the roaring growls of the Titan behind them, its colossal head and wide-open snout converging rapidly on the trio.

She quickly ordered them to run in opposite directions as dictated by Darwinian countermeasures to ensure that at least one would survive.

Without checking to see if they had obeyed, the Gorgo scrambled towards the incoming threat, her adaptive brain remembering the tactic she and her mate had used, her adrenaline-fueled senses rapidly converging on a single-Gorgo version of the attack.

The Titan stopped less than twenty feet from the Gorgo, who also paused, the muddy skin on her snout pulled back, exposing her own teeth. Her front fangs were a fraction of the size of the massive white daggers facing her.

She growled while planting her paws firmly on the sand, stiletto claws extended.

You will have to get past me to get to them.

The Titan roared back at the open challenge, standing on its hind legs, the massive head and neck, nearly a third of the beast's total mass, rose an impressive height, towering over the Gorgo, who remained still, in control, knowing precisely what would come next.

The Titan's attack tactics had never evolved, which explained why the Gorgo saw fewer of them each season.

Advancing towards her strong and confident, the hungry monster blocked the moonlight, sniffing the air, savoring the meal to come, its menacing shadow casting over the Gorgo, who stood her ground, biding her time.

The growls intensifying, claws at the end of muscular front legs slicing the air, the beast's oozing chemicals filled the Gorgo's senses, telegraphing its intentions.

Just a few yards in front of her, the Titan dropped to all fours with earthquake force, covering the remaining distance, jaws blossoming as it drove them with trained resolve precisely over the Gorgo.

Now!

The female rolled on her side once just as the massive snout stabbed the sand where she had stood an instant before. The sheer force of the Titan's muzzle cratered the Tundra with soul-trembling vigor felt beneath the Gorgo's paws as she surged from the quick roll.

The Gorgo's thigh muscles exploded into life, shooting her five-hundred-pound mass forward through the billowing cloud of debris, dashing around the Titan like a shadow while the massive animal tore into the Tundra's floor, still not realizing the trick.

291

The Gorgo leaped onto the Titan's back with elastic vigor before the Titan could lift its lopsided head, drilling her two-inch-long claws into the sides of the monster's neck, clamping on while tearing into the soft flesh just behind the creature's skull.

The Titan roared in anger, in pain, in agony, trying to stand on its hind legs while stabbing the night air with its front legs, jerking its head back, trying to cut itself loose from the Gorgo's deadly embrace.

Her fangs biting through layers of gray skin, blood spurting, the Gorgo dug deeper, the Titan's flesh warm, pulsating.

Nearly erect now, the Titan abruptly dropped back down on all fours while also thrusting its massive head forward, catapulting the Gorgo off just as it bit deep into the monster.

The Titan, the night air, and the sandy tundra exchanged places as she was flung nearly ten yards, but somewhere along the way her brain commanded her legs, and she landed right side up facing the threat.

The Titan growled, blood jetting from its neck, streaking down its sides in dark streams, as if it had just emerged from the water, staining the sand around it.

The sweet taste of flesh and blood alive in her snout, the Gorgo once more stood still, spitting a crimson ten-pound lump before leering, exposing bloody teeth at her much larger opponent, challenging it.

The Titan paused, confused, staring at the clump of meat by the Gorgo's front paws, finally realizing where it had come from.

Taking a step back, the Titan roared, standing semi-erect, soaring over the Gorgo, its head listing a little, muzzle wide open. The wounded beast's claws pierced the night as it closed the distance before dropping back down over her.

And once again she rolled on her side, but this time in the opposite direction, surging to her feet just as the Titan claimed another mouthful of sandy tundra.

An instant later she was back on top, landing on the same spot, skewering the sides of the Titan's neck with her claws before clamping her snout on the flesh from the same bleeding cavity, ripping madly, tearing, widening the wound with vicious bites, burrowing her entire head into the gash while trying to hang on as the Titan shook its body violently, threatening to fall on its back, crushing the Gorgo.

But she didn't let up; the Gorgo kept gnawing, ripping arteries and cartilage, her sharp fangs reaching the thick muscles controlling the massive head.

The Titan's roars increased in pitch, turning into deafening howls as the Gorgo sank her jaws into the muscles surrounding the vertebrae, triggering a massive seizure on the beast, which remained semi-erect, its head sagging to the right, front legs sticking straight ahead, stretched claws frozen.

The Gorgo clamped her snout of crimson steel over a thick muscle and pulled back hard, ripping it off the bone.

In a deafening howl, the Titan lifted its head straight up, quivering, and in doing so it lost its footing and began to topple backwards.

The Gorgo pulled her head out when realizing the beast was off balance.

Retrieving her claws, she pushed herself off, landing on all fours on the sand while rolling once, twice, scrambling to get out of the way of the collapsing giant, which struck the ground on its side with the force of a massive boulder, kicking up more sand and a boiling cloud of dust that shrouded its bulk as the Gorgo stepped back, once more placing herself between the threat and her cubs' escape route, poised for another strike.

She waited as the dust cleared, as the Titan slowly got up, its large round eyes, as dark as the sky, regaining focus, blood now pooling by its paws, flowing faster than the tundra could absorb.

The prehistoric hunters stared at each other.

The Gorgo growled. *I can do this all night long.*

Confused, the Titan shifted its head from side to side with obvious difficulty, confused; studying her opponent, uncertain how such a smaller creature had been able to inflict so much damage so quickly.

Slowly, the Titan snorted, oozing a cloud of chemicals that conveyed a new message to the Gorgo.

I'm finished here.

It then took a step back, and another, before painfully turning around, whimpering, having difficulty keeping the oversized head up, seeking the protection of the forest.

But the Gorgo wasn't finished. She had come here to hunt, to feed her cubs, and the formidable Titan had suddenly been transformed from a threat to a slow and weak meal.

The Gorgo sniffed, savoring the scent of the Titan's flesh, relishing the taste in her mouth, her stomach aching in deep hunger.

The wounded beast was not going anywhere.

The Titan's rear now exposed to her as it tried to retreat to the forest, the Gorgo charged, easily climbing on top, positioning herself, claws glistening, digging into tender flesh, securing herself.

The injured monster was too weakened to fight back, barely shaking, emitting a high-pitch cry as the Gorgo bit into a massive muscle, and shredding it with incessant bites, losing herself in a primordial frenzy of tearing, ripping, and digging.

Howling in agony while dragging its dying mass towards the forest step after agonizing step, the Titan made a final attempt to resist, jolting, shaking its back, but it could not break the Gorgo's vice-like grip.

The Gorgo's snout struck bone beneath strands of torn ligaments, exposing the vertebrae.

Clamping her jaws around it, she cracked it.

The whimpering beast collapsed on her belly while breathing in short sobbing gasps, foam and blood oozing from its nostrils, echoing across the quieted meadow, before all movement ceased.

Standing tall on top of the most feared creature of her time, the Gorgo raised her bloody muzzle to the star-filled sky, to the grey moon hanging full above her. For an instant becoming the top predator of this warming land, she growled twice in victory.

And it was at that moment of complete control, as the moonlight cast a grayish glow on her atop the Titan, that her nostrils detected a new chemical signature.

At the same time a gurgling sound erupted from the river, sweeping across the rolling tundra, followed by more eruptions, on water and then through the sand, irritating her nasal cavities, her eyes.

Her cubs cried out for her as the eruptions intensified, as a massive explosion in the distance shook the valley.

The wall of fire propagated across the meadows at lightning speed, incinerating everything in its wake.

The Gorgo tried to warn her cubs of the imminent danger as flames swallowed their world.

Book Club Discussion Points on Global Warming

"Greenhouse warming and other human alterations of the earth system may increase the possibility of large, abrupt, and unwelcome regional or global climatic events. Future abrupt changes cannot be predicted with confidence, and climate surprises are to be expected."
-- U.S. National Academy of Science.

- ## Permafrost.

    Global warming is thawing the permafrost in Siberia and Alaska, causing buildings to collapse and also creating "drunken trees" due to the softening of the soil in affected forested regions. The biggest threat, however, comes from the potential release of as much as 70,000 million tons of methane, an extremely effective greenhouse gas trapped beneath the permafrost since it was formed 11,000 years ago at the end of the last ice age. This release could take place over a very short period of time (a few years up to a decade), exponentially accelerating the rate of global warming. This has been hypothesized as a cause of past and possibly future climate changes. In addition, methane clathrate, also called methane hydrate, is a form of water ice that contains a large amount of methane within its crystal structure. Extremely large deposits of methane clathrate exist under sediments on the ocean floor. Increasing ocean temperatures can release large amounts of this runaway greenhouse gas and could increase the global temperature by an additional 5° C in itself (on top of the warming done by the released methane under the permafrost). The theory also predicts this massive methane release will greatly affect available oxygen content of the atmosphere. This theory has been proposed to explain the most severe mass extinction event on earth known as the

Permian-Triassic extinction event. This, I think, is a very intriguing inflection point.

- ## Rising Ocean Level.
  With increasing average global temperature, the water in the ocean expands in volume, and additional water enters them which had previously been locked up on land in glaciers. To put things in perspective, if all the ice on the polar ice caps were to melt away, the oceans of the world would rise an estimated 70 meters (229 feet). However, with little major credit melt expected in Antarctica, sea level rise of not more than 0.5 meters (1.6 feet) is expected through the 21st century. Thermal expansion of the world's oceans, however, will contribute independent of glacial melt, enough to double those figures. This means that at the current rate of global warming from carbon dioxide release into the atmosphere, sea levels could rise as much as 1.5 meters by the end of this century. The "methane event" could multiply this number by a factor of 5 or more while also pulling in the sea rise timetable. A sea level rise of three feet would cause much of Miami, Fort Myers, a large portion of the Everglades, and all of the Florida Keys to disappear.

- ## Storms.
  Hurricane power dissipation is highly correlated to temperature, reflecting global warming. Computer modeling has found that hurricanes under warmer, high carbon-dioxide conditions, are more intense that under present-day conditions. Hurricanes such as Katrina and Rita gathered most of its destructive power during their days traveling over the warm waters of the Gulf of Mexico. The "methane event" could result in much warmer waters, creating storms never yet experienced by modern civilization.

- ## Forest Fires.

  Rising global temperatures might cause forest fires to occur on larger scale and more regularly. This releases more stored carbon into the atmosphere than the carbon cycle can naturally re-absorb, as well as reducing the overall forest area on the planet, creating yet another positive feedback loop.

- ## Ocean Acidification.

  It is estimated that oceans have absorbed roughly half of all carbon dioxide generated by human activity since 1800 (around 120,000,000,000 tons, or 120 pentagrams of carbon). But in water, carbon dioxide becomes a weak carbonic acid, lowering the pH of the ocean. This acidification results in the methodical destruction of coral reefs, reduction in fish reproduction as well as the plankton on which they rely for food. Scientists are trying to assess the effect that the "methane event" would have on the ocean acidic level.

- ## Melting Polar Ice.

  There are large reductions in the Greenland and West Antarctic Ice Sheets. Excepting the ice caps and ice sheets of the Arctic and Antarctic, the total surface of glaciers worldwide has decreased by 50% since the end of the 19th century. The loss of glaciers not only directly causes landslides, flash floods, and glacial lake overflows, but also increases annual variation in water flows in rivers. The melting of glaciers at an accelerated rate in Venezuela and the Peruvian Andes is a particular concern because of the direct reliance on these glaciers for water supplies and hydroelectric power The sea absorbs the sun, while ice largely reflects the sun rays back to space. The retreating sea ice will allow the sun to warm the now exposed sea, contributing to further warming in yet another positive feedback loop. The "methane event" would be a significant accelerator.

- ## Droughts.
  Large-scale experiments have shown that rising atmospheric temperatures, longer droughts and side effects of both, such as higher levels of ground-level ozone gas, are likely to bring about a substantial reduction in crop yields in the coming decades. The "methane event" would also accelerate this.

- ## Heat Waves.
  Global warming leads to increasing frequency and strength of heat waves. The European heat wave of 2003 killed around 30,000 people. In the United States around 2000 people die each year due to extreme summer heat.

- ## Disease.
  Global warming is expected to extend the favorable zones for vectors conveying infectious disease such as malaria and west Nile virus. In poorer countries this may lead to higher incidence of such disease. By 2050, snow melting in the Himalayas and increased precipitation across northern India is likely to produce flooding in India, Nepal, Bangladesh, and Pakistan. Climate change is expected to increase the geographic range of infectious diseases such as malaria, dengue fever, schistosomiasis. Except for east central China and the highlands of west China, much as Asia Pacific region is exposed to malaria and dengue

- ## Insurance Companies.
  An industry very directly affected by the risks of global warming is the insurance industry. A June 2004 report by the Association of British Insurers declared, "Climate change is not a remote issue for future generations to deal with. It is, in various forms, here already, impacting on insurers' businesses now."

- ## Migrations.

  The U.S. and Europe may experience mounting pressure to accept large number of immigrant and refugee populations as drought increases and food production declines in Latin America and Africa. Numerous African countries suffer from famine and civil strife. Darfur, Ethiopia, Eritrea, Somalia, Angola, Nigeria, Cameroon, and Western Sahara hit hard by reduced water supplies, reductions in agriculture, triggering the instability on which warlords capitalized. Reduced rainfalls and increasing desertification of the sub-Saharan region will result in migrations to Europe. Increases in temperature can expand the latitude and altitude for malaria. Flooding is also conductive to cholera. The major impact on Europe from global climate change is likely to be migrations, now from the Maghreb (Northern Africa) and Turkey. Precipitation is expected to decrease in the central and eastern Mediterranean zones and south Russia, with acute water shortages projected in the Mediterranean area, especially in summer. Places like the Balkans, Moldova, and the Caucasus will be unable to cope with the droughts, resulting in massive migrations north. The Italians today already face a large Albanian immigration, and others may press north from the Balkans. The primary security threats to the U.S. arise from the potential demand for humanitarian aid and a likely increase in immigration from Latin America--all the while the U.S. is dealing with its own climate change issue. In the past, U.S. military forces have responded to natural disasters. The military was deployed to Central America after Hurricane Mitch in 1998 and to Haiti following the rain and mudslides of 2004.

- ## Water and the Middle East.
  In the Middle East, climate change has the potential to exacerbate tensions over water as precipitation patterns change, declining by as much as 60 percent in some areas. In addition, the region already suffers from fragile governments and infrastructures, as a result is

300

susceptible to natural disasters. Overlaying this is a long history of animosity among countries and religious groups. With most of the world's oil being in the Middle East and the industrialized nations competing for this resource, the potential for escalating tensions, economic disruption, and armed conflict is great.

- ## Critical Factors.

  The critical factors for economic and security stability in the 21st century are energy, water, and the environment. These three factors need to be balanced for people to achieve a reasonable quality of life. When they are not in balance, people live in poverty, suffer high death rates, or move toward armed conflict.

R. J. Pineiro

LaVergne, TN USA
27 October 2010
202493LV00009B/84/P